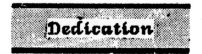

Dedication

To my mother
Mrs. Elizabeth Orji
my father, Chief Mathew Orji
My sisters, Theresa, Caro and Florence,
My brothers, Chike, Raphael, Chibuzor,
John and Chief Cyril Orji,
(Ideh of Ihitenansa). Dr. Ben Abadua
Friends, Buchi, Ifeoma, Legon, Inyang,
Onanwa, and Liz.

Chapter 1

The old chieftain sat himself on a deckchair in front of his bungalow and worried about the village of Nkwoko of which he was head, rumours, troubles and gossips were rife.

His wife had come back the other day to tell him that Emeruo was indicting Okani of stealing, that he was amassing evidence in order to arrest him.

Okpara had been furious with his wife and forbade her never to utter such words against Okani. Okpara was head of Nkwoko and it was unthinkable that such a matter would arise without Emeruo first complaining to him. It sounded incredible that a wealthy Chief of Okani's standing would steal palmheads so Okpara had commanded his wife to erase the thought from her mind.

"Yes our father', Olamma had replied and shut her mouth. That was three days ago.

Okpara's worries started this morning when passing through Emeruo's farm, he saw him vehemently pointing trees out to two strangers. From their stern rigid looks and behaviour, he surmised that they were people connected with the government. They were probably policemen. In a flash, his wife's remark the other day flew back to his mind. He had passed them unnoticed.

Now he was filled with exasperating thoughts considering the possibility of the truth of the rumour.

"This thing must stop", he said aloud. Olamma, inside the room was startled. "What is it papa? Is anything wrong?" She called from within.

"Sorry. I was just thinking", the Chief said.

Olamma laughed heartily, her husband when crazy could amuse. "That is violent thinking papa. You are no more strong for that kind of thinking. Remember what the doctor said the last time you saw him. It is this kind of grinding thinking he warned you against".

"What were you thinking of?", she asked him trying to change the subject. "Tell me do you want money for another wife or for a new house?".

This question threw the chief into other domains of thoughts. For Olamma, he thanked God everyday. Her presence, the joy and laughter she still brought to his lips often made him wonder what life was like for his fellow old men, widowers. Most of them like Okpara had children but no children. The quest for greener pastures had driven children from what they called village ways to the big cities where they had plenty of opportunities, thus leaving their parents in the villages companionless.

"Okpara" Olamma shouted when the chief refused to answer her. She had called his name to let him know that at this stage of their lives, she was never to be ignored.

I was thinking about Emeruo and Okani". He said and he told her about his experience this morning concluding that he now suspected that there were elements of truth in those rumours of hers. To his dismay she suggested that he call a meeting for settling the dispute. "It is the man with a boil that looks for the surgeon and not the other way round okay? How can I summon two people and declare that there is a dispute between them. What if they deny it? Many will think I am crazy."

"Then confirm first," She said. "This peace you talk about, to achieve it, we drop all the long ropes. When two brothers quarrel, their father does not wait until they come

2

to him to complain. He finds a way to settle the matter. Please papa, my fear is Okani. Call this meeting for my sake."

The old man, holding his jaw in his hand stared at his wife until she started laughing.

"Do you want something to eat?" She asked him.

* * *

The entire village assembled under the *udala* tree. The tree was mighty and looked more like the other two iroko trees in the village. It was a very ancient tree, was called the *udala omumu*, *udala* of fertility. During its season, the entire village partook of its numerous fruits for a very long time. A look at the clusters of the fruits on the tree, easily convinced one that the god of fertility really did work with the tree. Thus barren women and children competed on who would be there early in the morning to pick its fruits. It was a forbidden thing to pluck its fruits. Only the resourceful, persevering and patient people partook of its fruits. These were those who went early in the morning, or came at any time and of course the lucky ones. These people chanced upon the fallen fruits at any time of day and picked them.

It was under this tree that the village assembled.

Okpara stood up, a wooden bowl of kolanuts in his hand. Discussions gradually ceased from all sides. Only the intermittent hooting of the owl on the Iroko tree just outside the square could be heard.

Okpara stared at the bowl in his hand, his head inclined to one side, and he finally smiled, a disarming smile. No too much rhetoric, no elaborations, in this opening prayer, he thought. This matter should not be made to appear bigger than it really was. And so he called upon the name of the ancestors and broke the kolanuts.

When everybody had eaten, he rose again.

"Nkwoko *Kwenu*", he greeted them

"Eee i", responded the crowd.

"*Kwenu*"
Eei"
Kwezuenu"
"Eei"

"You all know why we are here. Two of our brothers, Emeruo and Okani have a matter which they want us to look into. We are not here to determine who is a better speaker between them. We are not necessarily here to blame them, but to make peace between them." The village head paused, solicitous for the understanding of the people of Nkwoko. They stared back at him understandingly. "A spit aimed at a brother's eyes touches his chest... his heart, and cools it. People are the pride of the king, and what makes people.. peace makes people. A thousand people who are not at peace are not a people. We have always been a people. We must know what to say in this matter today and how to say it. If one speaks right, may one reap fruits of blessings, but if one speaks wrong, may evil follow him to his house.

"I am saying this because our land is strong. It is a land that protects the weak and the strong. Lions and chicks live peacefully here. Our land does not condone intimidation. If a child uses the mortar well, his pestle falls into mortar, if otherwise he strikes his foot and perhaps learns to use it the hard way. Eem ...I think that we may start".

Okpara sat down and many of the elders shook his hands, showing approval for his opening remarks. He beckoned to Emeruo to stand up and present his case. Emeruo stood up and cleared his throat, anxious to make his case.

"Our fathers and our mothers, I should first thank you, especially the village head, for making it possible for me, and Okani to come before you to say what is causing trouble between us ..."

4

Okani was looking at Emeruo without knowing what to feel. This was a man he had always admired in the village, a man whose resourcefulness and hardwork were an inspiration to him as a young man. A man he had always regarded as his own father, a man he had confided in, many secrets that he could not tell his own wife. A man who the entire village believed was his favourite uncle, and the entire town thought was his father or brother depending on who was judging them. He just sat there waiting for what Emeruo would say was his reason for wanting to make trouble with him.

Until now, nobody had bothered to tell Okani what Emeruo said was his annoyance against him. Nobody could, not even Okani's wife, because Okani had a volcanic temper and nobody wanted to activate it. Because of his temper and his bluntness, he was usually kept out of village gossip, thus he had more time to work and enjoy the fruits of his labour. These qualities inevitably attracted a lot of respect for him. Now his best friend and brother was indicting him, of what? He was astonished, but at least this explained Emeruo's coldness towards him in recent times.

"... did you hear me?" echoed Emeruo's voice, " he and his daughter stole palmheads from my farm, as if that was not enough, they proceeded to kill the palmtree. I am not only annoyed that they carried off whole palmheads from my farm, but that they proceeded to kill the tree. Killing a palmtree belonging to somebody is evil in our place. Those trees gives us food and money and anybody who tampers with your means of livelihood wants you dead... therefore I want justice. I have irrefutable evidence of his assault on my farm, If I don't get justice here. I know where to get it". Emeruo's speech made the village shake. It whipped up several questions and sentiments in their hearts. Emeruo was a highly respected member of the village and so was Okani, but now what he said and the way he said it seemed odd and strange, incredible. Even if the facts were verified, they could never draw the same conclusions from them as Emeruo was drawing now. The people of Nkwoko were dying to get at the root of this matter,to find out what had prompted Emeruo to indict his best friend this way. Okani was not merely his friend, he was a titled man, a man who had won the respect of all Nkwokos and the surrounding villages. So many of them shook in anticipation of his reaction and the consequences of this matter for the entire village especially between Okani's and Emeruo's children.This was the mood of the people of Nkwoko when Emeruo came to a conclusion.

Before Emeruo could conclude his case, four elders were on their feet, including the venerable Ukpo and the village head. When the other chiefs saw the stout visage of the lordly Ukpo, they quietly sat down, but Okpara would not.

Ukpo was quick to speak.

"Okpara we understand your concern about this case, but I thought that it would be more appropriate for you to gather and join the threads of our discussions after —"

"No!" said Okpara in a surprisingly solid voice.

"No! Don't tell me when to speak and when not to speak Son of the Lion".

The crowd, not used to seeing the redoubtable Ukpo defeated in a situation like this, came to his aid. "He is right", they told the village head. "You should speak last on this issue".

The position of a village-head was a useless one, at least so thought many village-heads. The village-head was a kind of moderator at meetings like this,however, his views, arrived at after a careful consideration of the views of other elders on cultural matters, carried more weight than anybody else's. He was expected to interpret their culture and in this respect, it was understood that he would be the very last person to speak on specific issues.

Okpara was still on his feet, more thin than he looked when sitting. His pale wrinkled skin, a foil for his new vest. His *Osuba* which must have gone many rounds over his waist was too big for him. His gaunt hand was raised trying to quell the noisy reaction from the crowd.

Ukpo touched him and whispered something to him. Then he put down his hand.

"Let the old man speak", said Ukpo. The village responded with applause. He sat down.

Okpara was anything but a severe man. In fact he liked the conduct of the assembly to be friendly and light. Only old men like himself who tried to disrupt meetings like this could move him into a rage, and when he did, it was tumultous,so that he had waited to see Ukpo's reaction. If Ukpo had misbehaved, he would have shown him that a village-head had real powers. But he was never in doubt how Ukpo was going to handle the situation. So now that he had the stage again,he began to elaborate his speech.

"I am very glad that I am closer to my fathers. Our fathers understood brotherhood better. They had respect for our customs and kept themselves from recognised taboos. What can be worse than the unguarded remark made by Emeruo,that there is no justice here.

"Let me tell you. We could be anything, but brother-eaters. Even if anybody here wanted to, he could not be. We cannot afford that. We are a small people. We have more than paid the price of smallness through the terrible treatment the Ekemas have always given us. They invaded our land and chased our forefathers away for a very long time. We became refugees in the surrounding villages of our great town. I grew up in Umuoze. Emeruo's great-grandfather was a great warrior. His war-cry alone could infuse even cripples with the courage to make a go at their

7

enemies. To our enemies he was the killer. No man ever received his blow and survived it, so that it was said that he was a friend of the devil, otherwise, how could he survive all that dare-devilry?

"I also knew Emeruo's grandfather very well, a most accomplished wrestler,unchallenged after he threw the unconquerable Ojadiri of Oramba, three times on the same day. Ojadiri, the Unconquerable could not believe it, but each time, he threw him with more ease. Thereafter, it was said of him, that he used the indecipherable but powerful incantation of the great spirit, Nweze, in wrestling,for how could a mortal throw Ojadiri who was regarded as the son of a god? No man ever challenged him again till he died. "But the greatest feat, for which everybody, including his wife feared him, was that he could climb that mighty Iroko tree barehanded". He paused to point at the Iroko tree.

"During wars, he would climb that tree barehanded, with his gun slung on his shoulder, to shoot at our enemies. He was treated like a god by all, except the Ekemas, but they never dared go near him. These great men, Emeruo's great-grandfather and his grandfather, did not raise a finger against a brother".Okpara was now fully charged and he had the complete attention of the crowd. "We are all aware that Emeruo and his brother, Elesi, own more land than all of us here. Why?" he asked, looking at everybody as though expecting an answer from them. "Because", he continued "the most cowardly man in the village, Okani's grandfather coveted his land and the warrior was not quick to kill him. He did not even quarrel with him. Our grandfathers were so impressed by his behaviour that they gave him justice, even without his asking for it. This village gave him a quarter of all the land in this village in recognition of his contributions to the land. I want to tell everybody here that justice is here. Justice, we will give to whosever deserves it, whether it means taking the elders of this village to Gom, or any other place, to bear witness to that justice, I shall see to that".

Okpara now softened his voice.

"But this matter is not going anywhere. I only want us to be careful in our utterances".

He was finished and he sat down, feeling pleased with himself. He had spoken like a village head in a rather tortuous and superfluous way. This was why he was advised to be the very last person to speak on this matter.

The truth was, his speech had a salutary effect on everybody, the children mostly, who tittered in the realization that they had such heroes as progenitors. The mild rebuke also tempered Okani's reaction to Emeruo's speech.

Okani stood up to speak. He was taller than everybody in the assembly. He was huge, handsome and likeable. The name that his father gave him at birth was Ugochukwu. It literally meant "God's eagle". But it actually stood for the feather of the eagle with which the Igbos decorated a titled man. Ugochukwu meant that he was God's own choice. God had fastened his own feather for him, so that they said, whom God had chosen, no man could oppose or dethrone.

When he grew taller than every other person in the village, they called him Okani, an ambiguous name, meaning both "taller than all", and "greater than all".He accepted his nickname in this second sense. Thus, when he took the coveted Ozo title, he called himself Okani. People tended to construe his general bearing as having a relationship with greatness. Okani was indeed respected in Nkwoko. He was the classic example of the child who washed his hands very well and dined with the elders and kings.

In 1967 when he was fourteen, the deep animosity which had existed between the Nkwokos and the Ekemas culminated into another dangerous war. Boys of his age, on the advice of their parents, sought solace in their maternal uncles' homes, but Okani would not do that. When his father tried to force him, he told him, "but father, you told me that your father fought with the elders of this village at the age of twelve and made a name for himself as the indomitable Obejiri".

"That was when he was young. The fire in him died as he grew older ... He died a coward", replied his father.

"Please papa, let me stay. Look at my size, who would understand that I am fourteen? I would rather die here than go to my uncle's and make myself an object of laughter ... I feel overdue for this kind of adventure".

That was how Okani came to fight side by side with no less a man than the godlike Elesi. That was nineteen years ago. He had fired guns under his command, chased after men with his legs and brought them back to Elesi. He flogged them as Elesi directed.

The war automatically transformed him into a fully fledged man. The zenith of their exploits was the day that the unassailable Elesi took him into the enemy lines at a great risk. That day, there had been serious fighting, with the Ekemas besieging Elesi's house for over three hours. They were determined to bring the house down at all costs, as they sensed that it was their main obstacle to reannexing some of the lands already recovered from them.

Some Ekema boys, unknown to Elesi, were brandishing grenades which they stole from the army. Scores of them were deserting the army under one pretext or another in order to come back and join their brothers in the war with the Nkwokos.

From the balcony facing the main gate, Elesi was shooting into the air, at the multitude of Ekemas outside yearning for his blood. As long as they kept beyond the gates, he would continue shooting into the air, but anyone who ventured to the gate would surely die there.

Then, he saw a tiny object flash in the air and fall. The object started to smoke. The grim realization that this people had used a grenade on his house stiffened his fingers an instant. He held his breath, waiting for the explosion, but the smoking continued.

"Okani!" he yelled, a great urgency in his voice.

Okani heard his name from the other side of the balcony from where he had been shooting at the enemies. He had been shooting above the heads of two youngsters trying to enter the great compound with determination. With the urgency in Elesi's voice, he quickly loaded his two guns, balancing them on either side of the stomach, above the navel, he aimed at the two young men, and fired directly at them, determined to kill them. His ears rang from the explosions. When he opened his eyes, he saw the two young men running a great race, away from the house. This settled, he quickly rushed to the side from where Elesi had called. Elesi was looking like a hellcat when he saw him.

These bastards, these cowards want to see the end of this family. They threw a grenade here", he said between clenched teeth.

Okani did not know what to say, he was young and was disposed more to acting than to thinking. And even if he wanted to say something, conferring with Elesi was something he had never done before. He was not used to that.

"I am going to see the animal who threw grenade into this house, face to face. With my bare hands, I will strangle him ... Come with me!"

Elesi left his gun on the ground and started moving towards the staircase. Okani was seriously worried about him. In his eyes, he saw a supreme resolve to confront even the devil, at that time. This kind of hell-bent mission, this kind of courage had its disadvantages. He had thrown all caution to the winds. Okani picked up his gun and followed him, doubling his steps to catch up with him.

At the backyard, Elesi was filled with consternation when he saw almost all the Nkwokos, including women, gathered together, not battle-ready and looking like a people waiting for the end. When the women saw him, they raised their voices and cried in a gesture of seeking shelter in him. The men, their heads bent, were unable to look at him.

Their weakness, their faithlessness, their cowardice filled Elesi with the greatest scorn possible. He had always believed that the presence of an Nkwoko man had a dislocating effect on the Ekemas. He had seen this happen before, at least three times since the beginning of this violence.

In one such experience, he had taken three men to reconnoitre the enemy grounds,but unfortunately, they ran into a group of Ekema warriors, about twenty of them. His men had wanted to turn and flee, but a strange force had drawn Elesi to the warriors. From their position, the Ekemas could count the number of Elesi's men and yet they left their position and fled. He had begun to believe that with courage (which he thought that his people had), this would always happen. But where was courage today? To him, the only deserving way to talk to them was to shoot as many of them as possible, but then, he removed the idea from his mind.

"Okani", he finally called, "let us go". When Okani moved, Ukpo sprang to his feet and ran after him. The men of Nkwoko, imbued with fresh courage followed Elesi as he went to confront the Ekemas.

The Ekemas were confounded when they saw the great Elesi approaching them with his kinsmen. They could see that he had no gun. And the people with him also had no guns.

Perhaps they wanted to make peace thought the captain of the Ekemas. But the determined look in Elesi's eyes made him speak fast.

"Stop there Elesi or I will shoot and kill you".

Elesi, with his kinsmen continued moving towards the Ekemas. It would take any of them too much courage to kill him, he thought, but he was prepared to die anyway. The chapter on this war must be concluded today if there was need. Why had not anybody been killed since the outbreak of hostilities? Elesi thought. Seven months ago, the Ekemas had stormed their village, routed them and harrased them, but had not taken any victim. This was evidence of their cowardice. They broke the law and yet they were afraid of the law. Several times, they had gone to the police to allege that Nkwokos had kidnapped, killed or maimed one of their brothers. The police chief knew Elesi very well, and since investigations did not substantiate these claims, the chief had suggested to Elesi that the Ekemas trumped up the allegations for fear of actually wounding or killing an Nkwoko,so that they could plead retaliation. He therefore warned Elesi to be careful.

Elesi remembered the captain of the Ekemas very well. He remembered the day his mother came to him and fell on her knees to plead for the release of her son,this captain. Then, Elesi unable to cope with the alarming cases of wanton destruction meted on Nkwokos by Ekema youths, had arranged with his friend in the army to come and conscript them, and save the village of the vermin.

"Your son is in the service of government, and I have nothing to do with his being there", he told the captain's mother. He had let her go in peace because,once, about that time, she had cornered him by the stream and confessed her sympathy and those of other Ekema women with him. "I wish we were men! when we speak, they

13

dismiss us as worthless items," she had lamented. She even prayed for him that day.

This captain, her son, was as rotten, as bestial and as ruthless as the rest of their menfolk. Elesi could only feel hate for him as he approached. As if by a sign, the rest of the Nkwokos stopped about fifteen yards from the Ekemas. Only Okani and Elesi continued to advance towards the Ekemas. The Ekemas also stood a distance from their captain.

Elesi was big, but the captain of the Ekemas was a giant. No one was in doubt what would happen if he and Elesi engage in physical combat, but as they said, strength was of different varieties. Miracle was strength in its own right.

When Elesi and Okani came within three feet of the captain, Elesi jumped at him, going for his neck. But the captain was nimble. A sudden flash revealed a long knife in his hand. Without wasting a second, he hit Elesi with the knife.

Elesi tried to avert the blow, but it was hopeless. The knife caught his hip, but it did not open his body. The force of the blow threw the knife off the captain's hand. Elesi, disdaining pain, crouched as he was, dashed for the captain again. This time, he caught his huge legs and pulled him down.

As these two men struggled, Nkwokos and Ekemas watched with trepidation. It was as though their fates depended on the outcome of the clash between their captains. It was then that Okani moved.

He picked up the fallen sword. Moving straight to the struggling men, he struck the Ekema's captain a most deadly blow. The knife cut clean through the biceps to the bone. The sight was sickening, a demoralizing spectacle for Ekemas. Their captain was now hamstrung and was crying and writhing with pain.

14

Nkwokos made bold for the attack with their guns and knives which were strapped to their backs. The Ekemas fled before them, leaving behind their wounded captain. This was the last time that there was such a war. Ekemas learnt to resort to acceptable ways of dispute resolution,

And the people of Nkwoko sang with joy.

Ekema screams Elesi awake,
But when Okani wakes,
The earth shall quake,
Ekema stirs the lion from sleep,
But when Elesi yawns
Blood shall flow.

Elesi is a warrior
Okani is a wonder
Elesi is the battle
Okani is the baffle

Two men burdened with strain,
Men who won with strength.

Thus the people of Nkwoko rejoiced on their victory over Ekemas.

It was the far-sung Okani who now stood before the village assembly to defend himself against the charge of theft levelled against him by Emeruo, Elesi's brother. Everybody expected fire and brimestone, and would have understood it. But Okani spoke with his normal voice.

"My fathers", he began. "If I tell you that I am disturbed by Emeruo's allegations, then know that I am a fool. This is so because this village trusts in me. However, what bothers me is the possible motive behind it. Only a tree hears that it will be cut down and stands to see if the threat is real. When you wake up in the morning and the first thing you see is a cock pursuing after you, run my brother because cocks are known to spring teeth at night.

"That I sent my daughter to Emeruo's farm to pluck palm fruits on the day her suitors came is true. We had very little in the house, and that morning, I had seen two very ripe palmheads in Emeruo's farm. I asked his wife's permission before my daughter plucked them.

"I should say I am surprised hearing what Emeruo has just said. He is my favourite uncle among his mates living in the village here. I will not hide anything from all of you. I respect him and believe that everything for which I am known since the war, are as a result of his guidance. We have lent each other money, we transacted business together, and so many other things we have done together. What do these palmheads mean to the man who has in his chest all my secrets now as he sits there?

"There is more to this than meets the eye. Only one week ago, I would have said without exaggeration that I could trust Emeruo with my own life. And of course, he knows enough about me to cause me trouble if he want to, but I shall no more trust my safety with him unless we get at the root of this matter. We are a small people, a people hated for our industry and our will to survive. Divided, we will fall ... a great fall. I am prepared to make up with Emeruo, to call him brother to trust him again as before, for if I can't trust him again, it would be difficult to trust any other man again; if only he would say the motive behind his accusations". Okani was almost preaching a sermon.

"This village is built on love. Since I was born, I have never seen anybody called a rogue for taking palm fruits from his brother's farm. It is true that I plucked up to two palmheads. True it is big, but how couldn't I, knowing the man who owned it? I deny completely the allegation that I tried to kill the palm tree, neither did my daughter. That accusation, I do not know from where it came. My brothers, this is about all I have to say".

16

One woman was so moved by Okani's defence that she hissed loudly. "Ee wee" she said.

This incurred her the wrath of three chiefs.

"Who is this beast of the forest doing this?", they thundered. The other two chiefs backed off when they saw that Ukpo was also on his feet.

Ukpo combined charisma, and wealth to make a formidable force in Nkwoko. He was respected by everyone in the village and many feared him, including old men like himself. In the absence of Elesi, Ukpo represented the strongest force in this meeting.

He was still scowling at the woman who had hissed.

"Do you realise that people do not display such petty behaviour in the presence of elders and Nzes who hold the *ofos* of their fathers?". He shook his head,"Surely a man who plays with a hen matchès on excreta. Perhaps this was why our fathers forbade women from attending such assemblies, much more talking in them. Ask Ekemma what would have happened to you if it were in the olden days ..."

The old woman, Ekemma, made to support Ukpo, but he cut her short with a flick of his hand. Ukpo did not like interruption, when he was enforcing discipline. Not even when it was meant to support him.

The unfortunate woman felt the glare of eyes on her. Gradually her eyes misted and big tears rolled down her cheeks. She began to wipe them with the end of her wrapper, cutting a pitiable sight as she did.

Ukpo was perspicacious. Picking the cue of rising sympathy in favour of the woman, he said in a bland voice, "Woman, you may stay here, but we want no further trouble from you".

The woman nodded and cheered up with a good smile.

Ukpo saw Umeike, Okani's father waving his hand frantically, wanting to say something. Ukpo did not want to comment on this matter yet. There were so many things to it, hidden things which would surely come afloat if one had patience, for on the face of what had been said so far, this matter seemed ridiculous. But a frog did not jump in the afternoon for nothing.

" Yes Umeike," said Ukpo as he sat down. Umeike was a smallish man whose crass failure in life was an antithesis of Okani's life. He rarely spoke in village assemblies. This habit, he cultivated when he noticed that people did not pay attention when he spoke. If by coincidence, he stood up at the same time with another person to say something, he was expected to sit down. Nobody in this assembly except maybe his sons would defer to him under that circumstance, nor would they listen to him if he insisted on speaking. Nobody ever shouted at him, but through some secret sign, they diverted attention to the other man. Even Okani's greatness could not help his father. Umeike's unsuccessful attempt to change this situation made him to accept his position at the bottom of the pecking order. You could not fight a man who did not openly quarrel with you, much more an entire village. There was a time when the village pleaded with him to be moderate and tactful about the things that he said and the way he said them. When he did not listen to them, they lost interest in him. Because he was treated cavalierly, he became morose and taciturn, but that seemed to aggravate the situation further. People moved further away from him. "A silent man was as dangerous as a rattlesnake", said the village. It was his wife who warned him of the consequences of extreme retraction from the society. This problem, he solved by cultivating a comical manner of behaviour, such that the sight of him alone could amuse. Children thought him the happiest man in the world, but adults knew that he was foolish and billious.

"Wh-Wh-when we a-a-are ..." His attempt at speech **was a** fumbling attempt. Children giggled all around

18

thinking that he wanted to introduce some lightness into an already dense atmosphere.

"Shut up you rascally children". Okpara warned. The children could not understand that he was in difficulty, that this was not simulation, but real stammering. The older men who grew up with him and knew that he once stammered as a child waited for him, refusing to join in the laughter. Umeike took a deep breath, determined to relax, to go it more slowly, perhaps better this time.

Why not? He wanted to defend his only son who gave his life the little meaning that it had. A son who did virtually everything for him. It was Okani who gave him money with which he took the *ozo* title for which people at least had patience with him, and for which he could stand up without fear of being shouted down. It was because of his son that people greeted him and called him "Sir". A "Sir" was a "sir" whether you meant it or not.

"Is is not true", Umeike finally said "that only a stranger admires us for our lies? Sounding his finger for us? A brother does not admire his brother's lies, no matter how beautifully they are painted. Don't we know Emeruo and what he is capable of? We are in no doubt whatever about his abilities, but he has lied great lies today".

Umeike's voice was rising, beads of sweat forming on his brow and nose.

"To call my son a thief, a common thief who stole palm fruits in my very presence is the greatest insult I have suffered in my life. My son ... my great son calls him a friend, I think my son a fool to regard such a one as a friend. When we see greed and jealousy, don't we notice it anymore or are there no more people with eyes keen enough to see through this shameful show?

Everybody was worried about the direction in which Umeike's speech was going, but so far it was not offensive, perhaps merely chiding.

"W ...When I speak now, you will say that I have spoken again. Why are we wasting time on such a case. Nobody can stampede us with threats about going to court. If the scrotum itches too much, better take it out in the sun —"

"Stop it..." came a yell from among the crowd. Umeike was startled. It was Emeruo with murderous rage in his eyes.

"Stop that nonsense. Everybody in this village would learn from this. They will learn not to bandy words with me. I am going to teach Okani and his father a lesson they will never forget ..."

Umeike was still standing confused, unprotected by anybody against Emeruo's jarring voice.

"Emeruo ... stop that", Okpara said as he stood up to bring the situation under control.

"This has never happened before", said Ukpo as he stood up too. But Emeruo's voice towered above theirs.

"Who is Umeike that he should so address me? What makes his head swell like that? What has he and his family ever contributed to this village. Perhaps, only in the area of what the land forbids. Your great grandfather was a rogue, his son a nonentity", Emeruo said staring into Okani's eyes. "We have seen your father. How can people of such lowly bearing talk to me, and the elders of this village indulge them and listen to them. I know now what I must do. Everybody here must know that I don't need anybody's advice or guidance in doing what I must do, so let nobody at all bother me further". After this, he turned and walked out of the meeting.

While Emeruo was vituperating, Okani wanted to teach him a lesson. He wanted to give him the beating of his life. At his age, it must surely be the beating of his life. But, Yim, who sat close to Okani and saw him start to rise when Emeruo was staring at him, held him down.

"Be a man and sit still my son", Yim had told him. "Don't we know you in this village? There is something very dark in the sky. It is more than the coming of rain. Don't soil your hands with blood my son". Okani hardly heard Yim, but he took whatever he said and cooled off.

Before the assembly dispersed, the elders held that Okani was not guilty of Emeruo's charges against him, that Emeruo treated the village assembly with contempt, for which he was fined two hundred naira. He was mandated to apologise publicly to the village assembly and to Okani in particular.

But somehow, the entire assembly knew that that was not the end of the matter. It was obvious that Emeruo was not going to accept their ruling. But to speak the right thing was necessary to all of them. If a child had not yet seen something in a mysterious parcel, he would be anxious to see its contents, but when those mysteries were bared to his young eyes, he would beg that the parcel might be covered with speed.

Suddenly, the sky took on a bluish grey, growing darker, fast, until it thundered. Simultaneously the sky opened its lid to weep the failure of Nkwoko people. The pelting rain made them scamper to their homes, where they considered with heavy hearts, the import of the day's assembly.

Chapter 2

In his residence in Ikoyi, Chuby was lying on a divan, propped up on one elbow and staring at Betty, almost with hate. Betty's svelte body lay on the big brass bed in the centre of the room, a very big room and a very clean one. The dominant colour everywhere was grey. The rug, the wall, the paintings by Enweonwu, everything, except the contrast made by the brass and chrome finishings. The finishings and the huge mirror on the wall were polished to a brilliant sheen everyday. There were also beautiful flowers held by quaint looking pots. It was a room affordable only by the really affluent.

Today was another failure, Chuby thought as he looked at his watch. Shortly, he would be holding an important meeting with a friend.

Betty was slightly ruffled from the struggle which had been going on between them.

They had been lovers once in school, and later lost contact for no apparent reason. They just stopped seeing each other after they left school.

Since their re-union, this was Betty's fifth visit, and she had refused Chuby's advances of intimacy, to his amazement and discomfort.

She really loved and wanted him, but at her age, she could not afford a casual relationship with a man. There were also things on her mind. Stories from fellow high fliers, about Chuby's astonishing escapades with women. She also remembered how they met.

In school, Betty was a friend to Chuby's girlfriend, Rosa. It was during one of Rosa's long trips away from school that Chuby started dating Betty.

Betty mounted a campaign against Chuby. She avoided him in circumstances that might encourage him to press hard for her friendship. In fact she avoided both Chuby and Rosa.

His reaction was shocking but decisive. He severed his relationship with Rosa and came to Betty. But Betty would not hear of such a thing. The gossip would be too much for her to handle. Yet her decision had telling consequences on Chuby.

It was his long depression that made Betty come close to him again, a re-union that left Rosa without pride and without friends. She confided in a friend that God had created an empty world without Chuby. When Betty saw her after the last paper of their degree examination, she had sworn to make her pay for the gash she had opened in her very soul. Betty had stared at her, tongue-tied. It was the last time she ever saw her. She had left school with a phobia for men and she was determined to forget her and Chuby. Subsequent events in her life made her suspect that she was destined to a bad life. She began life as an actress in a T.V. soap, *The Raptures* in which she gained stardom. Thereafter, men buzzed about her the way bees buzzed about honey. Yet she had been successful in evading the most rapacious lechers in their business, her talent being her trump card.

One of her bosses nearly succeeded. Learning that she was the reserved type, he had conducted himself so well that Betty accepted attending dinners and parties with him. Things were working out for them until she caught him at the Holiday Inn, in the bossom of a notorious whore. That was it. And since then, Betty had kept to herself,

23

until one day she met Chuby's sister, Annie, while shopping around Tinubu Square. Through Annie, she had re-united with Chuby.

Up to her third visit, Chuby had played the gentleman to her delight. She would come, they would eat, talk, hug and kiss, watch television or video films if there was time, and he would take her home, after a slight hint which she usually put down. She was happy with him but she was not in a hurry to make love with him. But Chuby did not like playing the gentleman, not with a girl who had been his lover once. He played cool because of her highly reserved posturing.

As time wore on, he started having second thoughts. Did she mean that she had no boyfriend at that time, or even that she had had no boyfriend ever since she came to Lagos? This was unthinkable to him. People of Betty's standing, especially people in her line of business did not behave that way, especially those of them who lived in Lagos. Lagos could turn the most decent of men into unscrupulous porcupines. Saints became scoundrels there. It was the most active city in Africa. It reeked of everything, the high fliers and the high borns, the affluent with their high falutin manners, the intelligentsia with their pedantry. Businessmen, money bags, as they were called, diplomats, everything, not excluding the wretched who were in the majority. Lagos represented the centre of Nigeria's greedy money tradition.

Could Betty remain here and still be a saint? Here men were willing to pay any price for women that meant nothing to them, much more when it came to people who really mattered, and by every standard, Betty mattered.

For the most advanced lechers, love was unnecessary. What counted was how many women that one ravished. The ranks of the women also counted, for it could boost one's ego when mentioned in conversation with other men. A newly seduced lady meant another stripe to their

24

already overflowing and superfluous honours. An object of display which had long lost its meaning to the wearer.

Chuby not only felt rejected by Betty, he also felt dull with her. Experience, that reliable teacher, had taught him that a woman's "no" meant "yea". God! Women claimed to know everything that made a relationship work. One had tried to convince him that lovemaking was unnecessary in a relationship, but when they broke up without having made love, she went about town telling people that she was proud of one thing, that they did not really have a relationship, because he did not sleep with her. All this did not apply to Betty because they were once lovers, but it made Chuby confused how to decipher her true feelings.

During her third visit, Chuby had acted up, holding her hands down, pressuring her, trying to kiss or touch the erogenous zones of her body.

"Behave yourself Chuby", Betty had told him firmly. He still tried, but at the height it, it had been disastrous for both of them. Betty had called his behaviour immature and ungentlemanly. Then Chuby slipped into a silence that was strange even to his nature. For the first time since their re-union, the air about them was charged. That day however passed without a showdown.

Her fourth visit was even more strained. Somehow, in a complex inexplicable way, Chuby had developed an obsessive craving for this woman, an obsessive discomfort that only a sexual intimacy with her could quench. His inability to realize this goal put a question mark on his abilities. Everything he did this season was judged with regard to his success with Betty. That he loved her was undoubtable. He had not slept with another woman since she came back into his life, not even with the girl who had been his regular companion after he came to live in Lagos. He wanted more than just sleeping with her, but her behaviour gave him every reason to resent

25

her. He thought love was an understanding thing. This time again, the strange quietude surfaced. After she left, he promised himself to do it the next time and bear the consequences.

Today, which was her fifth visit, they had struggled so very greatly to a point where Chuby hated himself. He knew that he was making her uncomfortable, that he was not presenting a good image of himself, he wanted to stop, but it felt like losing a war. Betty's strongest weapon was her calculated criticisms of him. Chuby now so annoyed, lost his craving for her. He lost his erection. At this, he left her on the bed and went over to the divan.

She needed more than physical coercion to soften, he told himself. He stared at her vacuously. There was an unsettling emptiness about his face. His mouth was twisted and projected in a form that looked like self pity. He cut the image of a man decided on what to do. He even seemed relaxed now. It was the uncertainty of his feeling that worried Betty.

He turned his gaze on the thick grey carpet. This girl was beautiful and she had character. He never really admired a woman unless she possessed facial character. Betty had everything and more - a freshness of skin and sumptuousness of bearing that left him hungry.

She must make up her mind about it today ... or else ...

He looked at his watch. He had less than forty minutes before his friend would arrive.

He stood up and walked to the wardrobe and selected a fresh shirt without speaking to her. The expression on his face bothered her. Unconsciously, her face showed worry and fear. She was staring askance at him.

He quickly caught the change of expression and his mind began to search through their long ago relationship. He could not remember the exact event, but he remembered once, when she had made him to tell her, in a

26

fit of anger, to leave him and never see him again how she had literally knelt down to obtain his pardon. It was the look on her face that day that he saw her wearing now.

He poised for attack. Just as he wanted to speak, he heard her say, "why are you not talking to me again?"

"Please, leave me alone"

"What ?"

"Do not bother me with questions now, okay?" His voice was flat.

His reaction to her annoyed her. What kind of a man would behave this way simply because a woman refused to sleep with him, his former lover for that matter? Did not her constant visits prove that she liked him? loved him? Only she needed time to sort herself out. He should be tamed for their good.

"I don't really understand. It is simply difficult to reconcile your behaviour with you. This is the evidence of the communication gap between us. Can you not understand that I simply ... I do not feel the way you feel, at least for now. I need time to sort -"

"Let me tell you", he interrupted. ".Your homily about feeling is unnecessary. It is no reason at all. How can you reconcile your declaration of love for me and your persistent disregard for the things that I like?"

"I have no disregard whatever for the things you like Chuby. We are talking about only one thing". He ignored her, pursuing his trend of thought doggedly. "I say this because I know that if our feelings, our wishes were to be reversed, you would expect me to play along with you. I am certain that I will do it without much prompting from you, even though I might not necessarily want it at that time. You see, love is not something that one enters with preconceived notions and attitudes, or even with certain aims in mind. In relationships where purposes play a role, one could haggle over feelings and actions. We want to enter them from a position of strength.

27

"True love, Betty is flexibility, give and take. It is a preparedness to harmonize attitudes. Flexibility and preparedness are thus the only dispositions required, not tailored values and feelings."

Betty frowned, unprepared to suffer philosophical ambiguities. "I have learnt to respect the things that give me happiness Chuby. Perhaps that is the disposition that I have brought with me. Do not expect me to do things that would hurt me in order to please you... I don't want to please you and displease myself".

Now that they were talking, it pleased Chuby. If he could lay bare her selfishness, make her see it, it might help matters. But how long did they have? Not much time before his friend, Ikwu Otuonye, arrived.

"Lady, pleasing sounds frivolous. It is like attending to somebody's fancies. But helping somebody always involves some inconvenience on our part. Lovers always help each other in anything".

"Agreed Chuby, but where do you draw the line between pleasing and helping somebody. From your position it would seem that we inconvenience ourselves in helping people because we feel a great need, a great demand on us. But in this case, is your wish so important that it cannot wait?"

"Lovers are lovers because they construe their relationship in terms of help. This of course includes pleasing one's partner because those fancies, those cares are what really bring happiness. Look, love is not meaningful only when you enjoy it. I have seen people who would complain when invited to a party, but when dragged to it, they have a wonderful ball. In love, we learn to share experiences spontaneously".

How wrong he was, she thought. This was the problem with men who always mirrored life from a logical prism. Somehow however she was pleased for his patience and effort, trying to convince her about this, and

28

she loved his mind. Those complex connections that it made, always wriggling out of apparent absurdities. Yet this quality of mind was wickedness too. He often played fair and foul with it. She was still in thought when she heard him.

"Come let me take·you home". His tone was so detached, so unfamiliar that she was now ready to capitulate, to accept anything to save their relationship.That moment, her father's voice sounded in her ears. "Daughter, when you are tired in an effort, when you feel like giving up, that is the time of victory ... for you". For me? she thought. A click in her mind told her "yes"

She braced herself, stood up and walked to the huge mirror where she started combing out her hair.

They drove in silence all the way to her home, his face was solidly rooted on the road, unsmiling.

"When do I see you again?" she asked him as she opened the door to leave.

Silence.

"When are you seeing me? " she asked again.

Chuby was still sulking, expecting to be mothered and cradled.

"May be we should have a break Betty. I need time to sort myself out too. We need a break ..." he said roughly.

Betty didn't hear the last sentence. She eased herself out of the car, and gave the door a heavy slam. She walked off into her house, without looking back.

He came out of the car and rushed after her. Before he could reach her, she was already in her flat and her door was locked. He banged on it until she opened it.

"What is it Chuby? What do you want again?" She said with annoyance. He stared at her, an unbelieving expression on his face.

"I want to help you ..."

"I don't need your help ..."

"Stop it ... please. There is something wrong with you Chuby. When I once knew you, you were reckless, but not wicked. You have changed a lot, perhaps by letting your business mentality spill over into all your other relationships. You have shown me the worst kind of meanness today. But I want to tell you one last thing before you leave now".

Chuby's eyes opened wide, and gradually narrowed to slits as he started listening to this woman.

"Love and friendship do not mean different things to me Chu. Sometimes, I prefer friendship to love. A lover who is also a friend is best. It gives me a feeling of sobriety and safety. The giving notion of love, if taken to extreme amounts to craziness. A lover or friend is not someone who does not disagree with you. She is not someone who does the things that you like always. The true test of friendship is in the conflict of interests. Only people who trust each other can sail through at such times ... But even now, our interests do not conflict. I only asked for time, but you said you wanted it now... Now Chuby close that door.You are going to have me in so much quantity that you will tire ... Now Chuby".Betty challenged him.

Chuby looked at her face, it was filled with concern for him, but not enthusiasm. He felt ashamed for being so immature, so ungentlemanly. He tried so smile, he tried to move close to her, he tried to say something.

"I love you so much darling". He said in a contrite voice. Involuntarily, she reached out for his face, her two hands by his ears and kissed him. Their kiss had a salty taste. When they disentangled, they saw tears in their eyes.

"I am very sorry", he said again.

"Okay," she said with a beautiful smile. "I shall treat you here tomorrow since you must rush off to a meeting now or won't you"?

"Tomorrow darling". Replied Chuby.

He flew down the stairs. He was still singing "Tomorrow darling" when he entered his house.

*　　　　　*　　　　　*

"Sorry for being late", Chuby told a man seated in his sitting room, waiting for him. He seemed to have forgotten which of his friends had asked to see him today. But when the man spoke, the confusion was cleared.

"Oh! no problem sir" answered Ikwu Otuonye.

Chuby surveyed his friend as they shook hands. His thinness had caused Chuby not to recognize him when he entered. He did not like his condition. Should he tell him the truth and advise him to rest more and eat better food or should he take the traditional approach, and pretend that nothing was wrong and let him sort himself out for fear of aggravating his condition?

"Ha Ikwu! You have been running around without much rest. You don't look healthy to me at all. I am sure you need a lot of rest. I hope everything is alright?"

"My brother, what is mightier than the cricket has entered his hole. I am a troubled man ... on the run, my friend, and I won't stop till my pursuer stops".

"What is all this?", Chuby asked, feeling sorry for his friend. A torrent of words issued from Ikwu's mouth.

"I am sorry to be troubling you now, but it is the last thing left for me to do. I will not own a tomtom and yet for music, beat on my belly. When the skin itches an animal, it scratches it on a bark. But a man goes to a fellow man to scratch his body for him ....".

"Listen Ikwu ..." Chuby cut in, uncomfortable in his friend's repertoire of proverbs. In the village where oratory was greatly prized, where the wise and virtuous chiefs had the time and the patience to follow a man's trail of thought, no matter how he rigmaroled, proverbs were understood, in fact respected. Chuby preferred straight talk.

31

"... I received your letter, and accepted to see you", he told Ikwu. "I also, am a man. Position and money open doors, but I have problems also ... many that people solve for me. Now feel free to tell me everything on your mind".

Ikwu was encouraged, he cleared his throat. "It is the shrine".

"What about the shrine?"

"It has been pulled down, destroyed. Those four hefty cows, those cows which I grew to see were all murdered. The problem is, the god is missing".

For one minute, Chuby was confused and unable to think. He was stupefied. Then the full implication of this report hit him. This was the most heinous and atrocious crime imaginable. How could a human being for any reason attack a shrine? This was the sublimity of evil. Chuby was not a pagan. He was a Christian and he went to Church, yet he knew he could not have sanctioned the destruction of a sacred shrine.

Looking at Ikwu now, he pitied him. He could see why he was worried. A priest of a stolen god. The entire world would be waiting for the god to react; to fight for itself and the person that would be answering questions emanating from this universal expectation was Ikwu.

Chuby could now visualize the shrine well, even the village of Uda, Ikwu's home village. Ikwu's family had erected their houses right up to the brink of the only accessible side of the gully wherein Okpoko dwelt, from where they kept a strict watch against trespassers. The house of the priest was along the narrow and tortuous entrance path where stood an old rectangular mud building with thatches as covering. This building housed many of the important things with which the priest had ministered to Okpoko. Drums of great sizes, also *ekwe* and *ogene* with which different signals were sent to the villagers or litigants who always came for the judgment of the Oracle.

Further down, one reached a leafy bower under which Okpoko stayed. It was a remarkable sight hewn from a single block of iroko and showed sign of great age. At the back of Okpoko ran a stream which quenched the thirst of Uda people and cooked their food.

Chuby had gone to Uda because one of his business associates, an old man who had wanted to loan him money had insisted that they go to Uda to swear by Okpoko that none of them would disappoint each other. Chuby had suggested that a lawyer would not only give their agreement legal backing but would also reduce the strain and uncertainty of going to swear by a deity. But the man had stunned him when he told him that he hated seeing lawyers. "What we are going to do is more than an agreement, it binds us now and forever".

Chuby needed the money which he had tried to raise from other sources to no avail. And so had gone to Uda with the man. There, he saw a lot of things that appealed to his soul.

The shrine provided jobs to many sons and daughters of Uda who served as guides to myriad of visitors and litigants who flooded there; or they were hands of the priest. Followers of Okpoko had immense respect, trust and confidence in each other. This experience they shared with outsiders who visited the shrine. Because of the significance of the man who had taken Chuby to Uda, he was allowed to observe many aspects of life at the shrine. Chuby later became a frequent patron, anytime he was in the East. There, he promised Okpoko's ministers that they could always come to him for any help they felt he could render them. At that time Chuby had construed this in terms of money.

"What have your people done?"

"My people, you mean Uda people?" said Chuby, his eyes had suddenly turned bloodshot. He shook his head again and again. He was mad at his people. They had

33

behaved like the myopic fowl who forgot the man who had pulled its tail during the rainy season, and the consequences had become apparent. "We are suffering now. I fear that Okpoko's hand is upon us. When the shrine got destroyed, we were all with one heart determined to seek and find and destroy whosoever had done it. We all knew the importance of the god in our lives and so we went everywhere together searching, demanding for the denunciation and punishment of the evil doers. We went to the police, we went to the government, we took our case even to the churches. But there is this priest in Uda who suddenly saw in our effort an attempt to bring back paganism. This priest started preaching against our efforts to our people. 'If they are gods, let them save themselves' he had said. And he threatened to throw out of the church anybody who got involved in the attempt to recover Okpoko. Our people became afraid. They abandoned the course except a few elders who still fight with me. Even the chief of Uda who holds the *Ofo* of our ancestors was cowered by this pronouncement.

"But as I stand here talking to you, the stream of Uda is dried up. We now drink from muddy brooks which are fast drying up. This is happening in the midst of the rainy season. The old priest to whom I shifted my duty to Okpoko has since lost an eye in mysterious circumstances and our village is at the edge of war with our neighbours over a land dispute. My own business is completely shattered. Since that incident, I have not been able to sell a single article in my store. For this I have closed my business and I am now permanently in the village to look after this trouble. I feared for the worst. Some of us are beginning to see through these events, Okpoko's shadow. They come to me secretly and tell me to do something and I try. I really try but many people are unwilling to help. And then I remembered you as one of the few educated people who had visited the shrine. I remembered our relationship with you and I decided to write you to seek your help in solving this problem which is clearly bigger than my head.

"My mind tells me that this thing was done by the people of Ariobi. In the olden days, their Oracle was the most powerful god in all our tribe. People came from areas far beyond their influence, to worship him and had their cases decided by him. However, with the coming of *oyibo*, the Oracle lost its control over the people. But even with the loss of this control, no god was able to challenge him until the gods in their wisdom passed this control over to us, to Okpoko, the god of my fathers of which I am a priest, though I shifted the responsibility to another man in our village.

"Since the rise of Okpoko, people have come to tell me about plots by the people of Ariobi to destroy Okpoko in order to enthrone their god again. They could not accept the fact that a law did not rule forever. It changes with time, so is the wisdom of gods. The Ariobis, I think are responsible for this deed".

Chuby was greatly astounded by Ikwu's story but the story looked too neat to be true. "What makes you believe what you are saying is true? How can the destruction of Okpoko immediately enthrone the Ariobi shrine?" He asked.

Ikwu's answer contained some plausible clues. He seemed to have given a lot of thought to the problem. "First", he said, "the rumours. Then, they accused us of masterminding a malicious gossip against them; that we went about telling people that they murdered people in their shrine".

"How? Why?" Chuby inquired.

"Maybe it was guilt, more likely to discredit us by making us seem like liars. Funny, the same old system. Actually many, people who visited their shrine in the olden days never came back alive. Most of them were trapped by the deity ... you get?"

Chuby looked very ignorant.

"Have you ever visited Ariobi?" IKwu asked him.

"No". Chuby answered, momentarily uncomfortable with this enterprise which put him in the perspective of a dunce.

Ikwu seemed to have noticed this but he did not comment on it. It was absurd that he knew little or nothing of these matters. The Ariobi Oracle was clearly the most popular in their tribe. He was now determined to get to the point of his visit.

"There is no point telling you all this, only it may be difficult explaining these things to you. But I'll try".

"No please, tell me about the shrine, how it was in the olden days", said Chuby eagerly.

"Okay. In Ariobi, at the shrine, there are two mats on which disputants must sit where upon the case between them is determined. Today, you may be sure that these mats are spread on solid flooring. In the olden days, it was different. Then, one of the mats was a pitfall. Under this mat, some men supported an unfavoured client with a round table which they removed at an appropriate sign from their collaborators, thereby collecting the mat and the unfortunate victim in a deep pit. To the relations and enemies of the victim, they understood that their brother or contender was dead. People who died this way were believed to have told lies to the deity. So as their relatives left, seeing their blood flowing from a gutter on their way out, they mourned or despised them".

This story was as horrifying as it was disillusioning to Chuby. "Are you saying that this shrine regarded as the most powerful authority in our tribe at that time was all wicked and fake?" He asked.

"That is not it. I don't really know whether it was just fake, but remember that power and glory cover a lot

36

of dirty things. They might not have done that in all the cases. Usually one could do that where one party was more powerful than the other. That place was feared and revered because people died there. Many people who went there never suspected foul play. They were fascinated by the ability of the shrine to give instant justice. This in fact forced many people to speak the truth before they came to the shrine. Nobody wanted to die. The dirty lie which they told against us nearly destroyed our shrine. It cost us a lot to handle the matter".

"Since then, there have been rumours that the Ariobis planned to attack our shrine, but I found it difficult to believe, until it happened".

Chuby thought about what his friend said and shuddered. He had never heard of such things before. As a child, he had always detested stories about gods and tradition because it made him grope backward into his past which he never wanted to. This perhaps could explain his paucity of knowledge about these things. He could not believe that shrines and gods sanctioned wars against one another. But then, all of what Ikwu had said amounted to circumstantial evidence, a weighty one, he had to agree. Other possibilities struck him. "Have you thought about art syndicates, who might be interested in stealing your god?" He asked his friend.

That is out of the question", Ikwu replied. "Why would they want to destroy the shrine, to murder the sacred cows if all they came for was the god?" Ikwu asked tearfully. "This problem is larger than my head," he resumed, "and I have come to you to help me".

Chuby was thinking seriously. He knew that solving a problem like this involved understanding it properly, but no understanding came to his mind presently. He was still thinking when a door at the dining area opened and a creamy pretty girl emerged, and announced to Chuby that food was ready. To Ikwu she was the most beautiful woman in the world. Chuby immediately remembered that he had not offered Ikwu anything. "Oh! Forgive me Ikwu. We have been here all this time and I have not offered you anything even kolanut".

Before Ikwu could reply, – he would have protested that this matter did not permit kolanut or any refreshments, Chuby told his sister to bring them food, surprised that she was still in the house. He had expected to see Alex his cook and house boy as Annie had said she had a date with somebody.

As Annie placed the food on the table for them, Chuby said, "I thought you were supposed to be having fun with your friend somewhere, what happened?"

She giggled. "Well, it did not work out, I told you that it would not".

"He didn't turn up?"

"He did, but what I saw in his eyes frightened me". Chuby was utterly perplexed "What?" He asked his sister.

"Falcon, he had the eyes of a falcon".

"Where have you ever you seen a falcon?" Chuby asked his sister.

"I know what falcons are supposed to be, trained birds of prey. I don't need to see one to know one".

Was Annie normal at all? Chuby thought. Every other thing that she did, she did well, except relating with men. Since she graduated from university and came to stay with him, she had not been able to maintain a relationship with any man, acquiring and discarding them like a fastidious dresser, before he ever wore the clothes out. Chuby would have understood, but she was always finding faults with men, with almost all. A friend Chuby once confided in had said that she had a spirit husband that lived in the river bed and so the mysterious aquatic man would not let her keep a man above him. Annie never seemed worried, but it worried Chuby.

Her newest date, a strikingly handsome young man was good enough for any woman. This Annie told her brother when she first brought him to their house. Chuby was happy until she started visioning about his eyes. First she had come in one day and called him 'kite-eyes', Chuby had been confounded. What was wrong with his sister? Now, a falcon.

"What a beautiful sister you have!" Said Ikwu, interrupting Chuby's thoughts, "I wish I had a brother educated enough to marry her".

"As if you knew". Said Chuby. "She is really out for gentlemen".

When Annie left them, Chuby laughed inside. Despite everything, she still thought him a great man. She had once told him that she preferred gentlemen like him who can take care of their women. "What do you mean by gentlemen?" Chuby had asked. "I mean guys who can take care of their women".

"Yes, behave nicely, decently, with finesse and not run around with women". At this, Chuby had kept quiet. He was not sure whether he really fit the description. But Chuby knew that was not Annie's problem. She needed a trusting, respecting and friendly man.

The sweet aroma of the food in front of them made their stomachs rumble. They fell to the wholesome meal with determination as if Ikwu's problem had drained the blood out of them. He wished that Betty could cook like 'his even more. Well, he would try her out tomorrow. Chuby was really grateful for Ikwu's company. Tomorrow was a day too far, his day, "our day" Betty had told him. He needed something as serious as Ikwu's problem to keep his mind off her.

When they finished eating and were drinking, Chuby asked Ikwu to tell him how the whole thing happened.

"Ah! It was so very bad", Ikwu said. "We did not even know. If we had known, ah! We would have fought till the last drops of our blood. That morning, our wives and children went to the stream to fetch water and saw that the shrine had been pulled down. *Njinji jili, ebenebe gbulu.*

"No one knew what to do. It was an experience we had never witnessed before. Even the wise priests of the great gods and the all-knowing medicine men were unprepared for this.

As they talked, Chuby pondered on how best to be of help to his friend. He could understand his friend's feelings but he needed the support of an intellectual equal or a superior to consider this issue more closely. He needed somebody who nurtured interest in this kind of matter. Now he realized that nothing was left of all his grand dreams as a student, of how to help his society grow. He had not cared at all, and this proposition seemed a little idealistic, a little out of his scheme of operation, but he could not refuse this man.

This was an opportunity to reconnect with his old self. As a younger man, he had had great dreams. Dreams that still struck him as authentic. Dreams that dimmed all his material attainments, for by all standards, Chuby was a material success. He was the owner of a multi-million naira construction company, the Fonx International, and other associated businesses.

The disconnection with his old self made Chuby feel that he was a failure in a sense. He could not measure with men who in his younger days had fired his spirit to great thoughts and actions.

His great grandfather was his hero. He was a man loved, respected and hated by his people. He was compassionate. He loved the village and did everything to uplift it. He was wealthy. He had land and many wives and children. He was uncompromising in his beliefs. He single-handedly questioned the outright rejection of traditional values by colonial and missionary powers. He wanted western education for his children, but not western culture and religion. For all this, he came under the greatest ridicule for a man of his position. But he did not budge until his death.

This great man was ostracized by his society, he was deserted by his wives, he was repudiated and denied by his own children, but he kept on. He did not reject his society but still attended their meetings, their funerals, everything that they did, until he died. When he died, he was buried like a fowl.

But with time, with better education, his society's understanding and conception of him changed. They could now wistfully reminisce about his great virtues, his patience, steadfastness and consistency. Chuby's own father was poor, but his knowledge of his great grandfather enriched his soul and mind.

In school, Chuby had heard of the Mahatma Ghandis, the George Washingtons and so on. Thus he had set himself a target, a goal which was to be like these people. Now he could see he could not compete with these people. He had not even performed averagely. This was indeed an opportunity for rediscovery of self.

When Ikwu left, Chuby's mind was resolved to help him. He was determined to do something and fast. Presently, with anxiety caused by the strange nature of this phenomenon, nothing came to his mind. He eventually decided to sleep over the matter. To Chuby, sleep was the bridge between anxiety and solution. And so, he had slept, almost without remembering Betty. But he sure was glad of it.

Chapter 3

She surveyed herself in the mirror on her dressing table with excitement and satisfaction. Her skin was aglow after a long soak in soap mixed with sweet smelling herbs. As she creamed herself, she wished Chuby would come in now and tear off her dressing gown, doing with her whatsoever his mind would devise. Chances were, if he came in now, he would play cool, quelled by her yesterday's remarks, but he need not bother. He was hers to seduce and she waited for that moment with anticipation. She rolled her eyes amorously as she popped minty sweets into her mouth waiting for that ring which would usher him in.

She had left the studios early enough to come home and put things right; many bottles of champagne chilled in the freezer and she had gone to Chicken George on her way back and bought a large roasted chicken which was heating in the oven now. She had prepared salad and of course she had *ora*, *okro* and *egusi* soup in the fridge. There was also stew, so anything at all Chuby wanted, he would get, anything at all.

*   *   *

"You are a great cook" he told her as he ate the last arm of the chicken she had served him. He had commented effusively about the perfectness of everything she had served him and she felt very happy.

"Now let me feed you". She took the chicken from his hand and began feeding him. Chuby took full bites at the chicken which soon became bones.

"I think there's too much oil in it" she said, looking for a napkin to wipe out her hand. An idea suddenly entered her mind. "Suck this oil out darling. She popped a finger into his mouth and Chuby started sucking at the finger. Gradually she moved closer to him following the rhythm of his sucking until she started kissing his ears, cheek, nose and mouth. Soon she was kissing him all over.

Chuby suddenly retrieved himself and pushed her forward, gently but firmly so he could stand up.

"What now darling?" She said in an eager voice.

"My bladder, 'it's weak. Got to pee," he said as he stood up.

She chuckled mischievously as she watched his athletic frame move towards the bathroom. Immediately he entered it, she threw her skirt and shirt away and lay naked on the settee.

When he came back, his eyes were filled with the brightness of her skin.

"You won't leave me tonight?" She asked as he moved closer to her .

"No ...never tonight", he said as his mouth crushed upon hers, his eyes closed as their bodies united in the most electrifying reality of their beings.

*   *   *

Travelling to the East was always a great experience for Chimezie. An experience, leading to vistas of reveries of bygone times, a time he allowed his mind a free float on the events of his life.

Chimezie was Elesi's eldest son. He resided in the North, where he owned a hospital, the Rockfield Specialist Hospital. The hospital matched his earlier dreams of it, big, famous and a centre of excellence.

His vocation as a medical doctor had materialized on the day that the famed late Dr. Emeka Ojagwu came to visit his father at their house. Emeka's appearance was out of the way to his young mind. His dressing, which was very European, was very clean, and he had a flawless manner. Chimezie could not believe he was speaking Igbo, only because he understood him. Chimezie liked everything about the great doctor and more because the doctor showed a keen interest in him.

"What would you like to be my son?" Emeka had asked Chimezie.

"I want to be exactly like you ... I want to be a doctor and help others recover from sickness". Chimezie replied looking with wonder and admiration at Dr. Emeka.

When Elesi emerged from the pantry, where he had gone to fetch some kolanuts for his visitor, he was pleased to see his son seated on Emeka's shoulders, conversing with him.

"Wonderful friends you are!" Elesi exclaimed.

"The chap says that he wants to be a doctor, and he means it. Do encourage him Elesi. With his spirit, the concern I see in him for others, he would make a wonderful doctor".

"But he is only a child", Elesi said. Emeka laughed. "My great friend, how many times do I have to tell you that a man is but an amplification of all that he learnt and cherished as a child ... But you even say it ... that one does not learn to use one's left hand when one is an old man. With adequate and proper stimulation, this boy would be a great doctor".

Elesi respected Emeka's opinion, most of which sounded revolutionary, but were equally effective. often more effective.

Later, he stretched Chimezie's imagination as to the opportunities that would be open to him as a doctor. When he did well in the sciences at school, he showed more

44

enthusiasm. He invited his important friends, doctors and lawyers mostly, in order to solidify the image of the successful elite in Chimezie's mind. He engaged him in private classes and gave him access to all reasonable material comfort that he possessed, including a promise to enroll him in a driving school, so long as he took his studies seriously. Chimezie loved cars and was mad with joy when his father made this proposition. But the real attraction, the real crush was Emeka who held him spellbound and represented everything a man could aspire to and the key to this was education. Thus he took his studies seriously.

It was tough, having to master the intricate and the complex world of science, a difficulty not helped by the general apathy and lack of interest in it, by fellow students. But his father was always there to pep him up.

Once he had talked to him about the secret of success. " ... I became a success because I made people believe that I could accomplish virtually anything I set my mind on. Their belief in me, their expectation became my greatest strength. What I did not let them do was set goals for me, but I made them take it for granted that I would succeed in anything I intended to achieve".

When Chimezie finished his specialist course in Urology, in the United States, his father had helped him garner finances to set up the Rockfield Hospital. Today, he had many experts; doctors and technicians, who were as fascinated by medicine, and as dedicated and hardworking as himself. The Rockfield was Chimezie's dream and his life. They handled complex and complicated cases, mostly referred cases. The hospital was known as the place where possible miracles were possible.

But Chimezie had another passion which was tradition. He always wished that he understood his culture, that he could analyse it, unravel and solve its mysteries

45

and difficulties the way he analysed medical problems. In short, he did not know much of his tradition, but the occasional snippets from his acquaintances up North would make him compile a list of questions he felt could only be answered by his father, Elesi. It was this passion that made him accept to be initiated into the *Ozoebila*. A process of rebirth by a ceremonial death and resurrection into the society. A passion that made him travel down the East of the Niger every August for the New Yam Festival at Nkwoko. He always yearned for the wisdom of the *Ozoebila*, a wisdom that confronted a man unawares, leaving him sometimes with a feeling of knowledge, of truth and yet, fear. It was the *Ozoebila* who said that "Living is the truth", and Chimezie had sought to discover truth in the lives of men. This was another journey to living, to knowledge.

As far as Chimezie was concerned, his father was the pontiff of his culture. His father had liberal and objective approach to cultural analysis that laid the foundation for Chimezie's later attitude to life. Yet his dedication to his culture was unquestionable. It was a dedication founded on the link between the material and intellectual products of different cultures. Chimezie's career in the universities deepened his respect for his father and his culture.

He had learnt what self-esteem and self-image could mean to a man. One pedantic teacher who took him in psychology called it amour-propre. The general opinion in his class then had been that all men were the same, their differences did not have a biological basis but was traceable to environmental factors and the choices and interests of these races of men. He had come to believe in hardwork and he had succeeded. Chimezie was glad that his father was an African wiseman, because he drew the bulk of his strength from his Africanness. In their native expression, he was a man who knew his fathers. He understood his ancestors. Chimezie could always visualize his ancestors, he could always surmise what they could have said on important issues, from what his father said.

It was an eight hour journey from Jos, the trip a mixture of drudgery and joy, for although travelling long on a way replete with pot-holes was tiring, it was rewarding seeing the varied topography of the different states which he passed to reach Onitsha. And going to Onitsha had a special appeal. He loved Onitsha more than any city in the whole of Africa. He was born in that highly commercialized city, as such, he was an *Omata*. Despite the lack of vision of the so-called leaders and chairmen of Onitsha, despite their utter neglect of the infrastructure in this great town, the inhabitants of Onitsha continued to challenge and repudiate this negative image created by these detractors. For Chimezie, Onitsha held almost all the experiences and reminiscences that made him spry when he talked about them.

His best memories was of the time "before the war". A time when a lot of British influence could still be felt in Onitsha, a time when men dressed in suits and strutted the streets, when Chimezie's young eyes saw strange things. Despite the rapacious nature of the British colonial administration, they had a way of planning and administering the towns that Chimezie looked back on wistfully. He could remember that most of the streets were usually swept clean. He also remembered the well-covered drains and the strange slabs, with openings that scared him to death as he walked the sidewalks. His young feet seemed perpetually on a journey into them. He would stop, scared and crying, until someone older came to lift him through the rest of the nightmare.

It was a happy time too. He could still remember the mistakes and timidity of some of his friends. One of his friends, Chukwubundu Agbala, confronted with the water closet, for the first time had a great tale to tell of it.

"I nearly drowned in the Riverside Hospital yesterday" he had told Chimezie at school. Chimezie was surprised.

It turned out that the boy, with his mother had visited the Riverside Hospital, to commiserate with a woman who had lost her new born baby. While Chukwubundu's mother was bemoaning her friend's loss with her, Chukwubundu felt his stomach start to rumble. He felt a cooking sensation in his lower abdomen and his anus felt hot. He wanted to go to toilet. The Porter quickly led him to the Security Supervisor's toilet, a WC. "Sit there", he said pointing to what could have been a very clean bowl except that it was big and had a weird shape. "Just push this thing down when you finish okay?" he told Chukwubundu in an intimidating voice. He showed him the lever.

When Chukwubundu finished, he pulled the lever as commanded. The sudden gush of water from the sides of the bowl made him hopelessly afraid. It seemed to him that a hole had been struck on the great shell containing all the water in the world, and the world was going to be drowned. He stood petrified, unable to run. When the jet did not stop he let out a shrill scream.

The porter was waiting in anticipation of this and it gave him a great joy. He had done it to more boys than he could remember. He came in and closed the tap. Instead of telling the boy that after the toilet had ceased flushing, that water came from the pipes to refill the cistern, he told him that had he not come in time, water would have drowned him and the entire place. The boy kept wondering how reasonable people could install such a devilish toilet in a hospital like that.

But he dared not ask his mother, he could only talk to his best friend, Chimezie, about his ordeal, the following morning in school.

In Lafia, traffic was slow. The Governor of Plateau was on a working tour of the Local Governments and people had been mandated to come out en masse to welcome him as he passed in a cade. The city officials were now over-ambitious. For more than thirty minutes, they cut off traffic because they suspected that the Governor might be around any minute. Chimezie was very disappointed with this practice which often placed the potentate over and above every other individual in the society. While it did not enhance their credibility, it made the scramble for political power such a stiff and dangerous business.

In the centre of the town, he saw musical groups playing gaily on their instruments while local minstrels sang praises of the Governor. Lafia women sold cool potions of drinks for which the people were known. In this hot afternoon, *Fura* and *Kunu* featured greatly.

Chimezie was still reminiscing these experiences when he reached the Ninth Mile Corner. At a filling station where he refilled his tank, vendors besieged him with different kinds of wares, ranging from beancakes to delicious cookies. He bought some of the cookies and springwater to quench his thirst.

The way he was going, he would be in Onitsha in less than one hour. His feeling of nostalgia became heightened. Was it possible to recapture that "before the war", feeling again when he reached Onitsha? As an adult, his reactions to everything were different. A quest for the true, and a journey through different experiences would never allow him such experience of euphoria as he felt as a child. Everything had changed. But knowing the city that housed these experiences was still very sweet.

Soon Chimezie had traversed over eighty kilometres on the Enugu-Onitsha dual carriageway, to reach Nkpor. He was in fact now in Onitsha, for Nkpor was an extension of Onitsha city. The presence of new industries,

49

some of them claiming to manufacture auto spare-parts, others cosmetics, others still, in the agro-allied sector and so on brought him great mental relish.

This was progress, he thought. His scientific orientation always insisted on a leap from theoretical to practical proofs. It was not enough to say that all human beings were equal, this truth Chimezie accepted without doubt, but they should also be seen to show results for their efforts, especially if they believed in the same goals and means of attaining them.

He was doubly happy for the industry and strength exhibited by the people of Onitsha in the solid and powerful buildings that he saw as he sped through the Borromeo Roundabout. He could see the Inosi-Onira Retreat, the house of the great Zik, the first President of the Federal Republic of Nigeria, and the Owelle of Onitsha. He decided to enter through the expressway that led to Asaba, for on that road, the great River Niger gave a wonderful sight as one descended towards the flyover. But he did not reach the flyover. He turned right to enter MCC layout. The obvious evidence of activity, power and progress filled Chimezie with a new energy, wiping out at a moment all the fatigue he felt from the distant journey.

Once, he was discussing with his friends who shared an equal love for Onitsha, and one had opined that Onitsha might not boast of the brightest people in Nigeria, but it certainly boasted of the bravest. After the civil war, the businessmen in Onitsha, those who had bank accounts had started life again with twenty pounds each, a decision made by the then government to emphasize how worthless the Biafran pounds had become. It was these traders who now owned these magnificent buildings in Onitsha.

These traders did not just fight for their survival, they also fought to live. Armed robbery and other vices were natural hallmarks of a rich society like Onitsha. It became obvious that the police were hopelessly useless or willing accomplices. One fateful morning a group of traders were ambushed and robbed of a trailer- load of lace whereupon this news sparked off a spontaneous reaction from the traders. One giantlike man had stood at the centre of the market, his two fingers stuck in his ears, and shouted: "Traders are you still there? Are you still there?" The reaction was the famous "Oshebei" which caused the destruction of all those terrible organisations. In a week-long campaign, traders, disdaining hazards, harrassment from the police and attempts on their lives by desperate criminals, had flushed the town of all criminal elements. Onitsha became a safe haven for a long time. Even now, criminals knew that every wicked act committed against an inhabitant of Onitsha was a tick of the time bomb. These traders had resisted intimidation from the coercive instruments of government. The customs and the police especially had learnt to speak conciliatory language with them, so much so that business in Onitsha was as good as safe.

When he got to Onitsha, his father's gateman, Hamza, sighted him, and ran quickly into the house to inform his family before coming back to open the gate for him.

His wife, Lizzy, stood by the inner door, her eyes suffused with tears at the sight of him, waiting for his parents to finish hugging him. Chimezie was eager to reach her and was a little embarrassed that she stood still, not coming close. But then, he knew what she must feel.

Despite Chimezie's awareness of his father's stolidity in matters concerning sex, he grabbed his wife and kissed her long and deep in the mouth.

'Darling, I've missed you more than anything in the world," he said loud enough for Elesi to hear.

Lizzy's eyes were stars of love. Her face a symbol of happiness. She could only weep as she clung to him. She was waiting for the next sentence. He did not say it. Instead, he guided her to their rooms. As he opened the

51

door, he said, "No need asking whether you would pass my examination. You see, you've grown so beautiful I can hardly trust your answer".

"I can't wait for you to examine me" Lizzy said. He kissed and held her for long. "God Lizzy! You are the proof of life for me. From now on, it is living".

"Doctor, I am your patient tonight and I am in a serious condition. Don't make me wait too long ..."

"Darling, let me see Dad first. Chimezie told her after they had talked for a while.

"You are going to have dinner right away. The next time you come in here, you won't step out again okay?"

"Okay!" Chimezie said as he went back into the sitting room.

Everybody, Ibuego, Sylvester, Ejike, his father and mother were at table when he entered. After a lot of small talk, Elesi informed Chimezie of the chief events of the New Yam Festival. Chimezie was quite satisfied with his father's preparations for the festival. His grand plan seemed interesting as ever, however, Chimezie went back into his room with heavy heart at news of the deep animosity tearing Okani and Emeruo apart, an animosity threatening the very life of the village, its peace, its culture too.

"Papa I must go and relax", said Chimezie after their discussions which left him exhausted.

"Rest well and may the day break", they told him. Inside the room, Lizzy was almost falling asleep, but she came to full consciousness when the sound of the door moving on hinges announced Chimezie's entry.

Chimezie took his time to shave and sponge himself thoroughly before rousing his beautiful bride. They had a wonderful union. Before they slept he gave her an excellent mark. "As always darling, you are special". Her inner soul twinkled with her eyes as she lay on her back

52

listening to all those sweet words. He was the only man she believed.

"This time I am coming with you to Jos?" Lizzy asked him for the fourth time.

"That is why I have come, "he replied. Equivocal as his reply was, it was enough to make Lizzy sleep, and Lizzy of the blinking lids had a wonderful dream.

A bouncing baby boy for Chimezie. He looked so beautiful straddled on her back.

Chapter 4

"Our fathers", the great Chief began calling on his ancestors, the *Ofo* stick in his right hand and a small knife for the slaughter of the sacrificial fowls in his left. Today we eat the new yam as we remember your blessings on us, how you sit on us the way a hen sits on its eggs until they are hatched. We thank you for the protection you have given us. Our great town was once derided by others. They called us with such names as 'small', 'child', immature and so on. If we were once immature, we have grown. They have seen it that we have grown for anything that is small grows to become big as a child grows to become an adult. Our fathers, we ask for more of your blessings because you've made us heroes and you know that the shame of a hero is worse than his death. Take away what adds beauty to a man's life and his beauty dies.

"We are the great village that never played second fiddle to another. As far as history goes, there had never been a season when it was not an Nkwoko who pulled up the sacred knife at the market square after defeating our neighbours in wrestling contests. Today a new competition has risen. It is competition for development. We go abroad in order to acquire education and wealth necessary to achieve this development. Our fathers, we pray you to guide us in our goings and comings. What we think in our mind, help us achieve with our hands. We ask for the long stick so that where our height prevents us

54

from getting what we want, we may strike it down with the stick. If we pursue after something and can't get it, get it for us. We desire peace, peace in ourselves and peace with our neighbours for nothing works without peace. Enrich our understanding so that our appreciation of love is enhanced, so that we·see where and how we can help each other to achieve these great desires ..." Thus Elesi called on his ancestors until he had slaughtered all the sacrificial fowls in their individual names.

He was surprised to see that the children plucking the fowls were his own children as he was surprised in the morning when he found Chimezie in his *Obi*, ready to go to their ancesttral shrines with him for the sacrifice, Elesi ignored them, not even a word of encouragement to the children. In the past, he had always conducted this sacrifice with the help of children from pure pagan homes, with his wives and children far away from home for fear that he might send them on an errand that had to do with idol worship.

Excruciating and stressful as this experience was, Elesi endured it in the understanding that whatever would be would be. He still savoured the frightened voices of his children as they took flight now and then from the ancestral spirits, whose presence exacted and stretched their minds to their limits; these great spirits said to emerge from antholes at the break of an egg. The biggest of them, *Eze mmuo* always stood a distance from the people, including the *osukwu* and *otala*, filling the atmosphere with his ethereal songs. No earthly king could muster the grace with which this great spirit carried himself. He was guarded by the *Dimkpa mmuo* who always appeared spirited but cautious in his ways. The terror of the children was the *Akakpo* who would stop at nothing to get somebody unless he fell in his flight. It was the *Akakpo* who supplied the chills and the thrills which fed the imagination of the young.

Elesi now led Chimezie to Okpara's house where all the elders after their individual sacrifices to favourite ancestors in their own houses would gather together under Okpara's guidance to pray to all their ancestors collectively.

*   *   *

Elesi sat at the far end of the big oval table near the wall from where he presided over the dinner. Above his head was the portrait of his warrior father in oil. Flanking the portrait were two amorial bearings which looked as if carved from pure gold. They were gifts from the Chinese with whom he had done business for over thirty years and still remained their most trusted and important customer.

Today was the day on which the Elesis really enjoyed the New Yam Festival, the day after sacrifices were made, so that everybody, Christians and pagans were united once more in the celebration of a festival which meant much to them. Elesi's wives and children tried as much as possible to pacify him for the alienation they had wrought on him while he tried as much as possible not to make them feel guilty for it. He always had the events of the day well planned to give the very best to his children and his guests.

This morning, it was the fragrance from the near-done *suya* which Hamza, Elesi's night watchman was preparing that woke the entire village of Nkwoko. Hamza had had ample allowance for the *suya*, having purchased four rams of such sizes of which adult fingers could easily enter their nostrils and enough condiments for it. Hamza was from the North of the country, an excellent *suya*-maker, a skill for which Elesi paid him handsomely. He liked Elesi above any other man on earth and he liked to give him the best of everything. Elesi in turn liked him for his loyalty and strength. Standing above six feet, with wide heavy shoulders, he was very dark. His hands were his source of strength, big and taut as a hotelier's pestle. When he showed his calves, they were big yams, the type harvested from Abakaliki. This aura of invincibility always gave him employment with his peculiar masters, very tough and influential men.

There were those who had come to Nkwoko, to celebrate with Elesi and his family but had now gone because of other pressing matters. One of them was Major General Osita Oje. Another was the Amam royalty, His Royal Highness, Igwe Ojagwu II of Amam; a man whose wealth and influence made his people call him The Whale. He was late Dr. Emeka Ojagwu's younger brother. There was also Professor Paul Ukiwe who came from the neighbouring Isioma town. He was a professor of medicine and Ukiwe had tremendous respect for Elesi who had sponsored him through school and afterwards advanced him money for researches and experiments which gained him fame for which the Federal Government put him in charge of a fund of over fifty million naira, for conducting research into ways of managing and handling typhoid epidemics which had been the bane of many Nigerians in recent times. He paid his respects by never missing the Elesi August dinner. It was actually one of the few social events he attended in his life, fortunately for him, he always enjoyed it.

Now, at the other end of the table, opposite Elesi was the State's Attorney-General, Chukwurah Obiukwu. Elesi called him the Drizzles for he was full of drolleries. He was everything, sharp, blunt, sweet, bitter, hot but never cold. He always bragged to Elesi about his seemingly colossal powers. In many ways Elesi liked him. He was one of the most important pillars in his life, ever helpful with matters concerning the government and ever present in all his parties. He could see him now engrossed in conversation with Lizzy, Chimezie's wife who sat by his right. His eyes twinkled as she told him stories and

pointed at the traditional delicacy, *nfo ntakere* in front of
her. Elesi guessed she was explaining the recipe for the
cuisine to him. He was a connoisseur of gastronomy for
which Elesi was grateful. He ate well and commented on
practically everything he tasted or heard thus creating
conversation which made Elesi dig into his past to explain
to his children some of their traditional delicacies which
had been lost to European influences.

Elesi's heart grinned as he looked at one of the
special guests . They had been three but two of them
were missing, with them two of Elesi's sons, Ejike and
Ben. The special guests were Nkwoko girls whom Elesi
contrived to invite to these dinners in the hope that one of
his children might take fancy to one and marry her. The
alliances that resulted in such close marriages always
helped a man in his time of distress; His in-laws would
always be handy to help him in such times; a reality which
had confronted Elesi when he sought witnesses from
neighbouring towns during the dispute with the Ekemas.
In the past, the task of finding suitable girls was delegated
to one of Elesi's brothers, Dim Ezeala, who resided in
Nkwoko. It was the type of guests who Dim first invited
to dinner three years ago that earned them the appellation
"special guests". Dim claimed to have used one whole
year to select decent and good enough girls for Elesi's
children. Elesi would surely approve. His children would
definitely follow suit. No man rejected a wife approved by
his parents. Dim was encouraged by the fact that despite
Elesi's comely appearance, he was married to one of the
ugliest women in Nkwoko. She was his third wife, Njoka.
Dim's choices were not ugly by any standard, but they
were too simple and too crude compared to Elesi's worldly
children who had pretensions to education and breeding.
The artless bunch were so embarrassed that they remained
taciturn and immobile all through the dinner.

Subsequent years saw little or no improvement until this year when Elesi decided to handle the invitation himself. An old friend, a teacher was involved in the affair, for which three girls were invited today. They were really special for Elesi saw his sons trying hard to impress them. It seemed Ejike and Ben were luckier for they seemed to be making progress with their own guests. But this broom-thin girl here with Sylvester was giving him an iced shoulder. Elesi wondered what people of nowadays saw in thin women. In their own time, such women were referred to as prayingmantis, for they seemed to jerk with every effort they made.

*   *   *

Elesi looked at his watch it was 1.30 p.m. He stood up immediately. "Ladies and gentlemen", he began. He had already told most of his guests that he would not be with them beyond 2.00 p.m. He had to go to his maternal uncles' town, Umuawa to intervene in a chieftaincy squabble which had cost them lives and money. The President of Umuawa Development Union had personally pleaded with him to intervene in the matter, insisting that only Elesi was trusted by both parties in the dispute and therefore only his mediation would be effective. For this, Elesi had met with Okpara to have Okani versus Emeruo's dispute settlement shifted from 4.30 to 5.30, at which time he would have returned from Umuawa. Elesi now left his seat and walked to the back of Ibuego's seat, his hand resting on the back of the seat. "I would have loved to stay on and on, but unmanageable circumstances forces me to leave you". He began, patting Ibuego on the back. "You, those of you who miss me dearly and would like to hang me for it, I invite them to come with me".

Ibuego's face turned into a mass of contempt and everybody laughed. Elesi now began shaking hands with his friends, making brief conversation with each before he

59

left. When he came to where his brother Emeruo sat, he reminded him to attend the assembly for the settlement of his case with Okani. And thus Elesi left his children and friends to attend to other pressing matters which urgently needed his attention.

*　　　　　*　　　　　*

A brand new 505 Peugeot pulled up in front of their house. From where they were sitting, through the tinted glass, they could see the shining car roll to a halt. The right door of the rear opened and a handsome, elegantly dressed man in an English suit alighted from the car. He walked fast round the car to open the other door for whosever was with him. As he reached for the door, the person inside opened it. The man stood, his hands folded across his chest, his head swaying in delightful surrender, smiling.

"That man is not bad." said Ibuego. The lady that came out of the car looked like a mermaid in their eyes, a familiar mermaid.

"... No! But that's Betty of *Raptures*," the A.G. said. Her tight fitting dress with its rebellious cut revealed a lot of her womanhood; the sequined neck, shoulders and sleeves were a handful for the A.G.

"She is 'way out," said Ibuego.

"Wait till they come in," said Chimezie, uncomfortable with Ibuego's obsession with pleasure.

The lady looked at her watch and said something to the man, and they started to the main gate. Hamza was on hand to receive them. Just then, another car pulled up just by them.

A buxom lady, with a aura of a sybarite alighted from the passenger's seat. Another square man with a weather-beaten appearance alighted from the wheel. He followed the buxom lady who looked at her watch, and then at the elegant man apologetically. The elegant man kept smiling as the buxom lady closed up to him. As the mermaid watched them, he gave her a full hug of reassurance. Hamza led them into the house.

It was difficult to continue normal conversation, so everybody just waited. Chimezie tried to say something about their culture, but nobody listened to him. Ibuego was busy preening herself, pulling at her creased gown. Her compact flashed instantly and she undid one of the buttons just between her mounds, to give a killing effect. Few people noticed. All were expectant. The A.G., his nose crimson from excitement started to twitch. Lizzy could see him practice with his face to adjust to the feature best suited to welcome the visitors. Only the more mature men maintained their cool.

"Oga, some people look for you," Hamza told Chimezie who had now occupied his father's seat.

"Okay" Chimezie said, rising and walking with Hamza to the sitting room to welcome the visitors.

"You are welcome," Chimezie told the smart set, his hands spread apart in a gesture of total hospitality.

Chuby stood up as did the rest. He smiled at Chimezie and then lowered his head as if bowing to him. Then Chimezie saw the speckle above the lashes. That instant, a flash of recognition overwhelmed him. No, this could not be Chuby, his mind said.

"King Jaja! " Chuby yelled.

Chimezie was astounded.

"God of the Niger!" He yelled back, remembering the whimpering timid Chuby that he used to know; the boy who was scared to death by the sight of the W.C. They closed up in a friendly hug that nearly tripped them. Betty, Ikwu and Annie looked on as these two friends savoured each other. They had never seen Chuby in such a mood before. He was so happy, so uninhibited and played like a boy with his friend, which made him look very beautiful. They looked very much alike, tall, athletic and healthy.

The only remarkable difference in their appearance being Chuby's lighter skin.

"This is my fiancee Betty, my sister Annie, and my friend Ikwu." Chuby introduced his company.

"What a wonderful set you are. I believe I have seen your wife before ... on telly". Betty smiled and nodded.

"Welcome then once again madam. You are the most beautiful woman I have seen in years. And I love the *Raptures* a lot. I can't imagine what it would be like without you. Welcome Ikwu ... you are welcome to Nkwoko. Please join us at the dining room, we are having a dinner and I should say that your legs are good. Only one's best friends meet one eating ... please come and meet my family". At the table, Chimezie began to introduce everybody.

"My mother and my other brothers and sisters are having fun at different parts of the house. You will meet them later, and my father is out on a meeting". He finally said.

"Oh! Your thoroughbred of an old man, never tiring, even on a day like this. I admire him a lot ... I hope he is very fine?"

"Yes". Chimezie said nodding.

Chuby had a lot to say to Lizzy when he was introduced to her.

"... you are the lucky princess. So it is you who finally caught the whale, your husband is a wonderful man".

Lizzy was very delighted and she showed it with an indulgent smile. Her husband was not a man who had what she could call very close friends, not that she knew. He was friendly with everyone. But nothing could gainsay the bond between him and this man, and she liked Chuby greatly. A kind gentleman. Why had not Chimezie mentioned him before. Well how long had they even been together?

Betty surveyed the surroundings and was deeply impressed by the furnishing whimsicality of the house. From outside, it was not an architectural show, but its size and design said something about the owners. It talked about old money. Inside the house, almost everything was made of polished wood and brass. Art pieces stood everywhere, mostly works by Africans. Thick red carpet ran every inch of the house contrasting with the off white of the wall, maroon blinds and golden rollers. But the real show was the people.

Sylvester quickly stood up to let Annie sit besides him. He had been wearied to a point of exasperation by the thin girl's attitude. Her name was Clara. Ejike and Ben had succeeded in taking their own special guests out of the dinner, but Clara kept giving him a cold shoulder. This buxom girl was a smasher, with a lot of class. He prayed that she would be the salve for his already wounded soul. Even Ibuego had noticed his difficulties with Clara and had teased him about it.

Sylvester's simple deduction about female psychology was that making them feel insecure and jealous was a powerful weapon to hold them. But one could only achieve this when there were enough women, to pitch one against another. Thus, he had been stuck with Clara. Now, with Annie's presence, he was back in business, not for effects only but for real.

Even as Annie came to sit down, Sylvester saw Clara from the corner of his eyes, watching her full hips, tight in a black linen skirt and her clinging top with leopard designs which made her look like an amazon. Clara's eyes were green with envy. She started to attract Sylvester's attention, but he was already beaming at Annie.

Chimezie brought some kolanuts in a small bowl. He placed it in front of Emeruo who was the most-senior member of Nkwoko kindred present. "I have kola for our visitors", he said. It was the privilege of the most senior

63

member of a host· family to break kolanuts in such situations.

Emeruo's brow furrowed. His mood flew from hesitation, and resentment to rejection.

"I am not part of these things anymore", he said. "Part of what?" Asked Chimezie, surprised, thinking that his uncle was making some kind of joke.

"Rituals, incantations, kolanuts, all this is idol worship. I changed a long time ago".

"Changed what papa?" Chimezie said indignantly as he remembered some of the stories that he heard recently about Emeruo. "Just pray for the health of everyone and break the kolanut".

"Kolanut is unclean, didn't you hear that? It is the instrument of idol worship. People poison people easily with it. I don't eat it, so I cannot break it".

Chimezie guffawed, unconsciously, but it was a very dry laugh, though others laughed with him. The room was silent again as their visitors waited for them to resolve the kolanut issue, for once kolanut surfaced in any gathering, it took precedence over any other thing. Chimezie reached out for the bottle of scotch and poured himself his third drink. He gazed into his glass like a witch looking into a crystal ball in an attempt to see future events pictured there.

"... why should we worship wretched gods, such as Reverend Eze seizes everyday. Only thieves and wicked men can still pray to idols", said Emeruo again before Chimezie could find his voice. Chimezie was surprised at his uncle, at his denigrating remarks about their tradition which undoubtedly confirmed the stories making rounds that he was paranoid. He felt mortified at his uncle's behaviour.

He picked up his glass shaking it back and forth, but the liquid in it moved anti-clockwise, a habit he had practiced since childhood. He put it on the table and

64

wondered what to say. In that moment of concentration, he saw Emeruo in transparence. Only yesterday, he was telling him of the miracle-working Eze. The inexorable man of God.

"Remember that our chief has been worshipping in Okwu", he had said. "Ever since his son's misfortune, he often sleeps there, sometimes on just a mat. Everybody knew that the Reverend gave him a promise. Imagine! His son was sentenced to twenty years with hard labour ... but see, after the Reverend prayed, he was released in less than six months".

He proceeded to describe the calibre of men who worshipped there: engineers, doctors, traditional rulers etc. These lettered men came when the burden of living turned their unimaginative scepticism and atheism to realism.

Chimezie had avoided an argument with his uncle, because he understood that one could never win an argument with a man whose mind was already made up, so he had left him alone with his opinions.

Now Chimezie thought of that adage. That we were men was clear enough to him. That we have a superstitious nature was also true to him. That we had a greater tendency to superstition in times of trouble was most true. But whether superstitions were valid was another thing, and whether all of them were useful another. Chimezie concluded that superstition which led to blindness must be avoided, if we could not rid ourselves of all of it; for such superstitions destroyed reality and conscience; and conscience was simple logic deducible from experience. Who was the Chief's son for who Emeruo praised Eze greatly? An unrepentant drug runner whose trial and conviction was such that his father, a very influential man, could not bring himself to intercede with the authorities on his behalf. His mother had wearied him with tears and accusations of abandoning

65

their son to his terrible fate. The chief, like his fathers, believed that a man carried on his own head the consequences of his actions. It was his belief that even the mighty ocean did not drown a man whose feet it did not see.

That was not the first time that he had experienced so much shock because God blessed or punished him with children. Drugs had cost him one of his sons; the one he most loved. He was bedridden, before he died. He had watched him whither, shrink and die a most ungodly death. For the first time in his life, he saw death as glorious relief to the dead and anodyne to living relatives. That experience rankled in his mind. That another his sons could still get involved in drugs after that nightmare was unbelievable to him. Thus, he was convinced that their son was not a human being. But his wife eventually convinced him to go to his Reverend friend. Since it was the line of least resistance, and one most unlikely to work, he had agreed. But to his surprise, the Reverend had delivered. The Chief had shown his gratitude in ways that left no one in doubt; a largesse to the Reverend.

Chimezie reached in front of his uncle and carried the bowl of kolanuts. He selected the choicest kola from it and handed it to Chuby. "When kolanut reaches home, it says from whence it came", he told him. Chuby gave it to his wife who opened her bag and deposited it. She watched Chimezie very closely because Chuby had told great tales about him. He was a man after all.

"Almighty God, we thank you for this kolanut. It was you who created it, a most simple fruit and yet interesting. You saw fit to make it the head of all fruits. A man who offers kola offers life, he offers friendship and love.

"God bless all of us. Grant that if we eat this kola, we will be fulfilled with love, children and wealth. All this we ask in the name of Christ".

"Amen", echoed everybody except Emeruo.

Chapter 5

"This place is beautiful", Chuby told Chimezie as they waded further into the grove.

"I knew you would like it". After a moment's silence, Chuby spoke again, "guess where it makes me remember?"

"No-man's-land of course", Chimezie said quickly.

"You are a wizard".

"It is easy. I felt it the day my father brought us through here to show us our boundaries with the other villages. I was overwhelmed by this place".

"And so you always come here?"

"Anytime I can manage it. It is a place I once feared ... hated, but now I love it. This grove belongs to the goddess of fertility herself and villagers told stories of her frequent appearances to many whose heads filled out on seeing her in dazzling white. I never trod these paths until father brought us here. He responded to our fears by saying that the goddess was patient, caring and loving especially to young children. I felt the peace in this place that day. Later I was to come here at the barest opportunity for meditation. Everytime I am here I have a strange feeling that I know something or rather I feel at one with my people and I feel full in them".

"Something mysterious is happening today ... Something I can't quite understand", said Chuby.

"Ha ... you are mystified by this grove? I thought we shared a common affection for the sublime ... after your Riverside ordeal?" Teased Chimezie.

Chuby was nodding reflectively. "Yes ... always. It is not really the groves but your uncle. Is he well at all?"

"I am unsure of anything my friend. Forgive his rudeness I plead once again with you. I grew up holding that man in great esteem. I thought him one the most reliable men in the world, sometimes he showed more guts than my father. Whatever changed him ... religion perhaps. Being converted in old age tends to rob a man of all his elements. He is the blind zealot".

They walked in silence until they reached the face of the deity, a circular clearing that was neatly swept.

Chuby was impressed at the palpable neatness of the surroundings. "Do they sweep here every morning?"

"Osaka" Chimezie rounded at his friend, seeking to rebuke him for not knowing much about tradition and customs ..." Do you ever go home to see these things?" The moment Chimezie uttered these words, he flinched recollecting immediately that Chuby had been a run-away all his life. He never said glowing things about his family. his community of parents. He was such a poor lad, he could still visualize the look of wonderment on his face the day he took him to their house to demonstrate to him that the W.C. could not have drowned the entire Riverside Hospital. He remembered his dirty hungry hands that gulped his food that day. His susceptibilities must have been hurt, but it was inadvertent on Chimezie's part. Chimezie now walked faster, hoping that a little activity would dissipate the tension in the air.

Chuby was surprised at his friend's change of mood' and gradually caught up with him.

"Oh my heaven! Please, sit down, let us relax and talk. It's been a very long long time. How on earth did we lose contact until now?"

They found two stumps and lowered their buttocks on them.

"God of the Niger, how are you?" Chimezie said.

"Fine" Chuby said his gaze upon his friend's eyes.

"It's been long".

"Twenty-five years", said Chuby". You thought you hurt me when you mentioned my people. Jaja, you are wrong. All my life I've always believed in my people. I despised my parents and my family for letting my great grandfather's name slip the way it did, by letting his efforts die away unprotected and untended. I guess I was too hard on them because I know now that none except really strong people could have behaved otherwise under the pressures they felt".

"We had never discussed your people", stated Chimezie.

"Yes". Therefore, all you know about me is from your impression of me as a child. I grew up in poverty, true, yet everything I heard, everything I saw of my family spoke about greatness that was somehow stultified. The failure of my family made me seek refuge in education. I knew my father was poor, but I insisted on his sending me to school because in those classrooms, I mingled with the privileged such as you were. I discussed with the wisest of men through the books.

"My old man did not refuse my request, though he said it would be difficult. He believed in my vision. That day he told me things I never heard before about my family. I was to know that we were ostracized in our community because our great grandfather tried to protect his honour and beliefs". Chuby's eyes now shone , that man, he was everything to our village. He was its going and its coming. He hated the way European values trampled upon, eroded and suffocated our traditional values. He therefore decided that for his family, a cautious association with European culture was imperative. He

69

liked their education, but he rejected a wholesale assimilation of their culture especially their religion. What is the difference between the worship of saints and our ancestors. What difference does it make whether an image or a statue represents St. Michael or *Okorikata*. He felt it was double standards and therefore was uncompromising in upholding his traditional beliefs.

"But the very people he sought to protect from those influences took a dip at the religion and became stirred by its powers. The high point of it all was when one of his wives got involved. She was a dedicated Christian. She was married to my great grandfather at a very tender age of fifteen, so she perhaps did not fully appreciate the importance of what she was doing. The thing is she later realized she could never be admitted to receive the Holy Communion being a polygamist. She was also not baptized at the time, so she feared hell. Her craving for the body of Christ was such that she went berserk. She threatened to leave the old man if the old man did not take her to Church to wed, but the old man reasoned with her. It was unclear to the old man what the status of his other wives and children would be after the wedding, whether he could still regard them as his children and wives, that is, go into them as a husband normally goes into a wife. What was clear however was the rancour and misgivings the wedding would create in his household. So he explained to her that things had gone a mile too far, that the wedding proposition was an impossibility.

"The women's dilemma led her to denounce him. In her anguish and confusion, she came down with a serious ailment which saw her bedridden for long. On recovery, she left him for her father's house, where the household well aware of the genesis of her troubles refused her welcome. She fled her own household and ended up in a church where in a public testimony, she called her husband a wizard, poisoner and devil-incarnate.

70

"What irked the old man was that the church and the authorities sat on such a serious allegation, unprepared to investigate it, probably believing it, but what killed him was the faithlessness of his own friends, traditionalists like him who believed the story, frustrated his effort to go to the shrines of the gods and swear that he was innocent of the accusations and who tacitly ostracized him." Chuby was really filled now. "Nobody loves a strong man," he said "nobody loves a hero." The man took his troubles with equanimity. It was my father's weakness in the face of all this that I was running from in my childhood because I knew that water in the broken shard is for the dog.

"My struggle against poverty numbed my earlier desire for higher values. It made me forget, but things have changed," ended Chuby.

"What has changed?" Inquired Chimezie.

"I've grown. I am about getting married to one of the strongest women in the world, which leads me to why I am here. I want you to be my best man at my wedding, that's why I've come."

Chimezie broke into a belly laugh. "But I am married," he told his friend. "Can a married man stand in for you?" "I think of it in the context of its meaning, "Chuby said. "A best man is a best man and I thought seriously about it before I came to you. Anyway, the Reverend says the most important thing about wedding is the husband and wife. For me I want everything that happens that day to be real for me. Do you accept?"

"No" Chimezie said, "I commandeer, I seize no I beg ... I ... I am all for you."

"You old crook," Chuby said clasping his friend's hand. "I am very glad I was able to make it this season. Actually, we were going to Uda, to Ikwu's place when I decided to kill two birds with a stone. I reckoned you'd be home for the New-yam celebrations".

"That your friend," Chimezie cut in, "he looks like the entire world is on his shoulders. He never says anything ... hardly eats, no happiness".

"Leave Ikwu" said Chuby. "He is troubled, very troubled". He told Chimezie the story of the disappearance of the god, Okpoko. He told him of the mysterious events which had been happening to Uda people since the incident. The old priest who had ministered to Okpoko before its disappearance, who had later lost one of his eyes in mysterious circumstances had also lost a son. The young lad was said to have taken his own life when he failed in his bid to gain entrance into the university. A particularly poisonous type of snake had been known lately to have caused the death of two sons of Uda and many others had been bitten by them. And Uda had been deeply steeped in disputes with her neighbours." All these he attributes to Okpoko's wrath. He feels crushed by the experience because his family had also had to suffer terribly for seeking to uphold the traditional religion. His grandfather was accused of murdering twins in the name of sacrifice on the shrine of Okpoko. Ikwu says it's a complete falsehood. Despite the total lack of evidence to substantiate the allegation, the man was sentenced to a long prison sentence. The authorities eventually set him free, but on his way back, some people, probably Uda people waylaid him and killed him and spread the story that he was lynched by an angry mob because he stole out of hunger. His body was later found at the foot of Okpoko, but never the town where he was supposed to have committed the crime. You see, this story with the story of the murdered twins put Ikwu's family at the most disadvantaged position in their town until Okpoko became popular again. This popularity meant everything to Ikwu as he came to be respected, even feared once again. The desecration of the shrine again changed everything. Everybody expects the god to react, a curse or possibly death on his attackers. Ikwu himself is confused about the ways of the deities, their unpredictability. Their vengeance may take time, but he says when it comes, it sweeps an enemy inside out. He believes the oracle has already started dealing blows. For now, he is not content with leaving the whole affair to the god alone. As his priest, he wants to find him at all costs. The god may make his revenge when he pleases".

Chimezie now realized how uniform oppression was to all men. If he should tell Chuby of his family's sufferings under the Ekemas, he would undoubtedly shudder. In a way, their progenitors suffered that they might have a fuller life. They were oppressed that they may be loved. They took those sufferings that they may be free and freedom meant freedom from illwill towards others. Chimezie tried as much as possible not to let old events becloud his judgment of the present and future.

"What does Ikwu think happened to the god? He is a priest with a seeing eye I suppose?". Chimezie said with a tint of derision.

Chuby explained the Ariobi theory to him, concluding that Ikwu was fixated on the idea.

"It's possible, but highly improbable," Chimezie said. "Your friend sounds fanatical to me ... and vindictive ..."

"No. He is just desperate. Come to think of it, why would ordinary attackers go as far as killing the sacred cows and pulling the shrine down if all they wanted was merely the god?".

Chimezie had no ready answer to this question. It was hard to explain, but something else was on his mind. When Chuby was talking about the Ariobis being responsible for the crime. He mentioned that in the olden days, the Ariobi god killed a lot of people whose blood flushed through the gutter as their relations left the shrine. "Chuby, you mentioned that as relations and enemies of a man trapped by the deity left, they would see his blood

73

flowing in a gutter. That is not quite correct. The blood that was seen was actually the blood of a goat."

"What?" Chuby said in astonishment.

"Yes ... the pitfall as you described led to a tunnel from where supporters of the unfortunate victim of a conspiracy would carry him off to be sold into slavery. They rarely killed people, rather it was a veritable avenue for hunting slaves. The blood was a ruse to create an impression".

Chuby stared in wonderment at his friend.

"Were you going to Uda because of this?"

"Yes. I want a photograph of the god which Ikwu says is in his house and also to find things out for myself".

"Are you planning to get involved?"

"Yes ... very very involved. I once promised to help him in any situation when I visited his shrine. When he came and told me about this, I felt I owed him the help. My problem has been what to do. Honestly, I've felt most encouraged since our discussions today. I wish I had somebody like you to work with on this". On introspection, Chuby remembered Chimezie well in No-man's-land. It was a thick bush where they went to pick rubber seeds for their *pana* games. They often fought over the seeds, and it was there that children said things they would never ordinarily say in their houses. Chuby now recalled Chimezie's questions about the divinity of Christ, the existence of angels and the triune Godhead which used to shock them. He also remembered his clever proofs as to the authenticity of those claims.

"Chimezie, what am I gonna do?"

"I don't know. Chimezie said and stood up. His back now ached from sitting for long . "Let us leave before the villagers start coming with their sacrifices. We'll talk more about this later. As they found their way through the paths, Chuby thought for once in many years that he had a friend.

74

The last of the guests to leave the Elesi home was the A.G. Lizzy so fascinated him that he followed her about the house after Chuby and Chimezie had left for a drive around the village.

"Tell me more stories," he kept urging her, a strange glint in his eyes. "Your stories are exciting ... with a pungency favourable to intellectual minds".

"Thank you". Lizzy said, now edgy under his suspicious attention. He had in fact behaved in a way unbecoming of a man of his standing, more so, in his capacity as a very trusted friend of the family. During the dinner, while Lizzy told him stories, his hand had been crawling about her covered lap. Lizzy, unsure if the man was aware of the mission of his hand, had ignored it until the hand tried to force her laps open. She had been embarrassed beyond words and had flashed him her most baleful look which made him retract his hand, temporarily checked.

From the other side of the table, Chimezie had seen the strange look on his wife's face. He had cocked his eyes at her askance. She had smiled and shook her head meaning no danger. "I love you so much," she whispered across the table.

This exchange appeared to have incensed the A.G. "You are a rare beautiful woman," he told her. "You deserve everything ... in taste. I'll improve your career manifold. I'll do anything for you if you'd visit my office tomorrow".

Lizzy felt insulted, but she managed to keep talking with him. "You encourage adultery then?"

"My wife is what you would call a first class adventuress, but I still like her... a lot. I think the mistake we make is in being selfish about things. That I like her doesn't mean I love you less. In fact I've never met any woman I like as much as I love you. It is natural, those

75

drives we feel for our wives and our friends' wives and sometimes their daughters and nieces. I believe in a free world and that's the only way we can minimize frustration".

"Sir, I don't have to argue about what would happen when you have these drives directed at somebody and the person has her own drives pointed at another. There is no doubt that a lot of practical necessity abound when such conflicts of interests are avoided by making people stick to their wives and husbands. You believe in God, in His omniscience?"

"Of course, but we must always seek to discover the true will of God".

"It has already been revealed ... in the gospels, even in our traditional religions. What you profess is at best bohemian. It is dangerous". Said Lizzy.

"Don't be a slave to religion" he told her.

"Even in your law, your honour, it is a despicable act. Law itself is a kind of religion. And you cannot seriously say 'don't be a slave to the law'. The law is important, including the law on marriage. Most of all I believe God has created the best of all possible worlds as revealed in our religions".

"Liz darl, I must confess that I like whores more than I like saints. I am surprised at your shyness. You think too much about heaven, about hurting your husband. Those inhibitory tendencies are there when you've never ventured to live. Once the deed is done, the body is released from worry. It could even become a healthy habit. By heaven all married people in this country fuck ..."

Mr. Attorney-General, men who think like you are wicked and dangerous and I am going to tell my husband everything you said today. Perhaps he could help to convince you about the absurdity of it all". Lizzy said unsure how best to handle the A.G.

"You don't need to tell him," said the great lawyer. "I think I feel the truth of what you have been trying to say. "There is a saying we used to say when we were kids: my mother locked up my mouth and ears with padlock when she went to the market. You heard nothing from me today. I told you nothing".

Lizzy nodded with understanding.

The lawyer left fast, forgetting his long stem pipe.

*   *   *

Now the ladies were bringing some order into the sitting room again. They packed glasses and plates and cleaned the carpets. As they did this, Lizzy slotted a mellifluous soul-buster by Donna Summers.

Before long there was a heavy commotion outside which made these fair ladies rush out to the balcony, with Lizzy's words stuck in her chest.

In front of the house, they could see children jumping around some fighting men. It was as if the rest of them were fighting with one of them, the big one. As the ladies looked on, they saw Elesi's car pull up at the scene of action, and a police jeep pull up beside it. At this, they abandoned everything they were doing and hurtled downstairs.

The other men somehow had managed to escape and they saw Elesi instructing the police to arrest the other, who was fighting with them. When Ibuego saw that the man was Defo, her own brother and Elesi's son, she was weak. She could not even intercede for him because he had caused their father so much trouble. Defo was her favourite, of all her brothers and sisters. As she judged it, the only difference between them was that she had a university certificate, and that was a big consolation to her father, and it made him tolerate her. But Defo was a dropout. He had deserted university where he was studying Business Administration, and had joined the fast set, experimented with all sorts of drugs and got into all sorts of trouble except theft. His father had tried to motivate him in every conceivable way, but to no avail. He eventually decided that a detention centre was the best place for him. But Defo's mother was always protective of him. So that on the day that he was arraigned before the court for his parents to prove that he constituted a danger to the society, and therefore deserved to be detained, his mother had given an evidence contrary to Elesi's. On the strength of that, he had been discharged. His mother, sensing Elesi's disappointment, had sent Defo to her brother in the village. Since then, in a sense, Defo was dead to his family. His father had done everything to try to forget him, in the belief that he would one day be confronted with an experience which would either change or destroy him. Thus, Ibuego and Lizzy could imagine Elesi's feeling when he came back and saw Defo fighting in front of his house with some strange men, all of them wielding knives. Elesi had gone to bring the police as expected.

The Police were struggling with Defo when Chimezie and Chuby came back from the grove. Chimezie ran to his father, asking what the trouble was all about.

"I came back and found him fighting with some strange men. If you had seen these men, they looked like agents of the devil himself. And they all had knives .... This boy wants to soil our land with human blood. He wants to destroy a century long work accomplished by our ancestors, but God shall not permit it." Elesi answered.

"The policemen?" Said Chimezie, more of a question than a statement.

"I brought them to take care of him".

"Papa, please, forgive him this once".

"Shut up and sit down," Elesi retorted. He was rarely cross with Chimezie. Chimezie could sense his deep-seated hatred for Defo.

78

"Wait a minute," Chimezie called at the policemen, who were reluctant in their duty, realizing that this matter was a family affair. They waited.

Defo did not waste time in stating his defence. "Those men I found in front of this gate asking about a visitor in our house are rogues, real bad people who could kill. They have their hearts in their backs. I pursued them because I could not understand why in hell they were here".

"Don't listen to that animal," Elesi told Chimezie. "Thank Chimezie for your escape today, but don't think it a real escape because where I planned to keep you could have helped save you. Whatever you do, don't come into my house. Sometimes I wonder if you come from my stock or you have different blood in your veins".

"I am your son, I have the warrior in you," Defo shouted at his father.

Elesi left everything and turned to go inside the house, leaving Chimezie to work out anything with the police

"Papa ... please, forgive me." he heard his son say. "I have often come around this gate since your return, in the hope of finding you or any of my brothers or sisters, to explain my life to you," said Defo in a tearful voice.

Defo's voice stopped Elesi in his track. What he said touched his soul and he turned, for deep inside his heart, he loved Defo with all his mind. The policemen now freed him, aware of the new air which had built between him and his father.

"I have been bad. I have shamed you father, but now I have realized that none of these things pays. I have undergone suffering and I have realized that as your son, I deserve better out of life. Please, forgive me now and I'll show you what a son you've got". He was pleading with his father.

Elesi spoke no words for fear of weeping. He turned and embraced his son, patting his back with deep love.

Annie, Ibuego, Lizzy, Betty, Ben, Sylvester, Ejike and all others present had tears in their eyes.

Chimezie walked up to the police officers and chatted with them before they left in their jeep.

*   *   *

Elesi's wives had been conferring for long outside his Obi, his traditional temple and court which was adjacent to the main building. Their problem being how to make Elesi forgive Anyanwu, Defo's mother and Elesi's fourth wife, and accept back Defo whom Anyanwu had assured them had-mended his ways and was most desirous of peace with his father.

Iboma, Elesi's first wife and Chimezie's mother was mandated to broach the subject with Elesi and find out how deep his feelings ran about it, before all of them would together go to plead with him on Anyanwu's behalf. They eventually decided that confronting him all at a time within the period of the festivities and the presence of most of his other children would have a disarming effect.

They were still talking about this when Mgbocha, Ukpo's wife entered excited. "Why didn't you come to the village assembly?" she asked them. "You missed much".

The women all pouted in disgust.

"Assembly?" Iboma said derisively, "Is it a pronouncement of the gods?" Since meetings during festivities were not compulsory for women, they had decided not to attend in order not to give Emeruo occasion to insult them as he had insulted their guests in the house today.

"Emeruo is a coward," Iboma said.

"Warrior in a room ... in his own house, God! On his wife".

"Tell me! Iseke, Elesi's second wife exclaimed.

"Were you not in these parts when he locked Okani up, or am I to tell you how terribly he has punished his wife. Have you seen her face lately?"

"It is terrible, what did she do to him?" Iseke asked.

"What kind of offence would warrant such a treatment to his wife. The man is a coward. You know, during the war with the Ekemas, he ran to his maternal uncles".

"It was not because he was avoiding the war," Iseke said. "It was for a special reason".

"You call me a liar then?" Iboma asked aggressively. She was wondering why Iseke should bother to defend Emeruo, even if a lie was told against him. "What was the special mission? I am asking you. You who stay under the moon and picture the sun".

"Don't kill me mother". Iseke pleaded.

"How can he order the woman to stop talking to everybody in the village. The woman could not pass by our mothers and not greet them. She could not go to the stream and keep to herself. It was obvious she did not support his ways so he dealt with her, ate up her face like a witch. But his sister, Njataku is her father's daughter. She organised the entire womenfolk of Nkwoko and they went with pestles, knives, teeth, with every terrible tool, they cured him of the evil influence. They beat him out of his delirium. For a whole three weeks, he was in pain so great beyond expression. He paid for it".

"Will you all shut up and hear what happened today at the meeting," said Mgbocha. They now gave her attention. Mgbocha's face registered satisfaction when she said: "My husband thought Emeruo a lesson today". "He hasn't seen anything yet" Iboma said.

"By God, he did. He wept today. You could have seen him weep, crocodile tears, but they were tears. I thought he said he was greater than the village.".

"I have always known that Ukpo had been tolerating the stupid man ... Now he has seen what he has been wanting to see" Iboma concluded.

"When I said my husband, I wasn't talking about my Lord Ukpo. I meant Elesi, Oh! The gods could have been speaking through him today. It was a real show to watch. It is good to see the truth nicely told. My sisters, to say that all heads are equal is but a fart of the mouth. By the very vote of nature, some men are born great. My Lord Elesi told Emeruo plainly that it was because of him that people of Nkwoko had been condoning him. You should have seen him sweating and crying as Elesi pounded him like palm seeds. It is good to call evil evil. He rebuked him for disregarding what was a brotherly gesture of love from Okani, whom he said could have easily gotten palm-heads from any other person including his own father, Umeike or he could have bought a truck-load of it if he had wanted to. He said that Emeruo's action was motivated by illwill and jealousy.

"'If this were to be in days of our fathers, you would be sold into slavery,'" Mgbocha said to an imaginary Emeruo mimicking Elesi's guttural voice and gestures. His wives were thrown into laughter at the near accuracy of the mimickrey.

"'... or an *ofo* circled around your neck and you'd be sacrificed to the gods".

More laughter.

"'To win a case in truth is nobler than to kill in vengeance. When a lying mouth is exposed, the jaw sags. A person whose kinsmen curses on is dead already, notwithstanding that his empty body still walks the earth. You deserve to be cursed, but I will not curse you. Instead I plead with this assembly to forgive you'"

"Without an apology from him?" Iseke asked as if Elesi was present there.

"Ah ... why not! He apologised to the assembly. He knelt down before Okani and the elders.

"And where are the devourers of my fortune?" Elesi said as he strode up to his wives.

Nno nna anyi" they all greeted him. But Anyanwu was beginning to withdraw.

Mgbocha, audacious as ever ran up to him and embraced him. "Welcome my husband," she said again. She quickly started doing the *mpete* dance steps for him, her legs wagging like a dog's tail.

She first stamped her right foot on the ground with vigour, and then the left foot. She lifted her head and smiled at Elesi gradually turning her head until she had infected her audience with the smile and Elesi's wives began clapping their hands for her, producing the complex tune of *mpete*. Her two feet now spread apart, she began taking the refined steps of the original *mpete*, first she began by shuffling her feet, dragging one foot with the other like a dancer in an opera and gradually she rose to a twisting and breaking of shoulders and ribs which thrilled her audience. The clapping now assumed a faster rhythm, which judging from Mgbocha's closed eyes and the ethereal smile on her face had transported her to another world altogether. Suddenly her eyes flashed, her head shook wildly as she leaped into the air, momentarily defying the law of gravity. She landed on her toes and sprang up again, landing and springing, in a way her audience had never seen before. Even the great Elesi was so charmed that he ran to embrace her. He fumbled in his pocket until he found his purse. Pulling a wad of notes, twenties, he plastered Mgbocha with all of it.

"You are terrific," he told her. But Mgbocha was not finished. She gradually slowed her movement, almost to a walk now as she sang praises of Elesi. "The brave, the forthright, the strong, the saviour," she called him.

Elesi looked on and listened with real delight. It had been long that he had such a moment with Mgbocha. He could remember that during the investiture of one of the titles bestowed upon him by his town, he was required to send one of his wives at midnight, to fetch water from a nearby stream, that he might be "washed" with it. None of his wives could do it, not even Iboma whom he thought was the bravest woman alive. Elesi was not a man who pushed people beyond their will, he had waited, starved as he was, until one morning, when news reached him that Mgbocha had offered to go to the stream for him. That was how he was 'washed', and became Elesi. After that, he came to love Mgbocha as much as his own wives and mother. She liked him and prided herself as the only woman who played with him, the way she did now.

As his other wives stood, Anyanwu stood a distance from them, a poignant look on her face. Iboma decided that it was time to tell him about Defo, now that he was in a good mood and Mgbocha was here also with her strong charm and strong mouth to help them.

Mgbocha finished the *mpete* dance.

"We wanted to ask something of you," said Iboma with a meek voice.

Elesi looked at her. He could guess what she wanted to say, but he waited for her to say it. A slight nod signalled that she should go ahead and make her request.

"It's about Defo ..." Iboma started to say. All the women held their breath because Elesi had often lost his patience when matters concerning Defo were being discussed, especially if his mother tried to show concern.

"Defo is in the house," he announced to them.

They were utterly confounded. Elesi had never said anything in jest, yet it seemed unbelievable, judging from how he had felt since Defo left his house.

He moved forward, to his wife Anyanwu, who was Defo's mother. He disentangled her clasped hands and

84

embraced her and caressed her back. This was when the other three women rushed into the house to see Defo and welcome him back to their house.

"Thank you ... I hope that you have forgiven me". Anyanwu said to her husband.

Elesi smiled, still holding his wife's shoulders. "Tell Iboma that Defo's return must be celebrated ... anytime, before we go back to Onitsha. We must be happy for our son was dead, and is alive again. He was lost and is found".

*   *   *

Inside the house, Ibuego fawned all over Defo as he told them about his encounter with the three strange men. She seized him by the waist and dragged him into a chair, calling him evil superman.

"Those men are really very dangerous". Said Defo matter of factly

"But you gave them acid," interrupted Ibuego. "Why did you retire to the village with all this charm. Maybe it's the cronies who now hold your fancy!"

"Let's be serious". Said Chimezie in a serious tone. "Whom did you say those men were looking for?"

"A visitor here with a 505. Their description of whom they wanted matches your friend. I wonder what business he has with that kind of people". Defo said unemotionally.

He turned towards Chuby. "Do you know anybody around here?"

Chuby shrugged uncomfortably. What this handsome boy questioning him said and the way he said it made him resent him. He looked closely at Defo. He was like the Elesis, tall, athletic, but with bigger muscles that would have looked healthier if he took care of them. A permanent mist hung over his eyes, giving him an imperious bearing. He had very dark lips and beautiful

85

long nose. There was an unusual coolness about him that bordered on impertinence.

"How come they were asking of you?" Defo asked him again.

"Of who?" Chuby said, a bit alarmed.

"You live in Lagos and have a 505?"

"Yes?"

"Well it was you that they wanted. They were unfortunate that I was around the gate at the time, so I didn't even allow them near the gate. When the watchman saw me arguing with them, he came and started beating them with a heavy stick. We gave them the beating of their lives ..."

"We saw it all," said Ibuego. "I know women must be one of your inspirations".

"There was no woman there" said Defo.

"But we were watching through the window."

"I didn't know, I couldn't have seen you". He told her indulgently.

"Women like men like you ..." said Ibuego unconsciously.

"Ibuego!" Chimezie called his sister to her senses. "Forgive me Mr. Serious" she said and shut her mouth.

"Do you know any such people?" Defo continued with Chuby.

"I have told you that I don't know such people and there is no reason in the world to suppose that they were looking for me. There are thousands of people who own 505s and live in Lagos".

"But they did not all visit here." Defo interrupted. "Those men looked desperate. They are not the kind of people responsible people make friends with. Perhaps you have something that they want".

"I am sick of your ominous suggestions," Chuby retorted in obvious alarm. "What do you think you are doing saying those things?"

"Cool down Chuby," Chimezie advised his friend. "What you told me at the grove could be a factor. Perhaps some people are afraid that you have been making some moves to recover the missing god".

Chuby let reason penetrate him. "Yes, but I have told nobody about this since Ikwu came to tell me about it in Lagos, unless Annie, Betty or Ikwu did.

"I told Zuby," said Annie, Zuby was the boy dating her in Lagos. "He had always wanted to know why I could not keep appointments with him, so I told him I was helping you to look for the god without suspecting that it could possibly mean anything to him.

Suddenly, Chuby's mind was fixated on Zuby. He remembered what Annie said of him the last time he came up in their conversation. "Falcon eyes ... Falcons are supposed to be birds of prey," she had said. Chuby would have been bothered about this if Annie was reasonable about her castigation and rejection of men. Experience had thought Chuby that intuitive assessments of lovers was ninety percent correct. Women were better at this kind of assessment, but Annie always over-did hers.

"Where is Zuby from?" He asked his sister.

Annie was taken unawares "Oh ... sorry ... Aroh ... Arondizuogu ... sorry, I've forgotten".

"Please, try to remember" Chuby urged his sister.

"Ariobi," Annie said as if the word did not issue from her.

"Ariobi!" Ikwu said looking downcast at Chuby.

"Yes, I am sure," Annie said firmly.

"How long have you known him?" Chuby asked, his voice as scanty as a cop's.

"Why?" Annie asked feeling embarrassed.

"Sorry," Chuby told her "but the people of Ariobi are suspected to be responsible for the destruction of Ikwu's shrine".

Annie was perplexed. Zuby might know about this, she thought. He was always seeking information about Chuby, about his business, about his wife, about everything. The last time they were together, she had voiced her contempt for his probings, but he had argued that since he intended to keep her someday, he had a right to know of her family, and Annie had answered back. "You may ask or wish anything about me, but not about my brother". After that, the probings had simmered.

"Oh God! Annie said. "It's not really long. Maybe a month and ... We met at my favorite shop at Tinubu Square, and he gave me a flower and I liked him. That was it. Sometimes, I felt like an expensive piece of furniture he wanted to acquire, only to sit down with". Annie said hurtfully.

Lizzy, Ibuego, Ejike, Defo and Sylvester all looked confused. They wanted to be let into the secret manifesting in the discussion going on, but they did not interrupt the conversation.

The room felt silent for a few minutes. It was Chimezie who broke it.

"Well, we now know that this visit might be connected with Chuby's efforts in trying to find Ikwu's god. But even if we took that for granted, we don't know their aim. We will try to find out something about them while we can. How can we do this?" Defo spoke up immediately "who else but me?" He said. Somehow Chimezie understood what he meant. "It has to be fast" Chimezie told him. "We have barely a few days to spend here".

"I'll get you information by tomorrow evening". Defo said confidently.

"Meanwhile, let us propose a toast to Defo, to his continued peace with Dad" Chimezie said. They all drank to Defo's peace after which they retired to their respective rooms.

*   *   *

Chimezie's eyes had been closed, more than one hour, and yet, he could not sleep. Deep in his subconscious, he wondered what the visit by the three strange men could mean. Most of all, he could not explain or understand the fact that Zuby was an Ariobi. This night, he had not held his wife and cradled her till she went to sleep like he had always done since he came back. He was disturbed thinking about the possible consequence of the visit of the evil men to Chuby.

Lizzy had been tossing about in bed. Three times Chimezie wanted to wake her as she made movements that suggested that she was struggling with something. Now as he stared at her, she seemed very relaxed and she filled his heart with joy. The joy that she was his forever was so much that the bent on her, whispering in her ear "I love you". Lizzy did not hear. She continued the struggle. In the mystery world of dreams, she found herself in a darkened warehouse where some strangemen, looked side-long at her. There was hatred in their eyes. Their glare made her fidget. She became weak and felt that she was fainting. Then, the men started moving towards her. She wanted to scream and run, but her legs could not carry her. She could not call out. She was trapped, helpless, almost smothering when suddenly, she found the men in a circular fire. They were surrounded by the fire. All of them were in torment. Inside the fire was a huge frying-pan wheeling on its side like a hoop. Lizzy could not see what caused the movement of the pan. The pan was now wheeling so fast that her eyes could scarcely follow it. As it wheeled around the fire, it gathered heat until it began to glow. Now Lizzy could feel the heat from the fire like the strange men were who in deep torment.

As Lizzy looked down, she saw an ordinary kitchen knife. Instinctively, she picked up the knife and moved

89

towards the frying-pan. The moment tha. her hands touched the knife, the men screamed. As she moved closer to the frying-pan, the men pleaded for mercy. She edged on until she reached the now slow-moving, but exceedingly hot fry-pan. She stretched out her hand and touched it with the knife.

There was a shattering explosion as everything seemed to disintegrate. In her eyes, the men burst like balloons.

She was petrified with terror, unable to do anything as eddies of smoke rose to the dark clouds. She turned to flee. There was a man sitting on a table at the far end of the workshop. Her sight was blurred by smoke, thus she could not make out his face, but she saw his hair and eyes. His head was white and his eyes were burning. The man was wearing a stole. Lizzy realized that she still had the knife in her hand, she held out her hand, the knife in her right hand and moved towards the man. Before she could reach him, there was another explosion. She could not bear to look again at the spectacle. In her mind's eyes, his flesh was like fluff flying in all directions in the workshop.

"Oh God!" Lizzy screamed.

Chimezie quickly held his wife down and close to his body. "Oh! Darling, are you alright? It's okay now" he told her. She was weeping as she snuggled up deeper in his embrace.

He started kissing her face, her mouth and down her trunk and down. She responded with energy, shaking so violently that he had to hold her with great strength. "Darling please, calm down" he said between kisses.

"Chimezie ... hold me," she pleaded.

He got the message and held her. Gradually they rose to a refreshing coitus.

Chapter 6

Defo reached the quiet stream and waited. He wanted to make sure that nobody was following him, so he sat playing by himself to see if he would attract anybody's attention. He also had a good look at the trees, especially the palm trees. Palm wine tappers were the greatest security hazards or assets, depending on which side of the scale one sat. Perched on their coign of vantage and covered by foliage, they scanned the unsuspecting populace in a way that could make even people whose eyelids had been shaved to be chary and irritable. On a day like this, they saw men skulking to their neighbours' houses, staying too long with their neighbours' wives and leaving under circumstances that left no doubt in their minds. Children played the roughest and dirtiest games and cracksmen had a field day. All sorts of evil reared their heads under the quiet of the village. It was *Eke*, the most important market day for entire towns in their Local Government Area. In Nkwoko most people had gone to *Eke-ututu*, to buy and sell goods. Provisions and finances had been depleted as a result of the binge period of the New Yam Festival. People needed food and money, thus the village was almost empty of people. The stream was in fact deserted because the village folk who liked to swim and wash their clothes and foodstuffs here were in the market.

Satisfied that nobody was on his trail, Defo entered the stream. It was a shallow stream. He waded through it upstream, until he reached by his left, a track road which ended not more than four yards from its start. Beyond this point was a thicket of shrubs. The people of Nkwoko did not venture to this part of the stream, at least, not openly. The myth was that the track road led to the playing ground of the mother-of-the-water. Venturing into that area amounted to intrusion into her territory, and that could mean death or abduction by the mother of the water, into the deepest reaches of the waters where she used human beings as pillows.

Defo made two sharp sounds with his tongue and waited. After some four minutes, during which he was sure that his hosts were verifying who was visiting, there came a reply, two sharp sounds from within the thicket.

He met the bunch in a circular clearing, under a shade of trees. They were tough and muscular, reminding him of his days as a footballer in secondary school, when they relaxed as much as possible on a day of a match, until the games master came to loosen their muscles, calves and thighs, and to infuse morale into them.

The bunch did not normally eat today, so he could imagine hunger tearing their stomachs to pieces. He could remember the day they had tried to convince him that society made them what they were. He had not argued with them. He wanted to believe them, to feel what they felt. For him then, being bad was adventurous. It was a conscious turn that he made and he held nobody responsible for it. Now he could see them for what they really were – a hungry bunch; dangerous animals. He could imagine how his father, Chimezie or Ibuego would react if they knew that he consorted with this kind of people.

He had met them accidentally, one dead of night as he smoked *igbo* at Akonwa's joint. That night, they had

92

stormed the joint with bizarre shouts which had made every other person in the joint flee, except Defo. He had stayed, not out of courage, but because he was stupefied and his limbs were too weak to carry him. Akonwa did not have enough stuff for the group. This was when Defo offered them his personal stuff free. They offered him whisky. They drank, smoked and talked till morning.

Defo heard things he had never heard before. In his sizzled brain, his fascination for adventure turned the most heinous of acts into heroic marvels. Before morning, the gang had accepted him and they were really thrilled by his ways. They took him to their den, the very spot where Defo came to visit with them now. Defo was surprised when he learnt that such a place existed in Nkwoko near the heart of their shrine, Ogwugwu Omuma. The thought of the nearness of these people to his people worried him, but his thirst for adventure had overwhelmed him.

Their leader, Bide, had let him into most of their secrets. He talked for long and at the end of it all, Defo understood one thing about them. They were rogues who robbed people of precious things and lived by their loot. Their friendship with him was ratified and concluded by *igba-ndu*, (blood vow), in which they all pledged to protect each other, and to keep all their activities secret, even under pain of death.

He had hung out with them for three days. They had met on an *Eke* day, and he had stayed with them until another *Eke* day. In fact it was on the fourth day that he really learnt about their activities. Before then, they had a lot of whisky, cigarettes, marijuana and beer. They went out and bought roasted chicken and fried beef. Most of them went out at night to their women and came back in the morning. Only Bide had the privilege of going out of the den in the afternoon. This was important, as they did not want their den to be discovered. Defo also noticed that one of them, Charlie, had never left the den since his arrival. Since he and Charlie often found themselves alone together, they talked and soon became more intimate than the rest of the gang.

On the eve of the market day, they had eaten like some mad people. Every stock they had was depleted. It was as if there was a tacit injunction that nothing of what they had should be left over the *Eke*.

The morning of that *Eke* day was the worst morning Defo could remember in his life. He liked to have breakfast, but throughout that morning until 1.00 p.m., he tasted nothing. At 3.00 p.m., the gang left for "operation". He declined to follow them because he needed time to appreciate their business. Bide was not bothered about this. The important task of binding him over, by making him drink their blood, had been performed. He decided that the best way to win him over was to completely spoil him. After today's operation, he was going to spoil him once more until he got around to lead them into his father's house, that they might "operate" there. When a thief delivered his own home for operation, it was a manifestation of total commitment which gradually led to a total understanding of a brotherhood. Brothers were people whose interest had supremacy over all other interests.

It was when they came back in the night that Defo had an insight into what he had entered. They brought home goods, alcohol, clothes, and money. He saw how hard the business was. It was hard because it required a great deal of heartlessness. The operation was not even against the rich in the society who they had unconvincingly tried to indict. It was directed against the poor powerless villagers. It was against the people of Nkwoko. The rumpled and stained money they had brought with them was a proof of this. Defo hated himself for his myopia.

Somehow, he could not identify with the booty offered to him by Bide. He was surprised to find his maddening thirst for food significantly diminished. He found himself brooding most of the night and he drank a lot. In the morning, he felt sick enough to announce it. They all wanted to help him, and Charlie wanted to go with him when he insisted on going home. But he did not want to string him along.

When he reached his uncle's house, he found him sitting outside near the *ikwe-akwu*, with his hands on his jaw. All his children were around him, crying in a bid to comfort their father. When Defo looked into his uncle's eyes, they were bloodshot with streams of tears. He later learnt that the man was robbed yesterday evening of two thousand naira as he was coming home from the market. The thieves had slapped him so hard when he tried to resist them, that blood came out of his left ear.

Defo became positively sick. The rage inside him was suffocating. His uncle was like a father to him, even more, because he accepted him, despite all what he was up to. He would gladly have died in his defence, had he been there.

He lay on his bed, shaking with anger, and then, he remembered the gang. He remembered the dirty money. It was probably his uncle's. He hated the gang. He wanted to rush out to the den and burst all of them open with a gun, or probably tell on them, that they might be arrested. But he was also scared. Not so much because of what the gang would do to him, as the vow which they made him vow. Before Defo came to the village, he had no room for superstitions in his life. Even now, he still considered himself unsuperstitious, but now that he was confronted with this situation, he was full of doubts. A doubt worsened and magnified by an incident which took place three weeks after he settled in the village.

A certain man accused his neighbour and his wife of practicing witchcraft on him. The accused and his wife had been so enraged that they took the matter to court. As the case went on, certain members of the village started saying that there was a proper way of settling such disputes. And it was by the accuseds going to swear by the deity that they were innocent. When husband and wife heard this rumour, they took the matter out of court, to be settled in a way that would really clear them of the guilt in the eyes of fellow villagers. They went and swore by *Omuma*, and both died before the twenty-one day's "guilt period", could elapse. The event was too much for Defo. It shook the foundation of his skepticism against superstition.

But even now, he remembered what his father once told them. "Swearing by the deity is a hard thing," Elesi had said. "A careful man should normally not venture out of his house after swearing by a deity. He should not eat in the company of people he did not trust. His survival vindicated him and embarrassed his accusers. Therefore men often kill people who are under oath in order to save themselves from embarrassment and suffering, and forever tarnish the image of their enemies". This meant that people could have poisoned the man and his wife.

This thought brought Defo much intellectual succour, but no strength to act against his vow. One mind told him that *Omuma's* hands were real and long and would get him, while another mind dismissed this. Could the god really stand by evil men, aid them to fulfill evil schemes, just because their names had been mentioned in ignorance in a dirty vow. This invincibility claimed by many evil men, did it really come from the gods? Sure there must be good as well as wicked gods. Could *Omuma*, the protector of Nkwoko permit such a thing? The more Defo thought, the more weak he became. In his confusion, he decided not to visit the gang again, but neither was he going to divulge their secret. This way, he felt safe.

However, the incident in his father's house, the visit by the three strange men, and Chimezie's story about the stolen god, Okpoko, made him to go back to the gang to see if they could be of help. Aware that he no longer felt any fraternity for them and that his conduct by desertion left much to be desired.

He had prepared himself, in order not to show his hate and concern. He hoped that with a cheerful face he might get some vital information out of them.

But now, seeing them, their hungry faces and unkempt environment, he could only feel repulsion for them. A repulsion which was heightened by the tacit disapproval the group showed about his presence. Bide did not talk to him, and so every other person ignored him. Only Charles could manage a smile. Defo moved closer to him. He noticed his sallow face. He guessed that fasting since morning might have worsened the colour of his skin. The last time they were together, Charles had confided in him that he could not understand why they had to fast in order to do the devil's work. Defo had found out that Charles liked food. As he moved closer to his friend, a funny idea entered his head. He broke the silence by speaking to him.

"Are you sick?" Defo asked Charles.

"No just thinking and strengthening myself".

"For what ... in what way?"

"We all ask God to give us strength in everything we do ... or don't we?". Asked Charles, pretending to be serious.

"Then you are in the wrong house. You should ask the devil to help you, not God"

Bide had been angry the moment one of his men told him it was Defo waiting to enter. He was filled with the desire to chop off his head as soon as he entered. The boy

97

had embarrassed him terribly by deserting the gang. Moreso, he will put the security of the gang in jeopardy if he told on them, Bide's only consolation had been the vow which he made Defo vow. By every consideration, something told him Defo was not going to give them away. But he did not forgive him. He would be punished, his punishment depended on the mood engrossing him when he finally reached him. Now the stupid boy was here on an important day like this, a sacred day in which they prepared themselves, meditating and suffering themselves until consumed by anger and driven by hunger into the roads like marauding beasts ready to despoil any man of his property; there must never be a quarrel between them on such a day, the *odu-una* conjurer had cautioned and he was taunting them. With unbelievable patience, Bide restrained himself from the evil thoughts pricking his body.

"Some idiots checked my old man's nouse yesterday. I couldn't believe it. They were after a visitor in our house". Bide heard Defo say.

"How can?" Said Charles.

"I am telling you it happened and if I wasn't there, it would have been a different story".

There was a sudden bark from Bide. "Shut up you idiot son of big man." He said between clenched teeth, shattered by Defo's suggestion.

Defo smarted more as he remembered his uncle's ordeal with rogues, probably this gang. Again the visit by the dangerous men contrary to what Bide once told him, that no other group of bandits would work Nkwoko unless mercenaries, or they got the permission of the gang. "Are you hungry?" He told Bide pulling the tiger by the tail.

"I warn you. This no be place, no be time to play. Shut up or leave now. In fact leave here now". Bide ordered.

"I am not playing". Defo stated coolly. "I tell you that thieves invaded my house yesterday and all I get is a shout at me". He paused for a while looking really worried. "What is the gain in this gang? Is it not mutual help?"

Bide laughed dryly and then exploded. "If you think I am stupid or I dey mad, then you are a fool. You've never supported this gang once. You are not a member". He laughed loud now, mocking. "My house you call your father's house. I care nothing what happens to your dirty bottom father. Get away from here now".

His words slapped Defo's face. He was not one to swallow insult, not out of fear. Sure he was in the unsafest place on earth with this gang, but no man in it made him afraid including Bide. Yet if he started anything now, they would make mincemeat of him. A man alone cannot make a spectacle of a barn. Defo turned to leave.

"No move an inch," he heard Bide say. "You will stay here till I come back".

Defo's annoyance was expanded beyond limit. Inside his chest, one could almost here threatening growls. Again his mind told him to ignore Bide and move on. But the steam was too much now. His mouth burst open with words "No man can make me do anything against my will," he stated almost normally. His eyes were now covered with a great mist which seemed to defy every power in the world. "You stand in the very shrine of my ancestral gods and order me around. May the land on which you stand open up and swallow you .... You stupid animal who think of nothing except looting and eating".

Bide's men were shocked. Bide himself was astonished, but as a man with the perspective of more than a decade of crime, he considered Defo as at best a stubborn kid. He would surely learn his lesson now. "You won't get away with this," Bide promised. "I want you to know say thieving na man's job. Only people who can kill and draw blood succeed in it, not fools like you. You call me common ... Ha ... no man wey don see my face for operation wey never respect am. My wish na im be their command." Sunday!" He called on one of his men.

"Yes sir".

"You remember that man, that big man with his big FGN car whether na judge or ambassador 'im be, with his daughter. Tell him what we did to them".

Sunday, a dark lanky boy with the eyes of a rabbit cleared his throat and told a gruesome story of how they raped a girl at gunpoint in front of her father. "She be the sweetest crying thing I go ever use in m life". He concluded.

Defo was filled with disgust. "That is intimidation. That is evil forcing other people, cowering them with guns when they have no means of fighting back".

"Yes. I suspected that your stupidity has reached like this. I go give you a fair chance to fight me. Remember it is going to be the clash of thieves. You still remember what you said about how you nearly suck your papa to death, stealing his money and eating it. If I for get such papa to steal from, I no for de patrol the streets with guns. Have you gone back to your father's house?" He asked him in mockery. His men laughed in his support for his apparent brilliance in replying to Defo's accusations which put them all in a terrible light. Charles alone did not laugh. He feared for the consequences of that exchange. Bide definitely would hack his pound of flesh as warning to others who might think of such a behaviour in future,

Inside, Defo was very happy for his reconciliation with his father, but he did not mention it. Slowly he began to speak again. "Some children steal because most parents under-estimate their needs. If it were otherwise, I tell you many children wouldn't have stolen from their parents. But whatever a child does, there comes a time when the iron limitations of adulthood, of mental maturity must lift him beyond adolescent weaknesses. At that time we become responsible for our acts. Any child who steals beyond that point is a made rogue. I can tell you that I've crossed that stage. I stopped stealing my father's money a long time ago. He was even afraid when he noticed, that he thought I had started stealing from outsiders because he used to keep money for me so I could take or steal if you like. But you Bide, you are a faithless and treacherous thief. You are a liar. I am sure you knew those men were coming to our house and you kept that from me. I hereby disavow the vow that you made me vow in *Omuma's* name. I ask for her forgiveness. I have no portion with an idiot, the very gods are angry with you ..."

Defo spoke until Bide, unable to control himself any longer rushed at him. He seized him by the throat and began to choke him. Every second he tightened his grip until he felt that blood could no longer flow through Defo's veins. Defo had been taken off-guard. He was surprised at the strength of Bide's hands as they crushed his throat. He tried to push him away, but it felt like pushing a raw heavy rock.

When Bide saw Defo's eyes pop red with blood, he felt that it was time to hit. Then, with feline-agility, he delivered a crushing blow on Defo's head. Defo crashed to the red earth. Bide pursued him with vigour, pummeling on his head several times. Defo could no longer trust his "coconut-head". He was called "coconut-head," because as a child he often fell down from his crib, landing with his head without sustaining any injury. He was succumbing to Bide's savage barrage, almost about to succumb when Bide did something that brought him to full consciousness. If Bide had maintain his grip as before, Defo would gradually have passed out, but he so hated Defo that he brought his teeth down to his nose, to bite it off. It was then that visions of his own obsequies hit Defo. A tattered and nasty event it was. Death tasted morbid and frightful. He became determined to survive, to live again, the right way. He could now understand why some people were happy when they were dying.

Like a man holding a roof about to cave in on his children, he jerked Bide up a bit with his right knee. With his left hand, he stretched for his testicles. He squeezed them so hard that Bide let go of his throat as he winced with pain. Defo stood and swooned. He ignored the excruciating pain in his neck to pick up a heavy pole lying by. With a fast swish, he hit Bide across the face, blinding his eyes and consciousness. He kicked, clawed and bit at Bide, in a way only a wounded lion could do.

Before the members of the gang could collect themselves, Defo had dashed into the thicket. They immediately made for him, but none of them, except Charles was on his trail.

With a ventriloquism unimaginable to Defo, Charlie ran him to the track which he wanted him to follow, until he reached a quiet part of the grove.

"Defo ... stop, It's Charlie". Charlie shouted at his friend. When he heard Charlie's voice, he stopped, and turned.

"How many are you?" Defo asked Charlie, unsure of his circumstances.

"I am with nobody".

"But I heard more than four people following me just now".

"I was producing the sounds with my voice," Charlie told his friend.

Defo was baffled. He sat down for air, When no other person showed up, he began to relax more.

"Congratulations," Charlie told him, "I was afraid for you".

"He is a bastard," Defo said with hate in his voice.

"It does not matter now. What matters is the question you were asking Bide at the den. Let me quickly tell you what I heard about the coming of your three strange men.

It seems that Bide was aware that they would come, but he was not certain of their mission or when they were to come. You must understand that the organisation which Bide belongs to is very big ..." Thus he told Defo what he knew about the visit by the three strange men. Information he gathered from personal curiosity and research. "I must rush back to the den," he told Defo when he finished.

"Thank you," Defo told him.

"Take care," he said and disappeared into the grove.

*　　　　*　　　　*

Peter and Paul brought the navy blue van in which they drove to a halt, by the dune at the stream. It had been difficult tracing the road to this stream because they had met nobody on their way to the stream. Now here, they did not know what to do, how to locate the playing ground of the mother-of-the-water. The playing ground was a forbidden area to the people of Nkwoko. Peter and Paul waited patiently like a faithful waiting for a sign. Their attention was soon attracted by the excited voices of a group of children. The way they circled about each other told one that they were struggling over something. They observed that the children were fighting one another. As they watched them, they noticed the cause of the excitement at the centre of the crowd. Two boys were aiming sand at each other. They did this with a speed and co-ordination that fascinated every onlooker. Peter and Paul were the only adults around the stream and therefore the only adults interested in the fight.

The smaller of the two boys seemed a wizard in the sand war. Most of his aims hit his opponent *kataa* in the face. Under the barrage, the bigger boy became angered and confused from the jeers coming from his fellows. He abandoned the sand war and made for his opponent with clenched fists. The smaller boy, now filled with premonitory misgiving, became more aggressive. His shots became more rapid as he moved back and forth, dodging like a tactful boxer and yet delivering his shots. The bigger boy's head was now covered with sand and dust. He looked like somebody under an attack of measles. All his efforts to get his hands on the smaller boy failed. He was discouraged, disappointed and clobbered. As the men watched, they saw two lines form on either side of his cheeks. They were lines of tears and they made the boy look like *odogwu-anyammiri*, with the dust on his head.

"Obere, give it to him" the other kids encouraged the smaller boy. Their taunts were so sharp that it made the bigger boy collapse on the ground. All the boys deserted him, including the small boy. From a distance, Peter and Paul applauded.

"Great!" They hailed the small boy who now turned to notice them for the first time as they beckoned to him. Instinctively the boy took to his heels, with him all his friends. They had never seen more tough-looking humans. They ran like gazelles, but they were no match for the adults who had no trouble catching up with them. The twosome were interested in Obere, so they took him and let the rest go.

"Where is the playing ground of the mother of the water?" they asked him.

Obere was too frightened to understand anything they said. They held him with steel hands, squeezing his tender bones roughly, to communicate to him how stupid he was to think that he could run away from them. As they squeezed his hands, they repeated the question.

Obere now understood them, but he could not believe that human beings wanted anything to do with the play ground. Sometimes, in their adventures, they had tried to go there, they had in fact discovered many routes to the playing ground except go there. He told himself that he was sunk today. These men must be agents of the mother-of-the-water herself.

They swept him off his feet to the back of the Van. Peter was questioning him when Paul suddenly started up the car threatening to carry him off with them. Obere was so confused he could not remember where he was.

"Tell us and you'll go" he heard Peter say.

"But I've never gone up to that place," Obere replied.

"We are not telling you to take us to that place. Just show us which side of the stream leads to that place".

"Sir please I don't know".

"Up where did you say?"

"Sir please ..."

Peter gave him a heavy clout on the centre of his head and then rubbed his middle finger from that point to the centre of his forehead. The boy was dazed. After crying, he was more forthcoming.

"But the people here will shout at you if you start going to that place now". He told Peter.

"There is nobody here".

"Yes, but people say it's a bad road. People have been harassed ... along there. They say it's the mother-of-the-water".

"Just show us".

When the boy pointed out the road that connected the playground, he got a fiver and an order to go home immediately and not talk to anyone about their meeting. He obeyed the order to the last alphabet.

They sneaked their way until they came very close to the gang. They could hear the sound of agitated conversation. Nobody disturbed them until they were within a few yards of surfacing from the bush. It was Sunday who suddenly raised his left hand, bent his head and cocked his ear bringing everybody to alertness.

"Wetin?" bawled Bide in his confusion.

Sunday turned to face the verdant bush. He had never been afraid of this bush until now. When they first came here, they were often uncomfortable at the slightest sound, even the sound of falling leaves. But they gradually got used to those strange noises. They even made the place a safe haven by helping to give substance to the myth of mermaid activity. They made sure that the road closest to their den was cleared of people. They did this by playing all sorts of skullduggery on people. Their rule of thumb was pushing things down people's head. Women and children generally fled when confronted with such an experience. Their husbands and fathers always came back to collect those things without any molestation. So people were advised to leave that evil road alone for the soldiers of the mother-of-the-water. Thus the gang were left alone. They took exceptional care in coming in and going out.

But this noise that Sunday heard was either from a man or a very big animal.

"Why you de shake so?" asked Bide trying to sound calm, collected and in control.

Sunday turned and used his right index finger to cross his lips signalling silence. Before he could resume his posture, a heavy load of blows landed on his chest, crashing him into Bide. The two fell on the red earth with Bide on top of Sunday. When he looked up, all his twitty wit was gone. He saw with his two eyes the hitmen. They were the most dangerous elements in the Organisation. They did nothing else than pay visits to condemned men. When Bide saw them, he started praying his last. One of them held a pistol daring anybody to so much as shake a hair. The one that hit Sunday came forward and pulled Bide up by the collar.

"Our men came here and failed on a job. They say that they've been informed on".

"Oh God! Oga believe that?" Replied Bide. His men were surprised to learn that there was another oga. They now understood and stayed quiet and out of the exchange.

"Why I go inform on them? Believe me, they just fail because they meet tough people for the job. The boy who spoilt their business was here today. No ... I tried to deal with him today, but he escaped".

"We know all about that," answered his inquisitor. "All this must stop now. Because of your record, master decided that reduction would not be enforced on you for now. But you must in the shortest possible time enforce it on that boy and on the other man who chickened out on the plan to get *Omuma*".

"Yes sir," Bide answered.

"Whatever his name is".

"I know him" Bide said.

"Do that and leave this place immediately. Get down to base".

"Yes sir".

With this, the men quietly retracted their steps and vanished into the lush vegetation.

Chapter 7

They had just finished dinner when Defo entered. Everybody was excited to see him. All their efforts depended on the information that he was going to give them, at least for now.

Ibuego and Annie commented about his looks. He wore a white T-shirt, jean trouses and plimsolls. This outfit made him look bigger and more dangerous than ever. He appeared very reserved, without the boyish excitement he exuded yesterday after his reconciliation with his father. Ibuego insisted on sharing the same seat with him.

"Do you want a drink?" Chimezie asked Defo after observing the seriousness of his face.

"I don't mind, brother".

He passed the bottle of Glenfidich Scotch to him. Ibuego found a clean glass and poured him a large whisky. "Do you want ice cubes in it?" Annie asked Defo.

"Drink it straight," Ibuego said.

"I like it straight, thank you," Defo smiled at Annie. "What did you find?" Chimezie asked him.

"Yes ... I found out something. A certain friend of mine informed me that he heard that those men were coming from Aba to do a job in Nkwoko. He said that the men were supposed to perform a job in our house. When I told him about my encounter with the men and also about the missing goddess, and her connection with Ikwu and gods in recent times. My friend seems convinced that Odiari and his group destroyed Okpoko.

"God of Abiama," exclaimed Ikwu to the surprise of everybody. "For what? What did he want? Why? Why?".

"He hasn't finished with his findings yet", Chuby told his friend soothingly.

"They are probably art syndicates " Betty said.

"Let's hear from him first", Chuby said.

"Oh sorry", Betty said and kept quiet.

"No ... don't worry. Your question is pertinent," said Defo. "When I asked my friend that question, his answer was in the negative. He considers Chief Odiari a mad and dangerous criminal fixated on the idea of a modern crusade against idols".

"You believe your friend?" asked Chuby.

"Yes".

"I don't understand", Ikwu said as he came out of his murderous thought against these men who had visited destruction on his god. "You said the crusade is for what?"

"Against idol worship. From the look of it, it seems the man hates the use of images in religious worship, but my friend is convinced the man is a rogue".

"Quite terrible," Betty said.

"Odiari is not destroying images in the churches?" asked Chuby.

"There is an interesting angle to this story," said Defo "My friend suspects that they carry captured gods, amulets, charms and other things to Okwu".

"Where?" Shouted Ikwu.

"Okwu, I don't know where in Okwu".

"I have been to Okwu," said Betty.

"Me too," Lizzy said ... "to Reverend Eze's mission",

Chimezie was surprised. "But you've never told me". He told his wife.

"What is there to tell? Nothing, I just went there once to pray with my friends".

"He probably sends the things to Eze to burn, that's his specialty", Betty said. "He burns those things in public".

"If he burns them, then he is genuine," Ibuego said to Ikwu's disgust.

"He doesn't burn them anymore", Lizzy said. "He now has a museum, *The Triumph* where he exhibits them".

Everybody kept quiet until Defo spoke again. "Truly, information supports the theory that Odiari sends his loot to Eze where Eze uses them to dramatize his importance. Eze may be at the centre of ... what do you call it? ... the Crusade?"

"Using thieves as knights?" Sylvester said. "You shouldn't say much things against a servant of God, especially when you have nothing against him".

"I have a lot against them ..." Sylvester insisted. "A man of God doesn't take what doesn't belong to him".

"Not on this particular issue, I am sure," said Lizzy. "We need to investigate these facts before jumping to conclusions".

"Yes ... we should visit Eze's museum," said Chimezie, "to see if Ikwu's god is on his battlement".

"Odiari too." said Defo.

"Which way do we go now?" Ibuego asked.

"We go all the way. I'd volunteer to go to Odiari's place," Defo said.

"Okay" Chimezie said, knowing Defo had the best credentials amongst them to go to Odiari's place.

Chimezie volunteered to go to Okwu and Lizzy and Sylvester offered to go with him. Chuby was advised to go back to Lagos with his team and explore the Ariobi theory.

go back to Lagos with his team and explore the Ariobi theory.

But there was somebody who was unhappy about the whole arrangement; Ikwu. He was convinced that Odiari had destroyed his god and he was disappointed how lightly his companions took the matter.

"I don't think I like the way this whole thing is going," he said.

"What?" Asked Chuby.

"A god of the people is invaded, destroyed, and we find the evil doers, and you say that we should wait .... Wait for what? Why do we stay here acting like stupid policemen when we should be planning a way of making them pay with their lives? All of them must pay, whether they are thieves or Christian bastards. This is a war between us and them. As Chimezie said, our ancestors are not worse than their saints, and yet they had had to suffer a lot from them. We have shown enough cowardice All this must change. We must exterminate them – these Christians, these thieves," Ikwu was close to sobbing, "I have men who would do anything for me, anything I command". Ikwu's eyes were basilisk.

The ferocity of his outburst shocked everybody. Since his arrival some moments ago, he had done nothing more than listen to what was being said. Now, they had a glimpse of the content of his mind.

"What you are saying Ikwu, is that you want us to take the law into our hands?" Chimezie asked him.

'Doctor, I am the priest of Okpoko. The punishment for this act is death and Okpoko is already visiting us with death for neglecting him. It is my duty to see that it is carried out to the last.

Everybody was further taken aback, especially Chimezie. He had not suspected that the root of Ikwu's passions ran this deep. He had no doubt that the despoilers of Okpoko committed the greatest crime possible. A man

111

who destroyed a god would commit genocide if he had the opportunity. Such men, Chimezie recognised should be made to pay for their crime in order to protect the society from their harmful acts and influences. Chimezie felt a repulsion towards people who felt that their position allowed them to pass judgment on others with abandon. He considered the act worse than genocide. But he had always seen their role in this enterprise as merely auxilliary, to help garner evidence strong enough to help the police in their own investigations towards making the culprits pay through legal means. However, now Ikwu's pronouncement was worrying. Chimezie had never had the misfortune of being in a forum where a plot for the elimination of human life was being hatched. What did Ikwu think that they were? Barbarous warriors and priests thirsty for vengeance?

"Ikwu", Chimezie called him. "I take it that you don't realise the meaning of what you are proposing and so you don't realise the implications either. If you are thinking of war or a crusade for your faith, you have come to the wrong crowd. Personally, I believe in persuasion for inculcating religious precepts, especially in this era where people have a degree of freedom of expression. If people have made things difficult for you in life, I expect that such experiences should engender a more sympathetic feeling in you towards others. I think our duty is simply to help dig out the truth necessary for the police to take care of whoever was responsible for the destruction of Okpoko. As far as I am concerned, we don't even know them now".

"Oh Doctor! You are ignorant. Because your Christian faith has made you afraid, you miscalculate and misjudge everything. You can't see what Christianity did to my shrine. It killed me the day that it killed that shrine. It has killed the man in you and me. What has it been able to produce? Men who no longer believe in God, people who no longer recognise bonds of brotherhood, people who ride roughshod over taboos, people who keep interpreting evil and good according to their everyday fancies. It has destroyed our culture. It must go. Listen doctor, I am prepared to go it all alone if that is the way it must be".

Chimezie laughed, "Ikwu, I think you sentimentalize this issue a lot. Before now, it was the Ariobis, now it is the Christians. Look I have an unflinching belief in God, in religion if you like, but more I believe in truth. I am officially a Christian, but in many more ways, I am proud to say that I am a traditionalist. From the beginning, Christianity brought with it a lot of evil. Perhaps, it would be more correct to say that its propagators here were evil, not what they preached. They also brought a lot of good. It brought us closer and faster to education and civilization. Nothing could justify the institutions of slavery, the concepts of outcasts and such practices as the killing of twins. All this, Christianity helped us to scrap. Some of the early missionaries were really really brave ..."

Chimezie felt a need to clarify his points further.

"Christianity cannot be the factor responsible for today's moral decadence. The law has refused to enforce several moral injunctions. Politics, through its famous principle of democracy has sold popular ideas, and most of these ideas are highly detrimental to society. Our materialistic culture is not necessarily a product of Christianity or even religion. It would be attributed to economic and political factors which encourage people to be greedy and self centred. Perhaps the greatest failure of Christianity is its inability to touch us, to change us, even the very people who profess to be its ardent propagators. What we must do ultimately is to continue to encourage democracy because it helps in the creation and support of genius. If we use it to sell the right ideas, we will fare very well. We must accept its setbacks also, in the hope that the more we approximate truth, we get over the euphoria of false freedom for real freedom that is grounded in wisdom".

"Doctor, you seem to think too much of Christianity, such that you really prefer it to our traditional religion", Ikwu said. "I am sick of all this talk,"

Chimezie spoke patiently still. "No. You are wrong Ikwu. I live for truth, not for religion. If I find any truth in any religion, I take it. I said for instance that I respect the love and firmness with which many traditionalists interact with each other, and observe traditional taboos that are reasonable. In truth, I have not found such qualities in many of my Christian friends. What I find instead, is hypocrisy.. But there is also one great truth which Jesus the Christ taught me, and that is forgiveness. I have often thought about his prescription that we should turn the other cheek when a man slaps us. A seemingly ridiculous prescription. A prescription that men, especially Christians have ignored".

Chimezie was speaking with the confidence of an oracle and the fluency of his speech held everybody spellbound. "I remember once discussing this prescription with Sylvester. He thinks it is unfair for him to always have a good disposition towards others, to be always willing to forgive, to take shit from them while they feel free to do evil against him. For him, using evil to pay evil might be a better way to turn the world around. But I was able to make him see that that had always failed. It failed before Christ and has continued to fail. Christ was actually looking for an enduring universal ethical principle. Thus he substituted the forgiveness principle for blow for blow. He was not thinking of his followers alone at the time he created the rule, but of mankind generally. It is a principle that if all of us could practice, would bring everlasting peace in the world. We have all hailed the Golden Rule at one time or another in our lives, but none of us has been able to give a near valid example of such a rule, but Christ did when he preached forgiveness. It is true that it is difficult to practice this rule here in the world, but it provides us with a powerfully clear and justifiable criterion of judging our behaviour. In truth, experience and intuition has taught me that the man who forgives is closer to God; he is closer to peace.

"By way of summary Ikwu, I think it would serve you to have an open mind towards the world, towards people and other things. Try loving all men and avoid seeing people in stereotypes. There are evil men in every organisation in the world. Satan was in heaven though he had an evil disposition *but he was also evil*. Evil and good belong to the world, they are attributes of human thinking and conduct, not necessarily of groups of men. Individual men are moral agents capable of choosing what things to do not organisations. We will help you find these evil-doers and hand them over to the police, not help you to harm them, okay?

At this, Ikwu rushed out of the room to everybody's surprise. He felt completely disappointed. This was not the life he had been brought up to live; not the language he was born to speak as only a sharp knife could fell a hard wood. Like his people, Uda people, these people had disappointed him. They possessed the power to help him but they had been bewitched by a force strange to Ikwu.

Nobody made an attempt to stop him. Time would surely teach him the way of the new world.

"Thank you," Chuby told Chimezie. "I merely came to seek your advice, but see how far you've gone already. Thank you again".

"Ah! What are friends for? You are also helping your friend, doing this for him", Chimezie said.

"I'll leave tomorrow then".

"Okay", Chimezie said.

Every other person by now had left the room except Chimezie and Chuby.

"Let us go and talk some more sense into your friend," Chimezie told Chuby.

"You talk to him. I am disappointed, the way he is going about this thing".

"Let's see", Chimezie pressed on Chuby.

At Ikwu's door they rapped several times without a reply. Then Chimezie turned the door handle, but Ikwu was not there. There was an aura of emptiness, of desertion about the room which said Ikwu was no more in it. He opened the wardrobe. All of Ikwu's belongings had vanished with him.

They came out and searched for him everywhere in the house without finding him.

"What do we do now that he's gone?" Chimezie asked his friend.

"We continue naturally. Going by Defo's pronouncements, his enemies know we are on his side and they are after us. Carrying on is our only security".

Chimezie considered what his friend said. "Okay, we carry on," he told him as they walked into the house, thinking in their minds how long they would be carrying on and sweating about its consequences.

*   *   *

As Chimezie pulled over to let a lorry filled with people pass, he railed at the road.

"What are you grumbling about now?" Lizzy asked.

"It's just very bad how people make big thing of little things. I mean couldn't Mama Defo have told us the actual condition of this road? See how muddy and slippery it is. I bet we'll be lucky to get to the prayer ground today, let alone go back". Lizzy said nothing, afraid that she might encourage this sudden querulousness. Chimezie was not given to complaints, but now ...

116

"And the lousy priest, couldn't he use all his damned bucks to fix this road," said Sylvester from directly behind Lizzy. Lizzy slipped her hand through the gap between her seat and the door frame and touched Sylvester, telling him not to speak further. They drove in silence for sometime, jostled by potholes until they came to a point where they saw several cars stuck in thick slime, their passengers all bedraggled with mud. Chimezie shook his head in utter disappointment. Now he started to observe the people around him. Many of the drivers whose cars were stuck had managed to push them to the edge of the road so on-coming vehicles could pass, but it was no help, the road was too narrow. He now halted behind a 504 Peugeot, and progress become impossible.

For about twenty minutes they waited in the jam, then, Chimezie cut out the engine. Another ten minutes crawled by and not a shift of an inch. It was then that Chimezie called his brother, to come with him and find out what was wrong with the road.

The problem was at a point where a mighty tree grew on one side of the road, on the other side of the road on the left, a wide Mitsubishi van got stuck on that very spot, with these two objects standing side by side, the road was just too narrow for vehicles to pass through. When Chimezie reached the spot, he saw many people persuading the owner of a white Mercedes sports car at the the vanguard to drive through the narrow opening, telling him that many cars had passed through the opening before him. One of the drivers was saying that even a trailer could pass through that space. Chimezie and Sylvester could see that the Mercedes could make it as was being suggested but they stood and watched things.

The owner of the Mercedes was a robust young man. He could have been any age from twenty-five to thirty. He was attired in very fashionable and sophisticated dresses; cream silk shirt, brown silk tie, brown silk trousers and a pair of deep brown skin shoes. His haircut was neat and deep skin folds at the back of his head signified good living as people popularly construed it. He was talking with four other boys who apparently accompanied him. The boys looked equally gorgeous.

This party refused to acknowledge the appeals and howls that came from the crowd around them. The way they talked easily in the face of this pressure told Chimezie that they were neither push-overs nor gentlemen. They simply ignored everybody, talking and laughing, but their manners held a clear message "Come close and have a taste of granite".

Chimezie went in front of the Mercedes and surveyed the position of the car. It was clear that, the car would pass through the opening with little effort. The owner of the car suddenly looked at him and gave him a friendly smile. Chimezie smiled back and wanted to speak to him to tell him to take his car out of the road when another boy, wearing a rather superfluously designed and overstarched caftan called out to the owner of the car. "James, so you are the person blocking this road? Remove this tin from the road so I can pass".

"Obodo you shoot a lot with your mouth. I like men of action". "Have I ever given you cause to doubt me?" replied the owner of the mercedes car.

"I know the owner of the car you are driving in. It is the 760 Volvo, Pati's car, "he continued, "we bought our cars from the same dealer in Germany. He told me that he would be here for three days prayers, and that you would be coming today with this car so the Reverend could bless them for us".

Obodo was clearly discomfitted and did not know what else to say.

"I don't want this car scratched in any way, so the Reverend won't have any reason to tell me to park it in Okwu. I hear that he has grounded many cars there. I

118

really need to see Helen this night with this ride. .... I haven't seen her since I bought it. I'll make her eat money this time".

"Are you just coming from Lagos?" Obodo asked him in a less confident tone.

'Yeah . The Reverend sent for me. He had better get over this blessing thing in time".

Chimezie was astonished at what the robust young man said. He wondered what significance religion held for him and Okwu was supposed to be deep in religion.

The boy suddenly turned to Chimezie who had been looking at him for sometime. "Yes, gentleman, what can I do for you?"

"Get in your car and drive past", Chimezie said, good naturedly.

"You just think so?" Said the boy with a drawn face.

"Enter your car and try".

To everybody's surprise, the boy entered his car and without difficulty drove through the narrow passage.

*   *   *

Outside the big wall protecting the main prayer-ground of Okwu, there was a big market where all sorts of wares were sold. Plastic containers seemed to be the most ubiquitous commodity in the market. Chimezie was happy they were finally here. They could at least have some bottles of mineral water. They locked their doors and started walking in the direction of the bukas.

They were soon besieged by cadgers who rained every imaginable kind of prayers and blessings at them. They started giving them money and they came in their numbers. Soon they ran out of change, including five and ten naira notes.

Sylvester was exhausted by the unreality of it all. He considered some of the cadgers healthy enough to work and many of them came back after they had given them money. This caused him to become hostile and impolite to them. "Get out all of you," he charged back at them. His eyes glared.

At the gate leading into the prayer-ground, several cars were lined up, waiting to park inside the grounds. One of the gatemen approached each car whose passengers gave him some money before he stepped aside, nodding to his colleague who pulled the lever that raised the heavy iron bar that gave one access into the grounds. Chimezie watched the exchange between car owners and the gateman with interest, wondering if the Reverend knew about the extortion. The driver immediately before him refused to give money to one of the attendants who came to his window. The burly attendant simply ordered him out of line. When the driver hesitated, the attendant determinedly turned his wheel for him. Three other tough attendants came out of a shed, to the aid of **their** colleague and forced the man out of line.

Chimezie's turn came and Lizzy **quickly** gave the gateman a ten naira note, having fought hard to keep Sylvester who had been complaining about their methods from quarreling with them. When the attendant got the money, he frowned and hesitated a little and then looked at Lizzy again who did not say anything, before he stepped aside. The bar went up.

Inside the compound, there was an explosion of human beings. The arena was a medley of people. Those of them closest to the fence where Chimezie had parked their car were massed, most of them wearing tired and doleful looks. On closer inspection, they found that they were mostly sick and dying people with their relations. There were so many of them that Chimezie could not believe what he saw. It seemed that an epidemic had suddenly struck upon the populace. He felt that peculiar feeling which often made it impossible to leave the Rockfield even for a second. He wanted to help these people but they were many. Worse still, he was powerless without his paraphernalia.

Chimezie moved closer to a group of people who stood around a sick girl crying with pain. He could see a woman trying to help the girl, but the girl cried at every touch of her hand. The rest of the people stood and watched, unspeaking.

"Is there nobody who can help these people?" Chimezie asked a boy among those standing around the girl.

The boy immediately turned to him "I've gone there more than five times today to call them, but they won't come until they finish praying".

"Who?"

"I am talking of the attendants of the Reverend, the sisters and brothers here," said the boy wickedly, mockingly, "those whose job it is to care for us pray, while we die slowly ... It's not even a prayer. It's a meeting. I've told my mother that it's time we tried somewhere else ... oh God! She has faith like stone". The boy was crying now, "her faith is here. We've been here for three weeks and haven't been able to see the Reverend. His assistants come ... they are supposed to come but they don't ... they rarely do".

"This girl is your sister then?"

"Yes".

"You should move her into the shade, the heat is not good for her. She should have more air", Chimezie suggested.

The boy now looked at Chimezie with interest, "Is this your first time here?"

"Yes".

The boy nodded knowingly. "There are no rooms. We've been here under sun and rain since we came, it's the natural fate of search for salvation. Here is the best place, our only hope of catching the Reverend's attention in case he passes this way".

The boy was studying Chimezie closely and something about his manners told him he was privileged. "You are rich, "he said, "a nice rich man. Rich people have the world".

"In suffering, the rich and the poor are alike". Chimezie said soothingly.

"Even here, the boy continued ", they are sheltered in a dormitory. They have access to the Reverend when they desire and collect all the blessings. I guess heaven is the only sure place. But we must die first and the death of the poor is horrendous. Even death is not easy for the poor".

Sylvester saw one of the young men who had caused an obstruction on their way to this place. This one was rather laconic and hardly spoke, even when spoken to. This, Sylvester had observed when he watched him with his friends at the spot of the jam. Now, he was alone. He kept looking around, with his nose high, like a dog sniffing at the air when it senses a big find. He looked like he wanted to talk to somebody.

"Hello!", Sylvester called to him as their eyes met.

"Hello", he replied, raising his left hand in a gesture of further acknowledgment.

Slyvester quickly walked over to him.

"Man, there are so many broads here," the laconic one started to say.

"I am here to net a lot of them. My brother assured me that I would catch many of them here. See, there are really many. As a law student, a potential lawyer, I guess that I have an advantage".

This boy was full of surprises. Was he normal at all? Thought Sylvester. "Broads?" He asked him.

"Girls, you dumb bastard," Arnold shouted at him, thinking that he was really dull.

"You mean you deliberately came here just for girls?" Sylvester asked still surprised.

"The girls are here to pursue boys, so who is to blame?" asked the strange boy tartly.

"I don't understand".

Okay, look at these people in front of us".

Sylvester looked at the crowd of people and noticed that the number of girls and women far outstripped that of the males. The males were mainly young boys, snazzy in the best of outfits. And also there were numerous chiefs, many of them looking like businessmen in a court room over security matters. Many of the girls were really matured, agewise and otherwise.

"See what I mean. They are here looking for husbands, so any velvet-mouthed fellow is game for them. Will you accompany me for the chase?"

Sylvester ignored the invitation. "How do these girls succeed since many of the guys know what they are up to?"

"Well they succeed by doing anything possible. Some guys find some of them wholesome. Really many of them force their way into the hearts and houses of guys. But the big ones who are really desperate and know their way around, I mean those with connections just pick their men, mostly from devoted members of this congregation. The Reverend or any of his auxiliaries can easily arrange it. Just tell the guy that there's a strong spiritual drive toward the girl from his soul and he's hooked. Just like that buddy. Let's go now".

"No. This is so confusing", said Sylvester.

"Confusing... what? The Reverend is a hard man according to James. Their number used to be double what you see today, but the Reverend drove them".

"How?"

"Through a sermon. That day, he told them all he had on his mind. Well, can't say I blame him much ... on this

123

issue. So many girls, so many girls all demanding one thing, husbands, and this was becoming a sort of a red light district".

"So?"

"He told them that they were fools, opportunists who would stop at nothing to hook a man. He blamed them for their past mistakes, of not returning past love overtures because of their unrealistic dreams, and now that they were stuck, they had come to him to spring husbands with miracles. He called them Jezebels who would rather flock around one wealthy man than seek meaningful relationships with millions of men in the world".

"But I don't see how that chiding would drive reasonable people to form a congregation like this".

"Perhaps it was the response of the crowd as reported by my brother. The entire crowd howled at the girls. Dem don expire finish ... dem don expire, harlots, they called them. The worry about it all is that the girls who had a sense of decency were the ones that fled the congregation. The diehards, the frustrated bitches are still very much around and they are the people I am after, now let us go, will you?"

Lizzy and Chimezie finally caught up with Sylvester and his companion as they were edging forward towards the big crowd of people waiting for the Reverend to come for the afternoon prayers.

"Wouldn't you like to see the museum?" Said Chimezie to Sylvester.

"Ah ... I'd very much like to, but my friend here is explaining something to me. We'll join in a moment okay?"

"Okay", said Chmezie. He caught Lizzy's hand and they went looking for the museum. Somebody had told them that it is "Just at the back of the dormitory".

When they came upon the dormitory, a rectangular building with half walls, as the fat man described it. They were curious to have a look at it. Perhaps the privileged were housed in it as the distraught boy had said.

They discovered that from the side they were walking, there was no entrance into the building, so they had to walk round it to gain entrance. As they walked, Chimezie wondered how the priest was able to acquire this vast land. When they reached the side of the rectangular building, they were immediately confronted with trees, tall trees with long branches that grew sideways. The trees gave a pleasant shade in front of the dormitory, and somehow the noise from the prayer-ground was cut off. For a moment, Chimezie's mind felt peaceful and he wondered whether the sick girl's brother was not exaggerating things. He was savouring his new-found idyll when a male voice distracted him.

Oga, please, give me some money. I am very hungry," a dark, strongly built boy sitting on the floor in fetters said with a scowl. Chimezie gave him a ten naira note and the boy smiled.

As they walked towards the dormitory, they saw all kinds of crazy people who sneered, booed and shouted uncountable obscenities at them. Inside the dormitory, life was quieter, but the condition was squalid. No patient or the visitors there resembled a well to do man or woman. Chimezie knew on their way to the place that they would never find such people here. His eyes were suffused with compassion as he looked at the patients. Many of them understood and smiled at him encouragingly. Others ignored him and their eyes seemed to tell him to save his white – washed pity for some other people. After this exchange, they made for the museum.

The museum was a bungalow. There was a desk for a receptionist, but there was no receptionist. Chimezie and Lizzy entered the largest and the most important room of the museum. But he was unimpressed. He had construed the museum in the fashion of modern gentrified museums, but what he saw was a bad imitation of a museum. The shelves were constructed of rough planks and the objects they housed were so dusty that one could not have a good impression of them. Yet the forlorn and decrepit condition of things in this Okwu was an interest in itself to Chimezie.

They could see some clay pots with the faces of gods embossed on them. There were also wood carvings, most of them in small sizes, they looked authentically African. No serious attempt was made to beautify these objects by their creator. But one could never miss the ideas couched in the carvings. There were also pots of clay and cowrie shells. There were also masks, most of them resembled the type used by children for celebrating Christmas and new yam festivals. There was no trace of any village gods, nor did they find any works of excellent value here. Three other rooms in the building were empty while another was locked. Chimezie wondered what was inside there. As they walked back to the prayer ground, they could hear a rich cool voice over the tannoy.

"... and all of you who come here with peace and for peace shall have peace and happiness. But those of you who still think evil shall have wickedness upon their heads. The blessing of the Almighty is blowing upon the face of the earth now. Those with a good nature attract it. A good nature is hardwork. It is love, it is sacrifice..." Chimezie and Lizzy quickened their pace so that they might see what the Reverend looked like. "... The greatest evil in life is laziness. You must never steal from your fellows. But in everything you do, anything at all, ask God to help you for He alone knows what is good and what is bad. The laws of men are not always correct, that is why they change but the Almighty neither changes nor do His laws. And let me tell you, the Lord God never created anything bad in the world, for after creation, He saw that everything He created was good. Our problem is abuse.

We abuse every privilege and in so doing insult God's intelligence. Because of our own weakness, we imagine that God created evil, but look, look and you will soon find that almost everything we call evil becomes good some day..."

They found Sylvester and his companion at the very rear of the crowd.

"Brother, this priest is not bad o!, he raps very fine and I buy some of his ideas," Sylvester said to Chimezie.

"I heard some myself and I see some truth in them too Please skip the conversation until after the service".

"Man you tend to take everything on face value," said the laconic one to Sylvester, ignoring Chimezie.

"Let us pray," echoed the Reverend's voice over the tannoy. It was time for benediction and there was instantaneous silence so that even the laconic one saw how odd it would be to speak under the circumstance.

"... May the Almighty God through our persistent prayers grant us all that we ask from him and may he guide us to our respective homes in peace and in safety. All this we ask in the name of our Lord Jesus Christ".

"Amen" answered the crowd, which soon started to disperse, many of them pressing to catch a glimpse of the Reverend. The laconic one engaged Sylvester immediately, "Sylvester," he called him.

"Yes".

Did you notice implication that nothing is really bad in the world from the Reverend's sermon? He said, ask God to help you in everything you do including running drugs. Perhaps drug running is good because drug is used in some cases as anesthetic and for other purposes. These positive uses make it good therefore we are free to handle it. Only God can judge us. The Laws of World Government are sham. Nothing is really bad. And he forgets the human defect, whether psychological or anything, that makes us go back to evil again and again

127

like a goat driven from an assault on a yam tuber. The defect that led Adam and Eve astray. For me, a positive message is one that goes beyond idealizations to a positive remedy to problems. In this abuse, they should not handle drugs and all such dangerous things individually without supervision ... at least, for now".

"Why do you harp on this drug thing as if you can prove it," said Sylvester a little irritated. "You dumb lamb", Said the laconic one to Sylvester.

"I agree with your friend, what's his name?" said Chimezie.

"You agree with him that I am a dumb lamb?" Sylvester asked his brother.

"You are funny," said Chimezie a little more seriously. "We are talking about issues here, and I think that your friend's observation may have a lot of truth to it. We can't rule out the possibility that ..."

"Arnold!", called somebody. It was the robust young man with the mercedes, Arnold's brother.

The laconic one became quiet immediately. In a short while, he would relapse into melancholy and become unreachable again, thought Sylvester as the light in his face died.

"Arnold! The Reverend is blessing the car now, please come with me, you and your friends if they will be kind enough to come. The Reverend says there'll be little refreshment". The laconic one was hesitating when Lizzy gave him a gentle push and followed him up, marching all of them to the residence of none other than the Reverend Timothy Eze.

When they arrived, the Reverend had started blessing the cars. There were three other people who had brought their cars to be thus blessed, including Pati, the owner of the Volvo 760 and his poseur friend, Obodo. The priest requested that the bonnets and doors of the cars be opened, and this was done. He showered praises on their owners for their industry and urged them to look beyond their noses, in order that their wealth might be of use to the society. He appealed to God to thus bless others who wished for such things. With such prayers, he fortified the cars and personally fixed his stickers on all four cars. He did these things with the confidence and grace of a seraph, so that one who witnessed saw that God was solidly on his side and that whatever he bound on earth was bound in heaven and whatever he loosened on earth was loosened in heaven. The Reverend asked for water which an attendant brought in a glass jug. He told an anecdote of a man whose car was smashed five days after he had bought it. "When the man was asked to explain the cause of the accident, he said that the car had taken a lot of alcohol during the party for celebrating it". Now the Reverend was using water so that the cars would be cool-headed. This appealed to the crowd and they applauded by clapping their hands. After this, the Reverend invited them to his house for "a light refreshment".

The house was a bungalow, painted in simple white paint, so that it looked very ordinary. When Chimezie saw it, he wondered whether all that was said about the priest was true. Unless this priest had hidden motives, he seemed unassuming and simple enough to Chimezie. But when they entered the house, Chimezie's impression changed. From the corridor that led into the sitting room everywhere was covered with beautiful tiles and wood paneling. The sitting-room was large and lavishly furnished. Solid Italian marbles graced its floor. On top of this was a very thick carpet, on top of which was a table made of marble, glass and brass. There were lots of portraits and paintings, many of which were religious paintings of value. Chimezie did not know what particular thing to look at, since everything spoke of opulence. Even small objects on the table looked quite valuable, beautiful.

He tried to concentrate on the Reverend, and heard him say, "Welcome my dear friends ..."

"I like the art works in here," Chimezie complimented the Reverend.

"Thank you", he replied.

"What do we call this place Sylvester?" asked Lizzy with bated breath.

"Swish is the word".

Chimezie had noticed that the robust young man and the other groups were rather obsequious towards the Reverend. Everything he said was true to them. They knelt down and kissed his ring at the slightest opportunity. They laughed when he coughed and said sorry seven times at the slightest discomfiture that befell him. Chimezie felt slightly irritated by this kind of behaviour. But then he remembered his countrymen, how they worshipped the rich, the famous and the miracle workers. The less exposed they were, the more acute the problem. Somehow Chimezie saw that a man of this stature deserved to be fawned on. He realised that his irritation was a result of the fact that himself and his group looked odd, just sitting there and observing things without feeling the Reverend's power. He was used to important people and most of them he had met were humble and did not expect to be treated like God.

Lizzy was the only one who wore a brilliant smile, waiting for the Reverend's eyes to fix with hers. Sylvester tried not to show his scorn, he even tried to like the Reverend as objectively as possible, so he waited for an opportunity to talk with him. Chimezie noticed that he was not the only one who seemed aloof to the situation, at least there was also the laconic one.

Again he noticed that their sitting was peculiar. All the people who had brought their cars, for blessing and their families and friends sat on one side of the large sitting room, while somehow Chimezie, Lizzy, Sylvester and the laconic one shared the only settee in the room. From that position, and from their behaviour, they looked different from the rest of the group. The Reverend sat on a simple chair on one side of the room.

The robust young man stood up. "Please Reverend, permit me to introduce my brother and friends to you". They all stood up. Ever since Lizzy noticed a peculiarity of behaviour in Sylvester's friend, she started paying a close attention to him. It was she who gave him a surreptitious nudge that brought him to his feet.

"This is Arnold my brother, the one I told you about".

"How are you Arnold?" The Reverend inquired, his hand extended to him. The laconic one suddenly cried out with fright and slumped onto the settee. Everybody was surprised and quickly came to his aid. But Lizzy was doing her best to support him.

"I am okay now," said the laconic one as he tried to stand up again.

"No please sit," said Lizzy. But he was already on his feet, now with a cadaverous smile.

The robust young man was so embarrassed that he could not speak another word. The Reverend smiled at him encouragingly. The robust young man stared at Lizzy without uttering a word. It was Sylvester who realized that the robust young man did not know their names, and they did not even know his.

"My name is Sylvester, I am Arnold's friend, and Chimezie Elesi is my elder brother. This is his wife, Lizzy",

"Beautiful," said the priest as he extended his hand to them.

"What do you do for a living?" asked the Reverend, his gaze upon Sylvester.

"Well, I am trained as a zoologist but presently I am engaged in commerce. My brother's wife is the proprietor of the famous 'Lizzy Infantale'. My elder brother is the Director of Rockfield Specialist Hospital in Jos".

"Forgive me, but I am very impressed. I find it easier to converse with a man I know his trade", said the Reverend. He paused, and his eyes suddenly shined as if discovering something new.

"Did you say the Rockfield Specialist?" he asked Sylvester,

"Yes".

"Chimezie Elesi ... Oh! You are the good doctor who worked a miracle on my niece. I am sure you will remember that case. A small girl who was suffering from lead poisoning. When they brought her here, I tried my best for her, but it seemed that she was not destined to live. I nearly concluded that the Lord wanted her innocent soul, but then, I do ask people to find out what is wrong with them you know. You can't heal what you don't know. So they went back to Jos which was where they resided, only to write to tell me that after forty minutes of surgery performed on her by one wizard doctor, she recovered and was playing again. I later read in the papers that the baby's recovery was almost miraculous as the surgery usually caused one form of paralysis or another in people. You are the doctor?" the Reverend asked Chimezie.

"Yes," answered Chimezie a little elated and a little embarrassed.

"By God I am really privileged to welcome you. Welcome my dear", said the Reverend.

"These are my friends and members of the congregation," he continued pointing at the people on the other side of the room". Chimezie nodded at them and they responded with eager smiles. Here was another miracle worker. From that moment, he was something else.

They dined and wined for sometime until the Reverend said: "how do you like our place?" his gaze was upon Chimezie.

"It's nice in here I suppose".

"No, I mean the entire set-up, that's the entire healing mission".

"It's good again. I've heard people attest to the succour they've drawn from you. But there are also problems".

"Tell me please", the Reverend said humbly, an eager look in his eyes.

"It has to do mainly with the condition of all those sick people out there. There are some without shelter and even those with shelter live in unhygienic conditions. These things could aggravate disease rather than encourage its cure".

"You are right there dear doctor", said the priest, "people keep coming from far and near as they hear of the good work of our Lord Jesus Christ. We don't have the finances to manage all of them. The dormitory that we have now was possible when a group of good samaritans, members of this congregation, decided to build it for the sick. I even keep some of them in my house. There is also a big strain on our staff. For this, we are planning a big launching, a heavy tax drive to raise ten million naira in order to take care of these problems".

"That's a good idea. An idea I wanted to suggest to you. When is the launching?"

"It will be in September," the Reverend replied. Chimezie was now prepared to advise the Reverend the best way he could. The man proved to be good.

"Perhaps we will talk about this in private after ..."

"No," said the Reverend. "These people are my congregation. I want them to hear".

"Good", another thing Reverend, is that people have so much faith in you. They want to see more of you, but it

133

seems that many of them out there never get a chance to do so. You mentioned your staff, many of them contribute to this gap between you and the brothers out there who need your help. I met with a very sick girl outside there whose brother said they've been ignored because of a meeting going on here. The sick should get priority over everything". The Reverend's countenance changed.

"Doctor you've done some bit of eye and mind sampling already". The Reverend was not looking as cheerful as before. He was now scowling, looking at his fingers in a self conscious and conceited way, as if distancing himself from Chimezie. Chimezie felt this. It surprised him but he did not show it.

"Oh Reverend, what form is the launching going to take?" It was the robust young man.

"It will be a very big occasion, very big indeed. The Federal Government will send representatives. Most of the traditional rulers will be here ... in fact, it will be grand. My only prayer is the sky remains clear on that day," said the Reverend haughtily," as if to tell Chimezie that he could survive without him.

"Ah ... why not! We are waiting anxiously for that day. We hope there'll be dancing and enjoyment", said James Johnson.

"Why not, that's guaranteed", the Reverend reassured him.

"Well since I'll not be around then," said Chimezie, "I wish to give my own widow's mite. Please, I want this money used immediately to relieve the conditions of those people outside, especially in feeding them and providing some medical help before the launching is organised". He handed a cheque to the Reverend who opened it and looked at Chimezie in real surprise. He was smiling, now genuinely.

Chimezie spoke up again. "Please, one more thing, if you have some of them you think I can help, send them to

134

me. I suggest again that you engage the help of some doctors and other professionals, who will assist them in different capacities. What some of these people really need is medical help and also some form of rehabilitation. I thank you very much for your courage Reverend". Despite the Reverend's irritation, he managed to thank him with mirth and appreciation. "He just gave me a cheque of fifty thousand naira. I didn't know that doctors had this type of money", he joked. All the people in the room including Sylvester and Lizzy rose to thank Chimezie. They came and shook his hand. Lizzy embraced him. They were very impressed with his show of concern. Somebody made a noise indicating that he wanted to say something. He was one of the people who brought their cars to the Reverend for fortification.

"I am Pati Okonkwo, and I cannot say how happy I am about the exemplary performance of doctor. I wish to support his donation with the sum of twenty thousand naira". He sat down and there was a big applause for him. All four men who brought their cars for fortification towed his line, followed by their friends, until everybody had given something except the laconic one. He was regarded as insane in his family and James had brought him here so that the Reverend might pray for him, and if possible, treat him. He had arranged with the Reverend for this and the Reverend's attendants were waiting to take Arnold in after these ceremonies. Arnold would probably be put in chains for sometime until his madness left him.

"I really thank all of you ... I have always believed that what we sow is what we reap. The good lord shall give you manifold blessings ... Oh doctor, it's really a pity you can't join us that day. Well when you leave for Jos, it would be hitch free ride. Thank you", said the Reverend impatiently.

135

"Is there any special attraction on that day? I am not going to Jos. I can come and join," said Sylvester jokingly.

"I've always believed you would come Sylvester. But to tell you just in case you are interested, there'll be some form of art exhibition. That's why I think that doc. will really miss something, as he seems to have profound interest in art. Some of our members who used to combine heathen practices with Christian practices decided to give up their ungodly practices. They brought most of their fetish which had strong powers to me in order that I might destroy such powers and free them of their influences. This I used to do by praying and burning such objects. In some towns, people brought village gods, which I also burnt. But lately, some friends of mine felt that such objects could be useful for a better appreciation of our history. So they advised that we open a mini-museum for them. In order that we do not repeat mistakes of the past, I heeded their advice and opened a museum. However, important educational institutions and individuals have shown keen interest in some of these objects. They want to acquire them. We therefore decided that we could sell the salvaged ones to these institutions, to help ourselves, and also to help our country. Some of these works really depict the genius and excellence of character of their creators, only they were created for evil. Now they've been exorcised and they are merely objects of art. Other private dealers and artists would be bringing their works so it is not just what we have in the museum".

"I am really interested," said Sylvester.

Chimezie was surprised at himself for nearly forgetting his mission here. Perhaps it was the enormity of the sufferings of people here which needed immediate attention, or even, the priest's smooth ways. Chimezie regarded the priest in his soutane, a tall energetic looking man he was. He had a domed forehead, with cavernous eyes. The blinking of these eyes was very interesting. They looked like a crystal of light surrounded by water, a light which refused to be extinguished because of its deep origins. His face was without flesh, thereby projecting his cheek bones. This man could have been the perfect friar, or a dominee, don or even a descendant of the patriarchs, were he bearded. But somehow these qualities were overshadowed by a more aggressive nature. It was the look of plain ambition. A man who knew what he wanted and determined that nothing could stop him from getting it.

His manner told Chimezie that the Reverend was a man who was sure of himself. He knew where he was heading. His kind of ambition knew no limits. Chimezie remembered some of the stories that Emeruo told him about some of the Reverend's major miracles for which his flock respected him. One of the stories had it that the Reverend raised a woman from the dead. The said woman had had a stroke and was paralysed. Her condition had progressively degenerated to a coma until doctors gave up on her. Her young son, who had been attending to her in hospital, was summoned by the doctors and told to go and bring his family to come and take his mother home to die there, as she had no hope of surviving. The boy was said to have been shocked beyond words. All the while that his mother had been in hospital, he had ministered to her on the impression and belief that she was going to survive. He was so sure about it because in the congregation to which he belonged, in Reverend Eze's mission, he had been told that his mother would be alright and well again. Because of this, all the crises and commas his mother had had to suffer did not shake his belief that she would be well.

Thus when the doctors gave a verdict of "no hope," the young boy rushed into ward and cried to his mother not to give up on him. But his mother was as motionless as a stone. The boy, in panic then rushed out, reached their home and brought with him a jar of holy water blessed by none other than Reverend Eze, and a bell with which to pray for his mother.

When he came back, his mother was alone, abandoned to a hopeless fate. The young boy started praying, sprinkling the holy water on his mother and ringing the big bell while he called on the Lord to save her.

The hospital staff were attracted by the noise of the bell and came to quieten the hysterical boy. They led him out of the ward to console him, but the boy knelt down on the pavement and prayed, after which he went back, into the hospital ward, to see his mother. Inside there, behold his mother's eyes were opened, her mouth loosened and she called his name and her son helped her up from the bed, and noticed that her stroke and paralysis had left her. Specific medical tests confirmed these and the boy gave the entire credit to Reverend's holy water. Thus the Reverend's name loomed as large as Our Lord's ... He was the miracle working Eze, Emeruo had concluded.

Now as Chimezie observed the Reverend, he tried not to taint his impressions of him with bias. After all, the Reverend had just confirmed what Lizzy had told them about the museum. And they had found no gods in his museum. Chimezie decided that it might be good to warn the Reverend of the possibility of those private dealers bringing in stolen works in the exhibition.

"Reverend this exhibition is really a good idea, I mean transferring those objects to institutions which doubtless boast better facilities for conserving them. But lately, I've read of individuals who because of money have chased native gods into the villages, into their shrines, and carried them away, far across oceans where they build shelves for them in Italy and Spain. There's in fact one such unfortunate incident against a friend of mine and he's very determined to find the culprits ... I suggest you be careful Reverend, lest some individuals might dump such stolen objects here because of the exhibition. You know it's not good to fall into trouble because of the mistakes of others".

The Reverend was quick to reply.

"Doctor, I must tell you that I nurse some misgivings against your general conception of evangelism. Perhaps you are skilled in the art of laporatomy, but I am a priest of God. It behooves me to continue to guide your worried soul. Anything that must be done to strengthen the way, the faith, must be done. Have you ever considered the fact that those Europeans who came and carried Africans away as slaves were Christians? Did you ever believe that the great Washington of the United States was a slave owner? Perhaps you thought that slavery did not pose any moral problem for those who engaged in it. It did. Don't mind that some ruthless heathen among them tried to say that Africans were a sub-species of human beings. I am talking of the very intelligent ones among them. They did carry slaves because to them there was a good end in sight – the emancipation and the launching of the African soul to the way. Even the highest authority in the church gave a tacit support to this. For this noble end, they disregarded the difficult conditions under which slavery flourished. Now that the end has been achieved, the music has changed. Doctor, what we envisage is a new world, a world of one God. The residence of your village gods will never come in the way of this course. What I am saying is that I don't really give a damn if a god is dethroned if that would in the long run strengthen Christianity".

"No ... but ..." Chimezie made to interrupt, but the Reverend would not let him.

"Doctor, I've not finished. It seems to me that you are a prophet of doom, a trouble maker. It may be necessary to warn your friend that I don't care what he does. I am no coward. If I were doctor, I wouldn't be here today, and believe me I've grown strong in fighting too. I suggest that neither you nor your friend visit this place again. You saw those policemen outside, I could have asked them to arrest you, but I wouldn't. I am a fair man always, so now take your cheque and go". He threw the cheque on the floor.

Chimezie with everybody around was astonished beyond words. Such nonsense and impudence coming from a priest was unimaginable, and he could not think of a time when any man ever addressed him this way. He picked up his cheque and put it in his breast pocket.

"Reverend, your offensive words were quite unprovoked. As for the cheque, the poor will be worse off and I am sorry for them. However, I want you to know what I think of your little sermon. It's all a bundle of nonsense. You may be righteous or powerful, maybe too powerful ..."

"Doctor, I ...".

"No Reverend, allow me to finish. I gave you chance when you spoke. You may be too powerful I said, but remember that truth conquers in the end. You have merely stated relevant facts of history, but you did not bother yourself with how men have tried to resoive these issues since. That is an assignment for you. Know today however, that truth shall prevail".

The entire people present were completely confused, unable to trace where this quarrel started or even the bone of contention. They looked on in surprise as Chimezie and his party rose to go.

"Doctor if I may ask, what is this truth you talk about? Are they particular truths, events that you know to be true or are you constipated by philosophical speculations about truth?" In a sybyl-line burst, Chimezie made his reply. "Either way Reverend, truth is truth. You are a man of great experience and I am sure you have occasion to have swallowed a lot of philosophical junk which must have caused you constipation also. We recognise truth when we see it. We sometimes say it is straight and beautiful. Perhaps it was like that when the first man appeared on earth, but we have worked untold havoc on it. It is not straight, nor is it beautiful or sweet. Only wilful and courageous people recognise it when they see it, unless we are braggarts escorted beyond our humble homes. Its warning is mere music, a buzz to the ear of the complacent. But the wise sees the power in simplicity because after all the basic elements of our world is the simplest things, unbelievably simple things like atoms. Truth must be small, it must be trite but it has meaning because it is primary to growth, to survival. It is like music which men of different nations hear and like in its angelic melody; understandable as heaven's. But God has created many ways to it, its discovery, the heritage of the meek, the harmony of mankind. To the heathen, it is Ghost and drone to the skeptic".

The Reverend was now clearly perplexed but he still scrounged up courage to mock. "What were you babbling about doctor? You must be mad to think the way you think. You desire more than anybody else the healing hand of our Lord", he managed to conclude with concern.

"There is only one language meaningful to you Straight language. The language of the crock which always says doom ... doom ... doom. Bye Reverend". With this Chimezic and company walked out of the Reverend's house

Chapter 8

Egondu, Emeruo's wife had just finished washing the mound of clothes which she brought out in the morning. Looking at the line on which she spread them, she felt satisfied with herself. She had always dreaded the proverb that bringing out cocoa-yam seeds was not planting them. Washing was not something she enjoyed. Worse still, she hated the smell of sweat and dirt on her clothes, and worst the musty smell they acquired when her maid washed them for her. She had therefore cleared her wardrobe of all her dirty clothes and she had indeed washed all of them.

Now that the work was finished she felt serious pangs of hunger moving her bowels. While she was washing, she had felt the pang before, but she had decided to wait for her husband, who had gone to cut the morning palmwine. Now, it was nearing noon and he was not yet back. She thought, he might have stopped by one of his brothers' places for a chat, (even though this was unlikely since Emeruo had become morose after the settlement of his dispute with Okani).

She eventually ate without her husband. Afternoon came and she decided to look in on her brothers-in-law to see if Emeruo was in any of their houses. In front of Ukpo's house, she met Mgbocha, Ukpo's wife.

"Chei Egondu! Egondu! Now, you walk around looking like a mad woman. Is anything wrong?" Mgbocha asked her.

It was then Egondu realized she had left the house the way she had woken up in the morning. "Mama please stop looking at me. I just finished washing," she said, loosening the head of her wrapper to retie it.

"My Ibu, so you have already washed this morning?" Mgbocha said with pride in her voice.

"I am looking for Emeruo. Did he come to your place? He went to collect palmwine since morning and hasn't come back."

"You won't believe that I have not used my two eyes to see him for sometime now," said Mgbocha. "Is he well?"

"Yes Mama".

"He is probably drinking palmwine somewhere. I heard that he has developed the habit recently." Mgbocha's remark was clearly off-beat.

Egondu could not understand why she had suddenly started making fun of her husband for sometime now. To suggest that Emeruo would start drinking palmwine from early morning was absurd. She knew that Emeruo deserved to be treated with contempt, but the case was after all settled and she was not Emeruo, and she had never supported him all the time that he had had trouble with the village. Egondu felt angry with Mgbocha but instead she said "No mama. He drinks but never outside and not much. I am just worried because he made it look as if he was going to come back immediately. He actually wanted to go to the market with the palmwine."

"Ha! Emeruo become a wineseller?" Mgbocha said contemptuously. "Maybe he has already gone to the market."

Egondu, parboiled by Mgbocha's denigrating course, excused herself and went in search of Emeruo.

Thus she chatted with her relatives until she had covered nearly every house. Now that she was convinced that he had not gone into any of their houses, she found herself going to their farms where the palmtrees grew. The palmtrees here, *nkwu enu* (upwine), were tapped from the top and they came in drops unlike the stream of the raffia family which grew along the banks.

From afar, she could see her husband's gourds and plastic bottles still stuck in the trees, some of them trickling with wine. She was quite surprised, convinced that her husband had not come to the farm, and would have turned to go when her eyes caught her husband's big knife stuck in one of the trees. It was the knife that he had taken away with him that morning. A strange feeling suddenly overcame Egondu. Intuitively, she felt a great crack in her mind, a defeat. Not close enough to the trees, she called her husband by his name: "Emeruo" her voiced carried. The silence that greeted her was the loudest she ever heard.

"Emeruooo", she called again. There was still no reply. Her head suddenly filled out, but she kept on until she reached the very tree with the knife. Her nose picked up a maladorous smell and the buzz of flies attracted her attention to her left. What Egondu saw broke her very soul. She swooned, but somehow came to and ran like she never did before in her life. On the road, villagers called after her and ran after her in a bid to understand why she was flying the way she did, but she ran like the legendary Mgborie who refused to clothe herself as she ran from further punishment from her husband, until she reached her father's home. People who saw Egondu sent to inform the chiefs.

It was Ukpo who led the menfolk of Nkwoko to the scene of the tragedy. They saw a disembowelled Emeruo, his body was impaled on a bamboo stem. Flies were all over him, struggling in his mouth, crawling in his eyes

144

and filling his nostrils. It was apparent that he had taken his own life.

But when the chiefs found another corpse under a nearby tree, a complete stranger with bullet holes in his head, they lost their composure and were alarmed. It was difficult to accept the obvious conclusion the fresh evidence pointing at. A killer? In the village? In Nkwoko? There was only one thing that came to Ukpo's mind. "Okani" he yelled.

"Our father", answered Okani.

"Go and bring the police. My very eyes have seen my very ears today."

Nobody else said a word until Okani, grave of spirit, all alone went to bring the police, so that their illustrious son might be cleaned of the stench and shame that surrounded him, for flies ate him up and nobody had the heart to chase them away. Lions had been crippled today. They sat quietly, listening to the buzz and perceiving the stench as they awaited the arrival of the police.

      *   *   *

Chimezie was talking on the phone with somebody while his father relaxed on a settee in their spacious living-room at Onitsha. As he listened to the eager voice of his son on the phone, the power and strength of it, he could think more gleefully about the possibility of retirement to the village, to spend the rest of his life with his brothers and reminisce about experiences they alone could appreciate. He was surprised he did not see life as work and work again, as he used to.

Chimezie was telling his friend that he could not go back to Jos immediately because of some unfinished business. Elesi found it rather amusing, perhaps a bit incredible to think that Chimezie with his friends was wasting valuable time chasing after a god that was for all purposes probably in a museum in Europe or America on the conviction that they sought to redeem society. Elesi's judgement of the condition of his society was beyond redemption, a judgement made inevitable by prevailing realities of the time. Elesi had therefore long forsaken aspirations to political power and other situations which carried his sphere of influence beyond his family. He believed that the growth of a strong family helped children to easily articulate and appropriate such grand visions. As such, he had dedicated himself to building his family. His children had grown in intelligence, wealth, and power the way he had envisaged, and they were now beginning to seek and exert such influences which was not easy for their father to exert.

The truth was, Elesi cherished their quiet success, especially Chimezie's. He had always thought of him as a natural deputy to himself. He had not thought that Chimezie would begin to speak about societal reform the way he had spoken about it with him today. Elesi thought that such aspirations were best for the likes of Sylvester, Defo and other of his children whom he considered had more time to engage in such things.

Elesi was nevertheless happy over his discussions with his son. He had listened to his story about his encounter with the Reverend with relish. He had also savoured the bit about Defo's transformation and his near-heroic achievements. He longed to see him, but he was told that Defo had gone to Aba.

Chimezie brought exhilirating news from the phone. "My hospital has been voted the best hospital in Plateau," he told his father," it was on the network news and we didn't hear".

"That is really great my son", Elesi said with noble dignity. You've really worked hard there. You've given your life to it".

"There is a one hundred and fifty thousand naira grant from the State Government, for us to up-grade facilities

146

and the Minister of Health has promised to see how his ministry can help us grow". Elesi was really moved now. "It calls for a celebration son. Get a bottle of Dumon for us or do you prefer Dry Monopole?"

"Anytime the choice is mine, it's Dry."

"Dry then it is."

Chimezie went to the kitchen where his wife was preparing late breakfast, to get the wine. When Lizzy saw what he had taken, she was surprised, "what has gone into you this early morning?", she asked him.

"We want to celebrate and you are invited", he said boyishly. He made to turn off the cooker but she slapped his hand. "I don't know what you are turning into cooking breakfast at this time of the day".

Before Lizzy could reply to say he had caused it, he was gone.

"Liar", she called after him.

"Lizzy!" It was Elesi's voice and so she quickly turned off the cooker and rushed into the sitting room where she met father and son wearing shining faces.

"Where are Ibuego and Sylvester and the rest?"

"They all went out. Somebody please tell me what is going on?" Lizzy said.

"Sit down daughter," Elesi directed her.

She sat down and Elesi picked up the champagne. "It is unfortunate that a chief of my standing has to call upon my ancestors now not with kolanut but with wine, since I am told there is no kolanut in the house. But nothing has spoilt. Our ancestors eat kolanut and they also drink drinks. The brother of the monkey is the baboon. If one calls on a friend and instead meets his brother, his visit is equally fine. We thank God for the wonderful blessing which he has seen fit to shower on my family, especially on my son Chimezie today".

Lizzy was dying to hear what this blessing was. She had sensed that it was something big, the way her husband floated about his seat was evidence of it.

"God has made a promise to every struggling man, daily bread and progress on his part. God, your bounty today is testimony that hard work is not evil. We pray you that all struggling people may achieve success. A man who takes proper care and gives a good account of something entrusted in his care deserves a greater charge. God bless Chimezie the more. Bless my children and scatter your blessings upon the world. If we drink of this wine, we shall imbibe the blessings of long life, prosperity and peace in the name of our Lord."

"Amen" Lizzy and Chimezie said.

The cork of the wine went pop in the air and the golden liquid gushed out in bubbling splendour.

Lizzy was entranced at the news when Chimezie told it. She was happy for her husband. It was his kind of dream. Fame and credit attained on merit. They soon gulped all the wine and Lizzy went and brought another from the fridge. They were still drinking and talking when the door bell rang, and Lizzy went to open it. It was Elesi's brother in-law, resident in Aba.

"Guess who?" shouted Lizzy at Elesi and Chimezie.

"Who is that Lizzy", called Chimezie.

"It's Ezeama. Welcome Sir. You didn't come for the New Yam Festival".

"I couldn't make it", replied Ezeama murkily. Lizzy did not notice. The moment Elesis set his eyes on Ezeama's face, he knew that something terrible had happened. He welcomed him quietly and sat down waiting for the news.

"Why are you so dull?" inquired Lizzy from the man.

"It is not so good my daughter" replied Ezeama, grateful to Lizzy for the question. Elesi just sat there waiting for the news to come the way it was planned.

Picking news out of some**body's mouth** often had dangerous effects.

"It's Defo."

"Is he dead?" inquired Elesi calmly.

"No", Ezeama answered.

Elesi regarded Ezeama. "Tell me the truth now, Ezeama, the whole truth no matter how bad. I will not be happy with you if your report turns out to be different later."

"He is not dead sir", said Ezeama firmly.

"What happened then?"

"He was shot by armed robbers. It is a wonder that he survived, three bullets in his chest and one in the leg. Somehow, he managed to run with the wound to the General Hospital close by. That I believe saved him. He was lucky again that there was a doctor who gave him immediate attention. But he is still in very bad shape. The hospital saw my address in his pocket and came and told me. My wife is there now with him."

Ezeama's dilemma was a result of his report of a similar incident in the past. One of Elesi's drivers had had an accident with his van and died. Despite Elesi's request and plea for truth, Ezeama had made the matter seem light, insisting that the driver was well. When Elesi reached the scene and found the driver trapped inside the mangled van he was unprepared for the shock that confronted him. So now that this harbinger of bad news was here with another negative news, nobody was sure what the situation was. As Elesi prepared, he grieved for his dead son. When he came into the living room, Chimezie was also ready. They abandoned their drinks with their now mellowed sizzles. They also abandoned Lizzy who had become lachrymose.

*   *   *

Elesi stood by the door of the general ward, and tried to locate his son, but could not find him. A nurse at the head of the ward had assured them that this was the ward. This was the third time his eyes went round the ward without seeing his son. Then a woman sitting with a chair by the side of a bed just close to him, noticed him and quickly dropped the fan in her hand and went to greet him.

"Papa welcome," said Ezeama's wife.

"Thank you Isioma", replied Elesi as he moved closer to the bed on which his son lay. Defo was asleep. The sleep was death-like and it worried Elesi. It was one of those coma-like sleep men were in when they were on the threshold of death. Defo's chest was bandaged down to his abdomen. He was considerably emaciated and his body and face had lost colour.

His condition concentrated Elesi's mind. As a young man, he had few if anybody to call brother or son. At that time Nkwokos believed in monogamy, and a highly restricted polygamous relationship. Because of this, they were less populous than their neighbouring villages. Such was the thinness of their numbers that other villages saw a weakness and an opportunity to be exploited in that condition. The old generation Nkwokos were thus routed by their neighbours. They were chased away, out of their land. They became refugees in neighbouring towns. Elesi's parents had tried to put up a fight, but they were shamed beyond words. His father, a chief of no mean rank, had two of his toes cut off like an outcast. The warrior, unable to bear this, fought until he was beaten to death by nineteen men. His mother was raped and she lived a refugee in Umuoze. That was a time when Nkwoko was a ghost-town. His relatives scattered all over the country. Some migrated to Itsekiri, some to Abonima and some to Afikpo. But a good number of them, like Elesi, stayed in the neighbouring towns.

At that time, the land conquered by their enemy was quite large and they could not occupy all of it. Elesi swore to be like his father, a wealthy warrior. Thus, before he was twenty-eight in the land of his sojourn, he acquired some wealth. He came back and with the support of many chiefs of the surrounding towns and chiefs of Nkwoko, built a magnificient house in the unoccupied land, the first storey building in Nkwoko. At this time, Elesi had only one wife.

Then came one morning, when most chiefs and elders of Nkwoko and the surrounding villages came to Elesi's house to tell him that he could not succeed in this vast land with only a wife and no relations. Elesi had already encouraged his relatives sojourning close to Nkwoko to come back. The chiefs suggested that Elesi should marry as many wives as possible, and he should also encourage his brothers to do so in order that there may be people in their land, to serve as deterrent to jealousy motivated *onslaughts* against him. He should use his money if need be to marry for them. Elesi communicated this to his brothers, most of whom were willing to take other wives, but Elesi still hesitated.

His trial came when even the very chiefs who had rallied round him became jealous of his success and started opposing almost everything he did. In a way, Elesi was unperturbed nor was he flurried into taking many wives, knowing that in the conditions of modern times, jealousy and population did not count as much as truth, connection and money. But he was often humiliated in village assemblies. There, if he felt strongly about any issue and it was put to vote, he usually failed woefully. Elesi liked to sing during such meetings, but if he started a song, others let the song die like that. Elesi eventually took three other wives and did everything to bring back his relations living in other parts of the country.

It took long for their children to grow, but they did. In that growth, Elesi found respect in the eyes of the chiefs and elders. He came to be respected, and his power surpassed that of any other person **born in Nkwoko** and other neighbouring towns. **Children sang his name** in moonlight plays. He became **known as Elesi the** Great, Elesi the Wealthy, Elesi the Wise, **Elesi the Invincible,** the Unconquerable for on the day Nkwokos **had their** last fight with Ekemas, the captain of the Ekemas had struck Elesi full tilt with a knife, and the knife had failed to open his body. Elesi was completely rehabiliated. His town, three times offered him the highly coveted sceptre of kingship, and three times he refused. To Elesi, most of these things were accomplished as a result of the support his children gave him.

Elesi came to have the greatest value possible for life. It was a value doubled when it came to his own children. So now, as he looked at Defo and thought of these things, tears rolled down his cheeks. He stood there for long staring at his warrior son. The story of Defo's escape from death was in fact thrilling. How he longed to say a word to him.

The head nurse suddenly approached him.

"Mr. Elesi, we would like to attend to Defo now... please if you will go outside," she started to say. That moment, Defo's eyes flickered for a moment and focused on his father. Elesi looked into those eyes with wonder and gratefulness to God. For a moment he thought that he saw a ghost of a smile on Defo's face. That moment the eyes were shut and Defo continued sleeping.

Chimezie took his time to study Defo's **treatment** chart and assured his father that he was responding well to treatment, unless something dramatic suddenly happened. He opposed his father's suggestion that Defo be transferred to **their** doctor in Onitsha on the ground **that the** movement might do more harm than good **to Defo. Thereafter,** they left.

Elesi directed Chimezie to head to Nkwoko so he **could inform** Anyanwu, Defo's mother, who was still in

Nkwoko, of the unfortunate fate which had be fallen their son.

*　　　　　*　　　　　*

Nkwoko was in total confusion when they entered. Elesi's gateman was first to tell of the crisis in the village. Everywhere was deserted, so they drove to Okpara's house.

Elesi's entry was most comforting for most of his kinsmen who were neither prepared nor experienced enough to manage the kind of crisis which had overtaken the village. The police were their gravest plight. After asking questions and learning that Okani was the only one who had had a quarrel with Emeruo before his death, they had done everything possible to hang the two murders on Okani. Many times since Emeruo's demise, they had invited Okani for questioning. In fact Okani had just come from the station and it had cost the village a lot of money to secure his release. The village was thus thrown into confusion. They were convinced that Okani could never have done that and he had a valid alibi to press that point. But lately, because of lack of anything to hold on to, some elders, especially those jealous of Okani, had been heard to say that in this world, anything was possible. A thief they said, did not go to steal to be caught. The incident itself had brought Nkwoko to ridicule and they had been treated with contempt by neighbouring towns. They had called her a town controlled by the devil himself, a town booked for destruction. Anybody they said who had followed the history of her tribulations would certainly agree that ill-luck ran in her blood. The point of the contempt was when Chief Ukpo sent word to his daughter's suitors to postpone their dowry-payment ceremony till the illustrious Emeruo had been buried, but to his chagrin her daughter's suitors had sent word that the young girl was free to look for another husband, a fact which tore Mgbocha's heart to shreds.

153

"You are welcome," Okpara greeted father and son, while the rest of the village sat there sullen and immured in grotty feckless thoughts. It was obvious to Chimezie that these people were worn out to a frazzle and would give anything to end this macabrish chapter in their lives.

"Where is Ukpo?" Okpara inquired from Elesi.

"Ukpo?" Elesi said confused.

"We sent him to you this morning".

"Well, maybe I had already left when he called. I went to Aba", Elesi told the Chief and led him into the house. There he told him about Defo's problem. Despite assurances that Defo was still alive, the village head could not control himself for he let out an agonised wail, bemoaning Defo's misfortune. When Mgbocha heard the news, she flung herself to the ground with such force that made Nkwokos weep, thinking she had broken her neck as she lay on the ground motionless.

"Mgbocha! Mgbocha! Are you hurt?" Elesi who rushed out of the house when he heard their cry went to her. When Mgbocha heard Elesi's voice, she moved to a sitting position.

"So Defo my son is dead," she finally said.

"He is not dead yet," was the reply she got from more that a dozen women and men who now thought she had over-reacted to the news. Mgbocha became alert once more, confused and looked around. The other women came and helped her to her feet.

At this point, Ukpo entered with a tired look in his eyes. He kept gazing into Elesi's eyes as if yet another terrible thing had happened.

"Is there any trouble? asked Elesi, troubled by the way Ukpo was staring at him. "You are asking me Elesi? Tell me of the condition of my son. I have been in your house since hoping that you would come back with news of him so that I'd know the ultimate condition of things."

"Well, Defo is not dead, but he is in a very bad condition. I couldn't speak with him as he was sleeping when we saw him."

"Thank God," said the formidable Ukpo. He found a seat and lowered his frame onto it. He had lost most of his vitality and vigour for which his kinsmen revered him. Now he looked like an old rag.

Inside the house where the menfolk of Nkwoko conferred, Elesi was asked a lot of questions. When did the incident take place? Has the police identified the stranger who had died with Emeruo? Could the stranger have been fighting with Emeruo?

"The incident took place yesterday," Ukpo answered. The stranger and his mission there was still a mystery. Chimezie thought the fighting theory unlikely since the stranger spotted bullet wounds. Both of them must have been murdered, he said. "How could that be possible papa when Emeruo was killed by being pierced through a stalk and the stranger had bullet wounds? Somebody must have killed them. But what surprises me is Emeruo's connection with the stranger".

"Does anybody know whether Emeruo had been involved with some people lately, whether in business or anything at all?" inquired Elesi. He looked around and noticed that his brother, Dim, was not around, "Where's Dim?"

"Since the incident, he has locked himself up in his room," replied the village head. Elesi shook his head in understanding. He fought hard to suppress the tearful feeling welling up in him. How could their gallant sons come to this kind of fate? Himself and his brothers seemed to be the heads stringing the ears in this matter.

"Okani, I believe that you were closest to Emeruo in this village. You grew up almost as his own son. You did business together, almost everything. Don't you have an idea what could have cost him his life?" Chimezie paused, looking at Okani.

Okani was startled, for Chimezie had said the same thing the police had said to him. He instinctively resented the question, but when he saw the problem they were in, he thought well before answering that he did not know.

"What I mean is, it needs not be somebody you know or any particular thing, but something you noticed in him, or something he mentioned to you which we or you overlooked".

"Why are you questioning my son like that, is he in a court of law? He says he doesn't know. Isn't that enough?" It was Umeike. His sudden outburst was distasteful to all. Okpara ordered him out of the meeting, but Elesi intervened on his behalf. "My brothers, when we are searching for truth, it is like searching for an object in a river. There is no half measure to it, we take our shoes in order to feel it when we see it. Whatever made Umeike think Chimezie was questioning Okani in bad faith, I cannot understand, anyhow, so much for that". He signalled Chimezie to continue with his questions. But before Chimezie could speak, Okani, was talking. "My brothers, to be truthful, you remember my case with Emeruo. At the time we had that problem, I could not think of any reason in the world why he would suddenly want to make trouble with me. But with time, I remembered one encounter I had with him which I felt explained it". He paused, his chest heaving like a man who had carried a heavy load a long way and now desired rest.

"You all knew how hardworking he was in this village. I keep saying it, I am what I am today because I respected Emeruo's way of living. But, somewhere along the line, something happened. He became interested in keeping late nights. He was involved with one widow in Umuoze. His interest in work declined and he started having financial problems. In one month alone, he came

156

to me three times to borrow money. He managed to pay back all his debts, but I noticed that he was going down fast. I inquired into the situation and advised him to abandon the widow of Umuoze since I heard she was very wayward, but he would not listen to me. He kept telling me that he would be alright.

Then, one early morning, he came to my house to tell me of his plan of recovery. The plan was to favour me if I wanted, but he just wanted to bare his mind to me. The previous night Emeruo was approached in one of the bars at the market square, by some men who wanted him to help them to destroy Omuma's shrine".

"What! what did you say?" shouted the village head.

"The men wanted the shrine destroyed because they were on a kind of war against idol worship".

Elesi and Chimezie looked at each other. How things began to fall together!

"Why did they want to use Emeruo when they could have gone to the shrine to destroy it themselves ... at night maybe, and not run the risk of being found out, just the way Ogwugwu-Uda was treated?",asked Chimezie.

"God forbid," said Okpara his ears suppurating out of what he heard.

"The answer doctor, is that those who do these things believe in the power of idols. They are really agents of some people and they normally inquire from magicians and sorcerers on how best the task can be accomplished. With money, doctor, you can get some people to kill themselves. Well, Emeruo explained these things to me. He even mentioned Ogwugwu-Uda and said that nothing happened to those who destroyed or co-operated in the destruction of the shrine, but he did not mention the people involved. They were to pay him nine thousand naira for Omuma's head. Strangely, somehow he followed their argument.

"To tell you the truth, I didn't know what to feel after he told me about his plan. I couldn't believe my ears, however, I spoke to him as I would to my father and friend. I warned him that he could not do such a thing and bring on a great curse on our village. I told Emeruo, that if it was because of money that he wanted to destroy Omuma, I would give him three thousand naira to start a new business in palm-kernels. When he insisted, I threatened to reveal his plan to the elders. After our discussion, he started avoiding me, until he accused me of stealing from his farm."

"So what role was he to play?" Chimezie asked Okani.

"Well the opinion of the sorcerers according to him was that since human beings fashioned their own gods, they could also send them away without hurting themselves. What was needed for the operation was therefore the consent of the priest of a god, or any of his children. In Emeruo, the group found the perfect man, a man who was drowning fast, the son of the former priest of Omuma. They just wanted him around to say some incantations while they destroyed the shrine. This Emeruo told me with his mouth. Somehow he listened to me, but he was never happy again with me. Our discussion was an eye opener for him, but what he saw of himself was disgusting. I believe that he even considered killing himself.

"At the time we had this discussion, he gave the impression that he had finalized the arrangement with his friends. I believe they must have been annoyed with him when he changed his mind. I don't know, but I keep thinking that his death might have something to do with this. I believe that his later pretence about religion was probably to justify his action or seek protection in God".

At the end of Okani's speech, the menfolk of Nkwoko were stunned. How could anyone think of destroying

Omuma? To them, even though Emeruo did not fulfill his wish, he was a worthless fellow deserving no burial at all.

"The world has come to an end.", said Okpara. "That sorcerer, that wicked sorcerer is the devil's sorcerer. Does a man destroy his own house? Does a man steal his own goods? It is never right. Any man who has properly suckled on his mother's mammaries would never accept such a thing from a priest, unless a death - bound dog".

"But we don't know yet whether Emeruo's death was as result of this", said Elesi.

"We are not concerned about his death. We are concerned about his plan to destroy Omuma. A dog is more respectable than that worthless fellow", said Ukpo in a frisson of hate. "I see the hands of the gods in his death. They made him mad a long time ago and only killed him yesterday."

"True," said Okpara.

Elesi and his son felt sorry for Emeruo, but they did not say it. Elesi would rather that things become clearer to him. It was unlike his brother and perhaps Okpara had been right, a death - bound dog uninterested in the smell of faeces. He charged Okani to go to the police with Ukpo and give them his story to facilitate their investigation. He had a feeling that once Defo was up, things would be much better. His informant friend would be a great asset and Elesi was bent on getting at the root of this problem. Defo's accidental encounter with armed robbers ceased to be an accident in his mind but a deliberate attempt by unknown enemies to mow down his son. They would never get his son, not when he was alive. Even death respected the presence of fathers. He rarely killed children in the presence of their fathers. At the house, he picked Defo's mother, and headed back to Aba. He wanted his son out of the general hospital where there was little or no security. He wanted him in a private hospital, and he wanted him protected at all costs, he would see to that.

159

Chapter 9

Chief Oliver Odogwu Odiari sat in his plush office scanning the papers. He did not find his favourite paper, the *Trotting Vanguard* among them, not even the *New Concord*. He felt better when he saw the *International Champion*. He liked to feel that he had a liberal mind, a large mind so he liked to start with the national dailies.

As Odiari read the papers his visage changed from pompous delight to ghastly alarm.

"Seboo..."

"Sirrr," answered Sebo who had brought in the papers and knew that they contained disturbing news and was on hand to minister to his master.

"Get my car immediately."

Azinge who had called on Odiari was looking at his friend with understanding and concern, but Odiari failed to recognise his existence. He flounced out of his office, clenched his fist and brought it down on his desk, scattering most objects atop the table. "This bastard has failed me again", he cried. "Again."

"What is it Oliver?" asked Azinge.

"Nothing that will be of interest to you. I am sorry." Sebo put his head around the door, signalling that the car was ready. Odiari picked up his briefcase.

"Please come back another time for your deal. Something is creeping up my head," he said perfunctorily to Azinge and stormed out of the room, slamming the door behind him. When Chief Odiari left, Arinze walked to the huge desk and picked up the newspaper which his friend was reading that had so startled him. He looked at the handsome Chief and the caption below the photograph: Chief H.E.M. Elesi Offers N50,000.00 to Nab Murderers: Information needed urgently. Azinge wondered why this could possibly upset his friend the way it did. He read on -

Chief Elesi has finally come up with an idea on how to apprehend the gang responsible for the murder of his brother, Emeruo Dike, and a stranger whose body was discovered beside Emeruo's. It is believed by the police that this same gang with their wide network was responsible for shooting Elesi's son, Defo, at about the same period around the Aba, General Hospital.

As you may recall, Late Emeruo's body was discovered by his now distraught wife ... This story has long been confirmed by the Orlu Divisional Police. In his confirmation note, the Police P.R.O., Mr. Adoga Evonine stated that 'Emeruo's body was impaled on a spike after he was killed. His murderers made his death look like suicide, but autopsy reports revealed that he died of a bullet wound which punctured his heart. Mr. Evonine also confirmed the death of a stranger found beside Emeruo's body. According to the Police P.R.O., this stranger had a birth mark, or tattoo which resembled the map of Africa on his left cheek. 'Information that would lead to his identification might be useful in unravelling this mystery', stated the P.R.O.

Emeruo's demise according to police theory may be linked to his refusal to connive with some members of this gang to despoil the sacred shrine of his fathers, Ogwugwu Omuma. The police also indicated that there are clues which strongly suggest that these criminals were responsible for earlier attacks on shrines, including the attack on the mighty Okpoko.

Contrary to popular belief that these attacks on shrines were organised by fervid christians in the interest of christianity, the police says that these dastardly acts may be perpetrated by rogues who steal valuable objects from the shrines, including gods, themselves to sell abroad.

Serious police investigations have revealed a den in Nkwoko from where the murderers were suspected to have operated. The priest of Okpoko Uda has since been arrested and a key player in this drama, Mr. Ikwu Otuonye, has disappeared into the thin air.

The police believes that this laudable gesture by Chief Elesi, should spur patriotic citizens who have information vital for the solution of these crimes to pass them on, either through the Elesi offices or direct to the police at Orlu, or through any police station in the State, or through any other means they might device.

The police further advises that they can best protect the public interest when the public co-operates with them...

The full page report went on to report interviews with Chief Elesi, Emeruo's wife and others. Azinge dropped the newspaper and left for his house.

*   *   *

At the main gate leading to the prayer ground, gatemen and touts who had been beneficiaries of Odiari's largesse were quick to recognise him and they quickly raised the rail for him to pass. Many cars in front thus got entry without being subjected to extortion. Today, Odiari did

162

not even acknowledge their sycophantic bows. Sebo in an off-beat manner sped the car straight to the Reverend's house where a lot of people, mostly rich businessmen waited.

Odiari walked fast with a swagger to the small gate separating the Reverend's house from the rest of the grounds. His attitude earned him instantaneous attention from all and sundry who expected the policeman at the gate to fling the gate open for him. Odiari did not recognise the policeman at the gate. He was deeply disappointed, for despite his sombre mood, he was a man given to vanity. That the gate would not open immediately was for him a great misfortune, but he hoped that his show might impress the policeman. "I have something extremely urgent to discuss with the Reverend, something he must hear right now or things may go wrong. Open the gate", he ordered.

"Oga is very busy with some people, and he said no admission to any person till he finishes", answered the policeman.

"Go and call his houseboy for me. I have a very important message that he must hear right now," Odiari managed to sound persuasive.

"Oga," said the policeman "I won't leave here for anything in the world."

Odiari frowned. "You stupid policeman, haven't you heard of emergencies before? You are just an idiot. All of you policemen are idiots, especially you recruits. If you don't open this gate now, I'll open it myself". He could have been addressing the crowd for the stage was set for action and Odiari was not a man to be found wanting.

"Oga, you no fit o. I am only doing my duty, and I won't allow you or anybody to show me how best I go do am."

"Sebo," called Odiari. "For the last time you stupid policeman, tell Reverend Eze that Chief Oliver Odogwu Odiari is looking for him."

Most people in the crowd looked scornfully at Odiari's rather pompous behaviour while a few thought that the policeman should at least take his message to the servant or to the Reverend himself, but generally nobody interfered in the exchange. There were several seconds of tense silence during which Odiari paced the ground.

"Sebo," he called finally "break this gate if you must but open it now." Sebo walked coolly but confidently, emphasizing his huge arms as he reached the gate. He passed his hand through the bars of the gate and started to pull at the bolt when the policeman raised his baton and hit his fingers with it. Wicked pain instantly engulfed Sebo, jarring his brain. Had this not happened here, he would have retracted his hand in order to swing it for comfort. But he managed to open the gate. Sebo bit into his lips so hard that blood dripped. It was to balance the pain in his hand. When the policeman saw this, he drew back and looked back, as if soliciting for help. Sebo caught up with him. He slapped the policeman so hard that he fell on the ground. He pounced on him and throttled him so tight that out of fear, people started screaming. Several men tried but could not wrench the policeman's neck out of his hands. The frantic screams coming from outside brought Reverend Eze to the corridor to find out what was amiss.

At first, he had thought that it was a mad man, brought by a worried family. Madmen and patients could wait he thought, but when the screams continued frantically and without let, he decided to verify what was happening. As soon as the crowd of people saw the lordly priest, they genuflected by way of greeting. Then the priest saw Odiari presiding over the humiliation of his securityman.

164

"What is this Mr. Odiari?" asked Reverend Eze with annoyance.

"This bastard policeman won't get a message to you that there was something very important I wanted to discuss with you. Honest Reverend, it cannot wait. Can we see now?"

"Odiari, I hope that you are fully aware of what you are doing. How can you attack a policeman who is working under instructions?" said the Reverend with open irritation.

"There are emergencies Reverend. Even if he were standing at the gate of heaven he should know that." To forestall further embarrassment, the Reverend invited Odiari to a nearby room.

"What is this emergency, please make it brief, I am deeply tied up now with negotiation with executives of the RAMBLERS for the exhibition, and they will be going to Enugu for their flight to Lagos in little over two hours from now", Eze said impatiently.

"Did you see today's *International Champion*?" asked Odiari very angry inside that this priest was treating him as a mere appendage when he was the lynch-pin behind this exhibition.

"Please go straight to the point, Odiari. I told you I am busy unless you want appointment for another time." The Reverend managed to maintain a reasonable tone. Odiari fought hard to control his temper. "We are in danger of being discovered," he finally announced.

"Who are we ? For what?".

"You and I Reverend. I have come to tell you that you must suspend this exihibition... everything, for the time being. There may be a lot of stolen works among the lot you intend to exhibit. Forget this exhibition now."

"I think you are mad Odiari, remember that I am a priest of the Lord and I knew you in connection with helping you to become a good christian. The art works coming up for exhibition are mostly objects people willingly surrendered to the power of the Almighty God. I used to burn these objects until their educational and historical significance compelled certain academics to advise me to keep them for posterity. This exhibition will guarantee that these objects get to places where they will be better conserved, even for better glorification of our Lord's name".

"Reverend, I am sorry to say that this is no situation to be reduced to mere idiocy. I have put up enough with your lies and hypocrisy. I am a rogue, even now at my position, I still engage in deeds of darring do. I am better than you because I recognise it. I know myself for what I am and if I am caught anyday, I will pay the price gallantly, probably to the admiration of many decent people. You have completely shut out from your subconscious, your vile and ambitious nature which is the motivating factor in all your intrigues. You vainly imagine now that you are organising this exhibition out of charity. You imagine that you collected all the objects you want to exhibit. Let's go to your gimcrack of a museum. All that you've ever collected from your crusades are worthless amulets and pots. You leave them unguarded because you know that nobody is interested in them. Where are the works I've brought to you?

"Reverend can you swear that you did not know that everything I ever brought to you was stolen? To which village have you gone and they gave you the true god of their fathers? A god in which they have total belief in? I knew that you were very greedy and so I willingly diverted our loots from the shrines to you. I needed your influence on the people to keep up my attacks on these shrines, but you have so far shown me the worst kind of wickedness. What I ask you now is to save yourself and me from this rubbish. If it's money you want, I will give you money."

The Reverend was visibly shaken by Odiari's outburst. Imagine a common criminal like Odiari offering him money. Odiari clearly saw streaks of vulnerability in him and when the Reverend spoke, it was to hide his lies.

"Mr. Odiari, I feel greatly ashamed to be associated with a man like you. I must tell you one more time, I am doing God's job and I am bold about it. I don't care who comes here. One Dr. Elesi was here with all this crap about somebody looking for a god. I told him off. I tell you off now. However, know now that nothing can stop this exhibition from taking place. Even if I am framed up for doing God's work, I will be happier for it."

Odiari was determined to talk the Reverend out of his illusion.

"It is these Elesi s that are offering fifty thousand naira for information about who shot their relatives, one of them died and one is fighting death in hospital, the issue of stolen gods is prime in their mind. The way they are going I believe they will discover those gods if you stage this exhibition."

"I don't understand! What have these killings got to do with me. I've never killed before in my life."

"A lot", answered Odiari. "Because you consort with killers". The priest smiled mischeviously "which gods in particular?" he asked.

"I don't know. My boys do the job. But they call him Okpoko. I am sure that my men brought the god and other valuable articles from that shrine to me and I brought them to you. It doesn't matter which god. One single evidence is enough to land you in serious trouble".

The Reverend stood up as a gesture of dismissal. "Odiari, I'll see how best to organise my affairs. I beg you in the name of God to leave me alone."

Odiari had become alarmed by now. "Don't be a fool Reverend. I know why you are acting this way. You'd only constitute an embarrassment to your friends when

167

you are nabbed. They'll just wash their hands off you. They are all slaves to the law. Take my advice the way you took it before and obtained an illegal pistol from me. Remember that the gun once saved your life. What I am offering now may save you". Odiari was almost pleading with Eze now.

The Reverend had heard enough. "Good bye Mr. Odiari. Save your worries for yourself," and the Reverend walked out.

Odiari was completely perplexed as he sat alone inside the small room. He had not imagined that his meeting with the Reverend would turn out this way. He had thought as he was coming, that Eze would welcome his proposal with his two hands and with all his heart and thank him for his foresight. It had now become apparent that something was wrong.

On whose side was Eze? How could a reasonable man like him become totally indifferent and insensitive to danger? Was he working against Odiari or was it a case of who the gods wanted to kill they sealed his ears with wax and painted his brains with tar?

It looked now, like an arrangement of everyman on his own. There was still time. He still had about one week before the exhibition. He must survive. With these enervating thoughts, he stood up and walked wobbly to the waiting car outside. Everybody stared at him as the mercedes sped out of the compound.

*   *   *

Defo woke up this morning in high fettle. His mood was boosted by Ibuego's presence. She was unsparing in her shower of love and support. Everytime Defo looked at her, he regretted one thing – she was not a man. Ibuego was an amazingly diverse and inconsistent personality. Guaranteed, a handful for any parent any day. She was, by turns, saucy and kindly, cynical and righteous, materialist and devoted, careful and slovenly, she had all the qualities of an achiever.

Defo had always known the truth, that being a man was nothing special. But he also knew that being a woman meant certain limitations. Society and men could always pretend that a woman could be anything, but they were always afraid of what a woman was. A woman did not have the privilege of those painful but helpful pressures that culture always exerted on men. No woman was chided for not providing for the family where her husband was around. No woman was considered a failure for her inability to build a mansion. No woman was considered a coward for not contributing in town meetings. Men always had these pressure to push them. As Defo looked at his sister, he thought, many women were like water, we might never know their qualities unless we exposed them in the vicissitudes of nature, out in the cold. There, if water enters a rock, it freezes and breaks the rock, then we see the power of water.

"What's been going on? They don't tell me anything any more", Defo stated, yearning for some news.

"It's not good for your health ... but now that you are well, may be I should tell you everything tomorrow. Nothing much though," Ibuego replied unconvincingly.

"Now Ibu or never".

Ibuego looked into Defo's eyes for help. She was helpless with him. She had genuine affection for him and his character encouraged her to share reckless experiences with him.

"Ohooooooo". She began to protest.

"Okay, if you don't want to".

There was a rap on the door.

"Come in," Defo's voice boomed.

It was the hospital maid with the newspapers. Ibuego's eyes went straight to the *Champion*, for the man on the front page resembled his father.

"Defo look at her". She tried to divert his attention.

Defo snatched the newspaper from her hand.

To his surprise, it was none other than Chief H.E.M. Elesi, his father. The likeliness of the photograph was striking. He read the article below. As he read it, his face darkened. Ibuego tried to snatch the paper back, but he glowered at her like a dog. She became alarmed, but had to wait for him to finish reading.

"What is it? She asked when he had finished. Defo would not talk.

She pick up the newspaper and read the article. To her, there was nothing new about it except that she did not know that her father later changed his mind from thirty to fifty thousand naira.

"Oh ... I was going to tell you tomorrow". Said Ibuego defensively. Defo's head drooped sadly. Why Emeruo? he thought. Emeruo was the only person in Nkwoko who made life enjoyable for him while he stayed with his mother's brother in the village. Others treated him the way they expected his father to treat him – like an outlaw. The stranger with the birthmark was unmistakably his friend, Charlie. They killed him, probably because of his friendship with him. They must have found out that he had been passing information to him.

"Come on ... be a man Defo. What is it now?" Ibuego said.

"I want to get out of here right now".

"That is not the question. I support that, but we should wait till Dad arrives, and please try not to shout. I am sure he will understand".

"I am not going to listen to that doctor again". Defo said in an agonized voice.

"Why are you suddenly in a hurry Defo?"

"They killed Emeruo and my friend Charlie and you ask why I am in a hurry to go".

"Who is Charlie?" Ibuego asked his brother.

"The man they found beside Emeruo," answered Defo with tears in his eyes.

"You mean you knew the stranger?" Ibuego asked feeling almost happy that the mystery of the stranger was finally solved. Defo could not understand what kind of human being his sister was, but he was too downcast to care again.

"He was my friend. A bad guy who didn't mean to be bad. He was slower than all of them, but much smarter. He was a source of worry to them". Defo said as if saying this would help comfort his deceased friend. Now, the picture of his ordeal with his attacker hit him more clearly and made his heart jump. That fateful day, he had approached Odiari's house, near the General Hospital confidently believing that nobody there knew him. But to his surprise, he had seen Bide at the gate. He did not know what to tell him or what to do. They just stared at each other until Defo broke into a run and Bide started pursuing him. In broad daylight, with people passing by, Bide had shot at him twice and missed. The sound of the shots made people run into their houses. He ran and Bide pursued. Then he felt a sharp pain in his legs. That instant, it dawned on him that a slug had hit him. This weakened his agility, but he still ran. Looking back, he saw Bide still pursuing. Getting close to the General Hospital, people started making fun of the situation, thinking he was a thief being pursued by a policeman. More shots made them duck under benches. Bide had come closer now and fired another shot which struck him and brought him down. He then came very close and fired the last two shots into him. Defo had passed out, believing he was dead, until he woke up inside the General Hospital.

Defo started to weep as he visualized Emeruo being impaled on the spike, probably before he was shot. His body began to jerk and before Ibuego could do anything,

171

he threw up and continued to do so as he visualized them torturing Charlie. After this came relief. His taut muscles relaxed more and he went to sleep.

"How do you feel dear?", his father asked him when he woke up.

Elesi had been there for the past one and half hours. Defo rubbed at his eyes and his mouth tasted bad. He would have replied "terrible," but when he remembered that his discharge from the hospital depended on his bodily condition, he quickly sat up, smiled and opened his eyes, "Much better papa", He said.

"I am very sorry about the way you heard the news, I mean Emeruo's".

"Oh ... it's okay".

"We decided to offer a reward to witnesses who may be willing to come forward with facts. Sorry my son. I am very sorry. We wanted you to get well so we didn't want to bother you with all those horrible news". Elesi saw his son's face begin to change colour again.

"The doctor says that your temperature is up a little and your blood pressure rose slightly, but not to any dangerous level. You think you could stay here some more days?"

"No Papa. I want to go home. I am well. The home environment will help my recovery.

As Elesi listened to his son speak, he was convinced that Defo was well. Most importantly, the doctor had certified him well a long time ago. It was Elesi who told him to keep him in the hospital for security reasons. There was no reason now why the boy should not go if he strongly desired it. "The doctor thinks you are well Defo, so you can come with us". Defo was ecstatic with joy as he packed his belongings. Having been confined in hospital for long, he had come to appreciate the value of freedom. This he told the waving nurses as their car rolled out of the hospital.

That night two heavy gunmen came to the hospital and turned it upside down looking for Defo. The nurses were beaten blue and black to reveal his whereabouts. They took their sufferings with appreciation to God, that it was a miracle that the boy had left the hospital that night.

"His name is lucky," the matron had told the battered nurses when the gunmen left. They nursed their bruises with the consolation that Defo did not die before their very eyes.

Chapter 10

Chimezie and Chuby planned for the first exhibition at Eze's mission which from newspaper accounts was a matter of a few days. Chuby had come down to the East as soon as Chimezie phoned to tell him of the state of things. When he heard of Emeruo's death and Defo's miraculous survival, he felt that his inquiry had caused all of it and he said this to Chimezie. But when Chimezie talked about Emeruo's close connection with his murderers, Chuby was tongue-tied. Okani's information had led to a positive swing in police investigations. When Akonwa, the drug dealer at Nkwoko heard of Defo's trouble, he volunteered information freely, which led to the discovery of the den in the mother-of-the-water's playground. The gang had scuffled away before police could catch up with them. The priest of Okpoko, the old man who was standing in for Ikwu before the attack on Okpoko, was also arrested. Under questioning, he admitted that some men had approached him to help them destroy Okpoko, but that he had refused to have anything to do with it. He was detained for complicity and the search for Ikwu had produced no positive result. The police had also stormed Odiari's house with no results. Odiari had denied knowing any Bide and had demanded a public apology from the police for the embarrassment they caused him.

Chuby had agreed to attend the first exhibition in disguise. Chimezie was able to convince him to go. "It's the safest option," he had told him. "He knows you for sure or they wouldn't have been able to trail you to Nkwoko. But since you dropped out of sight, he must have shifted his attention from you, concentrating now on my family. Any how , we cannot take the risk of involving another person in this who cannot command our trust".

They had really tried to get a few responsible people to play some part in that game, but it had been obvious from the way the people declined and the things some of them had said before, that they thought the Reverend extremely powerful. One of Chimezie's acquaintances he asked to help had prayed in Chimezie's presence that the Reverend might not discover of their discussion through dream or any other way and thereby liquidate him with his immense powers.

They were still talking when Defo entered. The two men looked at him in acknowledgment of his presence, but Chuby's face was abeam with smiles. "The man who defied death," he called him. "You don't look bad at all, just as strong as a horse".

"If you say so", Defo said. He went to a chair and sat down.

"It's like we are heading to the end of this event without anything concrete ... yet," Chuby suddenly said.

Defo regarded him. "We know the people involved. All we need is strong evidence to nail them, which we are working up to. That to me is not exactly nonsense".

"You always sound too optimistic," Chuby said uncomfortably.

"Call it anything, if it is optimism, it is not unfounded. Our man there says Eze will likely walk into our trap, at least Eze for a start". He paused. "See ... understand that our sources, my sources of information there are very reliable. Odiari is not a religious man so what is his business with idols and Eze? Emeruo and Charlie's death and Bide's attempt to murder me in broad daylight are Odiari's schemes. Because of Eze's encounter

175

with Chimezie and very likely because of Odiari's visit there, the exhibition is now organised in two separate days, the first day, a feint of a day to cast us off his trail. Why does he take the trouble?"

Defo suddenly frowned, "they are very uncomfortable. How I would like to see their faces! ... Swains. But their discomfort bothers me. It is not Eze I fear. He is all mouth. Odiari is the problem. He feels like a caged animal now. I learnt that he tried to stop Eze from holding the exhibition at all costs and failed. He may try to stop us. Either way we stand to lose. But if Eze goes ahead with his plan, we may succeed. We may find something to hook him on. It is doubtful whether Eze even knows the gods".

"How do we even recognise Okpoko when we see him?" Chimezie asked diverting to a problem which had been bothering him.

"I've been there," Chuby quickly said, "though I am not sure I can still visualize the thing".

"I have a photograph of the oracle", said Defo fishing in his pocket. He brought the picture out and handed it to Chuby.

"How did you get it?" Chuby asked as he examined the photograph intently. He finally shook his head and handed the photograph to Chimezie. It was a large rather grotesque image, a combination of natural and supernatural forms. Half man and half angel, heavy of body but winged, seated, but looking as if resting between flights.

"I had a great difficulty getting that photograph. On my way to Odiari's place, I had gone through Uda hoping to find Ikwu that we might go to Odiari together. Ikwu was not there but I met his uncle who gave me that photograph after I told him that I needed it to identify Okpoko in case I found him. He took it from a large frame which Uda people had placed on Okpoko's altar. They had been worshipping the photograph since the bad incident or as the man said, since the mysterious turn of events in the town'. So many bad things happening many of them ending in death ..."

"Ikwu said so", said Chimezie.

"Don't believe those crap. All that are just coincidences". Chuby said.

Defo took the photograph from his brother and smiled in a strange way. "Somehow I believe that photograph saved me at Aba. I had it in my pocket when Bide shot at me. I just can't explain how I survived that incident".

Chimezie had been staring at the table in front of them. From the corner of his eye, he saw Chuby look in his direction.

"This world is really mysterious," Chimezie said. "It is mysterious how good things happen to some and bad things to others. Since Ajie was murdered in his own house with his own children present, Papa has been arming himself seriously. He even expressed satisfaction that all of us could shoot. I think he is taking care of that. If we are attacked, we may not be an easy army to assail. The only problem is walking around town because we can't carry gun".

"Who is Ajie?" Chuby asked.

"Papa's friend. Thieves went to his house one night and cut his throat in the presence of his children. It was terrible".

"Horrible".

"Good", Chimezie cut in. "Chuby shall go for the first exhibition".

"He'll need a cover, policemen. Eze's people won't know him, but if Odiari's guys are there, they may spot him and that may be trouble. Two policemen in mufty with a gun hidden somewhere will be enough to check them".

Chuby thought about the protection of the gun. "Good idea Defo" he said.

"Very good", Chimezie said.

When they had discussed other important details, Chimezie suggested that they caught some sleep since it was near midnight. They all rose and bid each other goodnight and left for their respective rooms to ponder and to sleep over the impending events.

*   *   *

"I said don't ever see my face until you've carried out those assignments", Odiari barked at his two hitmen. They stared back at him, making no effort to move, even if they had moved out of his presence, it was very unlikely that they would carry out his orders. For the first time since they came into his service, they were challenging his orders and judgment.

It was the one called Peter who finally broke the silence. "Will this be our last job? The very last? We have your last promise in our hearts and we already made arrangements to enjoy our retirement".

Odiari was galled by this new audacity, for never before had these two men dallied to execute his orders. They were actually giving him conditions now. Odiari had been annoyed with them for on the day that he saw the article in the *Champion*, he had first rushed to their flat and told them to immediately track Elesi down, but they had conspired and had forced him to go to talk to Eze first.

Odiari had promised them retirement after the last job they did for him, so that younger men in the organisation would take up the exacting task of hitmen while they concerned themselves with aspects of his businesses according as their specific interests dictated, until they gained enough to set up on their own. But could they not have seen that the organisation was in a crisis that only the sturdiest of them could handle?

Odiari prized discipline in the organisation. Whether he was in breach of his promise or not, obedience was the first rule; the leader of the organisation being the absolute source of orders. The punishment for disobedience was reduction. Odiari felt a desire to pull his revolver and make mincemeat of these stupid traitors. It would have brought him sublime relish. He knew they were unarmed as Sebo had been under instruction to whisk anybody that came to see him since this problem started.

The fact was, Odiari needed these men now. Pressure was on from the press and police, only the hardest of his men could be relied upon. These men had been tested over time and proved by all standards the sturdiest of the bunch. Each in his different way had never bungled a job. Together, they were predictable dynamite. They performed excellently because they were great optimists. Odiari repented of the murderous feeling rooted in his mind. He even called to mind the warning of his friend, Ovie Soza, who operated from Benin City. Ovie had said that "a man who rides the back of hungry lion should be very careful".

"This is no job for amateurs," he suddenly said. "It is kind of special and needs talent". Whenever he said a job was special, it was implied there was special gratification in it.

"You've been my most trusted friends ... see, just as we all planned for retirement, this ugly situation reared its head to destroy a life-long work". He talked in a floundering manner. His words were the song of the drowning. "I've known suffering. I've known hardship more than any of you. In that I've also learnt that I am a man. Yes, I am the architect of my destiny. A man is a great thing. It is he who takes a god to the market place. Even the Ark of the covenant did not walk into the battlefield. Men carried it. My friends, rats do not despoil a man who is wide awake. Gods do not exert their

179

influence beyond lands where they have control. I am the hand of the gods, their schemer. They need me as much as I need them, therefore I am free, free to defend myself and to dispense justice as I deem fit. We are the very gods who kill a man the day his life is sweetest to him. We are wisdom unknown," he was staring ahead trance-like as words poured out of his mouth. His audience listened as though under a hypnotic spell.

"You cannot forget the goddess. You are still under my covenant. Strength is the suppression of fear because fear makes men mess their lives. Men ... you are afraid. Admit it, admit your faithlessness. You fear for the consequences of your actions".

"We are never afraid. We are not afraid now". It was Paul from an exhausted and tortured spirit . "We will do your job ... this once".

"Go now. It is your last job and you will have a befitting reward". The two men agreed and left. They were determined to get the job done with immediately. Tonight.

*   *   *

Hamza used his left hand to try to control his twitching eyelids. For three days now, they had been twitching without left, and for Hamza, this was a bad omen. It filled him with a strong presentiment of danger. But on the surface, everything seemed under control.

This twitching had not come even before Defo had been shot. Its presence to Hamza meant that something terrible was about to happen to somebody very close to him. He had not been home to the North, for three years, but his brother, Garba, who had visited two months ago had assured him that his wife and two children were faring perfecly. What could it be? Who could it be? He thought.

180

He had begun to worry for his master too. The man had been overstraining himself for sometime now, sometimes coming home very late at night. He was generally uncomfortable. More discomforting were the strange sounds that he heard around the house. This was the fourth time he would scout round the house to make sure that nobody was lurking around. The house was now very quiet. Thus, Hamza struggled at his desk until he started dozing.

He was suddenly startled by the sound of a car which pulled up at a distance from their house. He looked at his watch, it was 2.15 in the morning. Another car joined the first one. Hamza heard the doors of the cars open and close. He counted eight of them. He was tempted to go outside and see who they were but he found himself sitting where he was wondering what to do, wishing that whoever they were, they were either friends of his master, or they did not come for him at all.

When Hamza did not hear the sound of footsteps, he became apprehensive. He quietly opened the door of his room and moved towards the house to alert his master of these insidious movements for his master had ordered him to report, without delay, any unusual movements or objects that he might notice around the house. The front entrance to the main building was already locked. It was a huge iron door buried in ferron concrete closed from the outside and from the inside. He moved to the back of the house, about to call his master through window when he heard the heavy latch of the steel door which gradually opened. Inside was none other than Elesi. His eyes were bloodshot.

"Come with me" he told Hamza. They ran up the stairs into the sitting room where Defo, Ibuego and Lizzy sat. Lizzy's eyes were filled with tears, Hamza observed. "Hamza," Elesi called his watchman. He now spoke in Hausa. "We are surrounded by enemies, possibly killers. I want you to stay here with Defo and help him anyway you can to ensure that these people don't enter this house". Elesi's eyes shifted to Defo, "see them before you fire at them". He told Defo who was now provided with a machine gun. Elesi looked disappointedly at Lizzy who had been crying most of the time. Lizzy stared back at him like a stranger.

About five minutes ago, Elesi had come into the room where she had been sleeping with Chimezie and awakened them looking like the god of war, he had announced that the house was being besieged by some strange men. He had wasted no time in deploying Chuby, Chimezie and Sylvester, all well armed to the roof which was constructed like a battlement. His long experience of war with the Ekemas made him to build the roofs of all his houses like that. Lizzy was experiencing that part of her life which had always been a legend to her since her entry into his household.

Elesi had come down from the roof to call the police for help. The duty-Sergeant had replied that the station had neither men nor vehicles to handle the situation in Elesi's house. He promised to do something as soon as he could organise his men. Elesi had been furious with the man. "You mean you sit down there doing nothing while we are here ready to meet death any minute from now?" He had retorted.

The Sergeant had promptly replaced the receiver but not before he had taunted Elesi to defend himself.

"I want you to watch the backyard to avoid our being surprised", Elesi spoke to Hamza again. "If anything unexpected happens, don't forget to climb up to the roof. It is the safest place in this house unless it is burnt down". He now paused. "You must all be careful. Lizzy and Ibuego, you may lie down on the carpet to avoid being hit by a bullet. No, better go into Chimezie's room. You'll be much safer there. Their main target will be here if they have guns".

"God forbid" Ibuego said. "I am staying here". Elesi looked at Lizzy.

"I'm staying too". She said more confidently.

As soon as Elesi left, Lizzy stared at Defo in bewilderment. "Can you shoot? Can you kill?"

"I can shoot, but I've never killed a man before. Who knows when my life is endangered?"

"My father taught us all to shoot". Ibuego told Lizzy as she now looked outside the front gate through the glass window. Hamza was stationed by one of the windows. He had moved furniture to give room for movement as the room was now dark. He had a good view of the gate as all the flood lights were on.

*   *   *

The roof of Elesi's house was crenellated, the parapet was low with discreet holes that served both as drainage and as a cover from where one could shoot at an intruder without being observed. It was by these holes that Elesi, Chuby, Chimezie and Sylvester took positions. The Elesi s covered all four sides of the building.

Elesi who was at the frontage could see the men, about five of them making for Hamza's room. He watched them push the door open and simultaneously fired shots into the room. He became convinced that they had come to liquidate him and his family. Elesi was not surprised that he was not shaken in the least. It was just another battle and the more he thought about it, the more he thought about the Ekemas, a crueller set of Ekemas. Elesi exerted pressure on the trigger of his gun. The explosion from it jolted him a little. Four bullets released in quick succession.

183

The reply from the invaders was dramatic. Bullets rained from all sides of the building, the unexpected bursts overwhelmed the Elesis, all of who dropped their guns and covered their ears as they listened to the nerve-wracking shatter of windows below. The explosions continued rhythmically for about one minute. The moment the shots ceased, Elesi fired directly at the direction where the man on the frontage had fired. Chimezie, Sylvester and Chuby had made similar observations and with their fifteen round rifles followed up the assault. The effect was comforting, ruffling of leaves and flowers as the invaders changed positions.

Whoever was firing at the house had not spotted any particular target. They fired heavily at the house in order to assail and penetrate it. A lot of damage had been done to the house already. All the windows had been broken and Defo had been driven from his former position by the window to the vent on the staircase. He had been lucky because as soon as he heard the first shots, he had ducked down. He was preparing himself to shoot when the glass window above him fell on top of him. His new position by the vent was very dangerous, a position his father would have disapproved if he knew Defo was kneeling there now, the machine gun between his arms. He could see very clearly because of the many openings in the wall, but these openings also meant he would easily be killed anytime an enemy directed his shot there.

The sporadic shootings had been going on for sometime without much progress on either side. The Elesis stoutly defended their house, hoping that the agents of death might give up and let them alone. But the invaders were not through yet.

After Chimezie finished loading his gun, he looked up to see three men shooting and moving up to the fence, through the back. He quickly fired at them, but they kept moving towards the fence. Chimezie kept firing at them and as if by a spell of magic, they were undaunted by his shots.

"Come here Sylvester", Chimezie called to his brother. "Come and give me help," he said urgently.

Sylvester quickly came to his brother's side and together they started firing at the men who now took cover and continued firing back.

More people were now firing at the house and the shots came from the side of the house where Sylvester was covering. Soon again, the house was drowned by the ring of gun shots. Chuby could see some of the invaders start to scale the wall into the house. "They've started coming in," he shouted at Elesi.

The Chief rolled up to Chuby's side and saw the men as they tried to climb the wall. Together, himself and Chuby fired at them, he following up each time after Chuby. As soon as the men gave up, Elesi crawled to the opening that led into the house and called Defo to come up immediately.

Now, the Elesis had a man to cover every side of the building and Defo to help whenever there was serious offensive from any particular side. The advantage the Elesis had were an ample supply of arms and the discreetness of their positions.

For some minutes, nobody heard anything until suddenly the invaders all started firing at the closed gate. They fired at it until the heavy steel gate opened. Soon shots were heard from the back of the house and the sides where Chuby and Sylvester covered. The invaders seemed to have assessed the strength of activities in the house. Thus, they used some men to keep Chuby, Sylvester and Chimezie busy while the main body of the invasion had concentrated on the gate. When the gate opened, Elesi was shaken and so were his children. Even then, they were running out of bullets and somebody had to go down to get more of it. But they were all rooted where they were with Defo shooting by his father's side to see if they could stop them from entering through the gate.

Then, some men spirited through the gate into the house and disappeared immediately. Elesi's heart pounded heavily now and so was Defo's who like his father had observed the movement of the invaders. Before Elesi could say a word to Defo, he was startled by the explosion of fire right under him in his very sitting room. Bullets continued to sound from the sitting room. For more than one minute, pouring until it stopped abruptly. Everywhere became silent, the Elesis neither moved nor did they say anything until a whistle was heard in the distance where the invaders had parked their cars. Soon, the cars started up and drove away.

After sometime, the Elesis could hear somebody weeping in the sitting room. The weeping gradually rose to a loud hysterical cry.

"That's Ibuego", Defo said and immediately stood up to go down. Before Chimezie could restrain him, he wanted to tell him to be careful as he might walk into a trap, Defo had reached the sitting room.

He was confounded by the condition of the sitting room which he had left not long ago. The once orderly and lush sitting room was completely disfigured. Defo saw Hamza and Lizzy trying to help a struggling Ibuego to a sitting position. When Lizzy saw him, she quickly ran to him and embraced him, weeping on his neck. Defo gently pushed her aside and went to his sister. "Ibuego... Ibuego... what is it?" The girl continued to sob.

When Elesi, Chuby, Chimezie and Sylvester came down from the roof, Hamza explained to them that Ibuego had operated the machine gun which had decidedly chased the invaders away.

Elesi shook his head and said. "My daughter" with supreme delight.

The Elesis did not sleep again. They maintained their ... positions till 7.00 a.m., not wanting to be victims of a surprise attack.

As dawn arrived, neighbours besieged the Elesi residence, but could not gain entrance into the house because the gate was still locked. Elesi wanted the police to be the first to enter his premises. They must have an unaltered impression of last night's events. Also, now that the machine guns and automatic rifles for which government supplied no licenses had been safely put away, leaving them with only "two round" double barrelled guns, Elesi did not want his family to come out to any surprise because some die-hards might still be mixed with the crowd outside. If the police arrived with their security machinery, they would come out.

Through the ventilator in the staircase, they could see their neighbours and passers-by come and go. They came and wept and they all seemed to imprecate on some objects in front of the gate. Elesi suspected that Ibuego's fire might have taken victims. His closest neighbour, Doctor Obolo came and called his name several times. Elesi would have come out then to let them know that he was safe and sound with his family, but checked the impulse.

In the distance, they could hear sirens wailing, so that the crowd outside started dispersing in different directions, to avoid being arrested by the police. As one man ran, he shouted, "nobody get N200.00 to settle this people". His friend who ran side by side with him said, "see when them de come, after people don die finish. I sure say nobody survive for that house. These bastards tear the house to pieces".

Only Obolo was around when the police arrived. Hamza and Defo were the first people to come out to meet them. The inspector on duty surveyed Obolo, and decided that he was not going to enter the house with them.

"Oga, remain here till we commot okay? We need to concentrate when we do our job", disappointed as Obolo was and annoyed as he was, he did not enter the house with them. However, Defo's report was most comforting to Obolo. His father was alive with his family.

When the policemen left, with the two corpses killed by Ibuego's fire, Obolo was overjoyed to be reunited with his friend and his family as many other neighbours. Obolo was touched by the total destruction which the invaders had wrought on the house and so were their other neighbours who knew well how lavishly furnished the sitting room was. Several gashes exhibited themselves on the wall and the nakedness of the tube of the big TV set on one side of the room was an eyesore. All this the neighbours decried and bemoaned.

Inside Chimezie's room, which was the only room in the entire house that did not exhibit bullet gashes, Obolo greeted his friend.

"Onwa," he called Elesi by his title name, "this is most unfortunate". As he said this, he continued to look around the room, at Elesis children who wore, tired looks, and yet determined from the look of the guns in their hands to defend themselves and their father.

"My sons, you are great warriors".

"It is God," replied Elesi.

"The warrior!"

"It is God".

Obolo moved close to Elesi and used the back of his right hand to greet him three times. It was to encourage him in his ordeal.

"Whoever says that we will not sleep, may he roost before the hens ... may night come to his eyes in broad daylight ... these evil men, what now? Hei ... God has shown his greatness once more". Obolo continued exclaiming, utterly surprised at what he considered a miracle that the Elesis were safe.

"It is God," said Elesi.

Elesi looked around the room, satisfied that only Obolo was an outsider with them, he instructed Sylvester to tell Hamza to stand guard by the door and not let anybody in meanwhile. They made a quick review of all their plans on how best to contain Eze and Odiari. The issue was no more a child's play. It was a matter of life and death.

*   *   *

Sylvester surveyed himself in the huge mirror inside his room, one of the few rooms in the house that escaped destruction, and felt satisfied with himself. His disguise was good. The traditional caftan and the fez had added years to his age. He never believed a dress could confer so much authority in so few seconds. He had considered wearing one of his father's Biafran suits with a bowler. But Chimezie had suggested the caftan. As Sylvester strode the floor, he widened his jowl as he laughed, to give it a heavy look.

It was all part of the decision they took the morning of the invasion of their house. Chuby had been dissuaded from going for the exhibition as some of Odiari's men might recognise him. He could still attend on the second day if everything turned out fine. They had decided to keep the press out of what happened in their house so as not to encourage Eze to tighten security at the exhibition or even to hide the works which might implicate him. Inside the sitting room, Chimezie handed Sylvester a newspaper with a report of an attack on Reverend Eze's mission in Okwu the very night Elesi's house was attacked. It was confirmed in the newspaper that the museum and the Reverend were hale and hearty. Eze was quoted as saying that the attack on his mission was "to frustrate the ten million naira launching planned by his mission in order to provide relief for the needy". He

189

reassured all invitees that everything was unaltered as God was on his side and not much damage was done to the museum or to his person or property. The plan for the exhibition was unchanged.

At table, the Elesis considered the effect of this new development. Chimezie was of the opinion that Sylvester still go. They all agreed that he should go. When Sylvester was ready to leave, they all bid him goodluck. At the Central Police Station in Orlu, Sylvester stopped to pick the three detectives who were to accompany him to the exhibition.

*   *   *

Okwu was jampacked with people. The old, the young, the high and the low. But noticeable today were the high, moneymen who came to pay their respects to the Reverend. Cars were not allowed close to the prayer-ground today, so that the people thronged to behold those powerful men of whom so much had been said in the newspapers.

At the museum, everything seemed normal, except that there were considerable changes in the appearance of the place. It was newly painted in white and inlaid with encaustic bricks. The counters inside had been polished and looked more respectable than Chimezie had described them the last time. As Sylvester scanned the counter, he wondered whether the newspaper reports about the blaze was true. Was it another of Eze's off-the-trail gimmicks? Why did nobody show interest in the museum?

He could not help laughing inside at the cheapness and the banality of the so-called works of art on the counters. The Reverend had given the impression that what he was going to offer in this exhibition were going to be works of great value. Thus Sylvester had come expecting to see quaint and odd works that would really excite him. But what he saw were the kind of masks used

190

by children in playing *Odogwuanyammiri*. Other objects included carvings of elephants, rats, antelopes, stools etc. The prices attached to them were simply outrageous, the rat for instance sold for eight thousand eight hundred naira, and it had another tag SOLD placed on it.

Sylvester surveyed the museum until he came to the passage which led to the other rooms, the stores of the museum. His nose picked up the smell of burning wood, and in that split second, he thought that the museum was on fire. Then he noticed that despite repeated coatings of paint on the walls of these inner rooms, signs of the blaze that consumed them remained. Thus, he understood that Eze had hurriedly repaired the museum in order not to postpone the exhibition.

Finding nothing of interest or of value inside the museum, Sylvester decided to go out to the prayer ground where the launching was being held to see if he could pick up some information before leaving.

The men at the high table had ruddy cheeks and hearty laughs. Somebody was holding the microphone, waiting for the noise to subside. Sylvester thought that he knew him and racked his brain to recollect where. The Reverend, in a dazzling cassock, had a halo of discreet vengeance that people mistook for a kind of piety. He was the centre of attraction. People came to obtain permission from him in order to go out to do such simple things as peeing. They wanted him to know they were there to promote his interests. The Reverend suddenly stood up and beckoned to the man with the microphone to continue with his speech while he went to his house to attend to something important. The man with the microphone quickly dropped it and sat down.

As the Reverend moved to his house, the multitude of people who had been watching the launching followed him. The afflicted and the infirmed tried to force their way up to him, that they might be healed by his presence or his

191

touch. Their desire for his touch was frenetic. But the Reverend touched nobody. The noise was rising as the multitude pushed. Sylvester could see the look of alarm cover the Reverend's face. With a movement of his hand, he ordered the police to push back the multitude. The police tried to form a thicket to hold back the crowd, but they were very few for that to be effective. Defeated, they became tough on the crowd. Then, they raised their batons and hit at the multitude, pushing them farther back. One old man's head was broken and he lay there on the ground crying to the Reverend for help but the Reverend ordered the police to carry him off.

"I warned them not to come today. I knew that some people would use this occasion to embarrass me," said the Reverend to most peoples' hearing. At his words, the enthusiasm of the multitude mellowed but was unquenched. They were still pushing, unable to reach the Reverend with the police, but when it dawned on them that the Reverend was not stopping the Police from punishing them, they backed off.

Sylvester wondered why the Reverend was that much alarmed. Perhaps his nerves were jumpy after the recent attempt to burn him in his bedroom. The more Sylvester considered this, the more he saw that the Reverend was not and could never be the man of the multitude. The more a man thought of his own safety, the more he was unable to lead a people, much less the weak, the downtrodden and the needy.

When the Reverend returned to his seat, the man who was holding the microphone before he left picked it up again.

"Reverend, I want you to excuse me. I have other pressing matters I must attend to as soon as I leave here. Before I do, I wish to give you the sum of forty-five thousand naira..." There was a thunderous applause from the crowd. The Reverend merely laughed and nodded his head several times. Sylvester wondered whether he was not satisfied with the sum, or whether he was trying hard to hide his excitement. Whatever it was, he could stand all this no more.

"Come sergeant... let's go!" he called at the three detectives who were by his side, fantasizing about what they could do with so much money. As they left, Sylvester wished that all of this was over and done with. He wanted no part of men like Eze again in his life.

Chapter 11

At the Savonri Hotel in Ihiala, Paul waited for Peter to show up. It was now close to ten hours and Peter had not turned up. They had decided to meet here after their operation, before going back to Odiari. Paul had arrived here at 2.15 a.m., and he had expected that at most, before 5.00 a.m., Peter would arrive, but it was now close to noon without any sign of Peter. He was now quite worried. Never in their seven years of working together had Peter kept him so long before showing up. He could not even remember ever having to wait for Peter. It was always Peter waiting for him after assignments like this. The highest time lapse ever recorded was when he had to join Peter in Onitsha from Benin. It had been only three hours and Peter had worried greatly.

Yesterday, in Okwu, Paul had found his own angle of the operation very simple by their standards. He had gone to Okwu, with his men and had discovered little or no security activities from Eze's men as impediment. Paul's men had worked very fast, strewing gun powder from their "anchor" into the Reverend's bedroom and the museum. Inside these buildings they left large quantities of gunpowder. The lines of the gunpowder had been an awkward V with the hand leading into the Reverend's room longer. They ignited the gunpowder from their "anchor" and watched as the flames snaked into the buildings. The museum was first to go up in flames. Within a fraction of a second, the Reverend's house went up in flames too. Their mission thus successful, they had scurried away. On the way, Paul dismissed all of his men, most of them hired hands, and drove straight to this place.

Peter had gone with the main body of the organisation, because Odiari had figured that with the tension everywhere, the Elesis might take some time to crack. All of Peter's hands had guns. It was a perfect outfit and yet they had not come back.

Paul thought of going back to Odiari. Again he considered that Odiari was not one to hear any news half and half. He wanted it straight and complete. Paul's mind was flickering. How could he forget ... the old man?

Peter had once taken him to a town, Atina, near Asaba to an old man whom he claimed was magic come true. The man's name was Onyedo. Peter had said that the man could use a single herb to raise a dying man. He had once extracted six bullets from Peter's body by just applying those herbs. Then Peter had told Paul that if ever they had any problem that no orthodox doctor could handle because of its nature, they would come to Onyedo, because he asked no questions. He knew his clients well.

"So anytime you suspect that I am in trouble, look for me in Onyedo's place first," he had said.

Paul was dirty after the operation and he needed a shave and a bath to look respectable and avoid suspicion from the large number of policemen on the roads that led to Atina. Inside Onitsha, around the flyover, traffic was painfully slow. Paul could see hordes of hawkers pestering people with their wares. He wound up his window to avoid them yet, many of them came knocking on his window to attract his attention. Paul's mind dwelt on the possibility that Peter was in serious trouble, perhaps he was dead. This caused him great discomfort. It was a great relief when the traffic eventually eased up and the rest of the journey to Atina, took him less than fifteen minutes.

The old man sat on a reclining chair in front of his bungalow, his two hands over his head. He seemed completely unaware that there was life around him, let alone that somebody had entered his house. Paul made a beastly kind of noise to attract his attention. He did not stir but said, "What do you want?"

"Can I come closer? I am a friend of Peter's ... I don't know if you still remember me?" The old man sprang up from his seat.

"Yes come in ... come here ... Paul?"

"Yes," said Paul utterly confounded. How could he remember his name? His visit here was four years ago. The old man's face had an unnatural whiteness. He looked more lifeless than alive.

Inside his sitting room, he pointed Paul to one of the three benches around. There was a motorcycle at the far end of the wall. Paul wondered whether Onyedo still rode on it. Out of a bland face, the old man spoke.

"It is good that you came, your friends are in a very bad condition, so bad that I had to keep them at the backyard ... something I had never done before ... but because of Peter — "

"Baba, please tell me, is he dead?" The old man sized Paul up. "Perhaps worse than dead son. He is in pain and short of breath, but he refuses to die. He's been expecting you." Paul shot up from his seat "where is the backyard?"

"Son ... you must be prepared for what you are going to see. There is a great job ahead and I am afraid it rests entirely on your shoulders. You must be composed," said the old man without making any effort to lead Paul to the backyard.

"Their operation was a total failure, with almost all of his men dead. Only two of them are preserved, but they are shocked out of their senses. Peter was able to talk to me when he drove that car to this place. He said that he lost two men to the people they went to attack. About six of his men died here in my house, in my hands, including the boy that drove the other car. A tough boy, but destined to die."

Paul was completely unhinged. He listened to Onyedo without understanding anything he said. Could it be that Sunday Jaguer, Bosah, Ovie, Jack, Vincent, all of them were dead? What was death by the way?

"... Their corpses are in the backyard. Peter hasn't said anything since, but I guess he is conserving his strength to use to speak to you. He is fatally wounded. This is his time, so be composed and listen to all he has to say. The prospect of death concentrates a man's mind ... now let's go and see them."

Until now, Paul had imagined himself a tough son of the devil. But now, trepidation gave him a turbidity of mind that was immobilizing. Odiari's ghoulish tastes had turned violence into a game. Paul's loss of ability to feel pity had become a source of pride to him. He could do what other men could not, kill a child who was begging him to spare his life. Until now, he had construed pity as a farfetched concept. His present realization was killing.

The old man had been on his feet for two minutes and Paul made no move to join him. Onyedo came close and slapped his back, hard. Paul stood up and reluctantly followed him.

What happened to Paul was like an *Ogbedi* with big ears running into the ancestral spirits. He was trying hard not to look at the corpses of his colleagues, but the first thing he saw was a heap of corpses with white legs poking out of the scanty canvas covering them. He wished that he had no nose. At the far corner were three men lying on a mat. One was propped up on pillows. He looked anything but alive.

197

"Peter ... Peter," called the old man in a firm low tone of voice. Peter turned his head from the pillow, his face was a drawing of agony.

"Has Paul come? I feel very tired inside".

"Peter, I am here ... you will be alright," said Paul in uncertain tones.

Peter's face lit up on recognising his best friend's voice.

"Give me your hand Paul." He raised his left hand that was besmeared with coagulated blood. Paul squatted and took it in both his hands comfortingly.

"Have you seen what happened to all of us? Only Jude and Obuekwe survived.

"You also," said Obuekwe and Jude.

Solid chills ran up Paul's spine. He had imagined that the men lying with Peter on the mat were dead. He was unaware that they had became fully conscious and had been listening to his exchange with Peter. Their speaking was a big jolt to him.

"Keep quiet two of you," said Peter, a tremor in his voice, "and listen carefully for you are going to end all this for us... Paul, I've always known that our games with Odiari would lead to this. I knew you trusted me most, but I didn't warn you. I also knew that Odiari respected my opinion even though he didn't care much. I also failed to challenge his lies. Things were going fine for us and I began to convince myself that there were many mysteries to life, and Odiari's creation could be one of them. At a point Paul, I didn't know what to believe. I was ready to pay any price; that was why I... we took great risks.

"But how could a people disregard the gods? In our vain ways, we imagined that we could play divide and rule with the gods. We asked for the protection of one god in order to destroy another. But we forgot that the ways of gods are not the ways of men, gods don't fight with each

198

other, neither for man's sake nor for their own sake. But they all play pranks with us. We always imagine that they are fighting. In this case Paul, when we destroyed and stole those carvings, we thought that we had pitched one god against another as Odiari made us believe.

"We forgot that gods are spirits and therefore do not permanently inhabit wood and metal. They answer us through such mediums, because it is useful to us, it helps our understanding. When we call their names through such mediums, they answer us not because they live there, but because we are accustomed to that system. Afterall, didn't we make those things. We stole not a single god but ordinary wood. In doing that, we antagonise the entire pantheon of gods. Our attitude and behaviour were like a child's, who after making an effigy of his father dragged it in dust. I am sure you would appreciate his father's feeling. They never gave us their blessing, but left us, knowing that like all swelling things, when we reach our capacity, we would burst," Peter's face contorted with serious pain. He pulled his hand away from Paul's and pressed it on his chest where a heavy bandage held a large wound.

"We have made a mistake, but we must try and remedy it the little that we can. I want to die with a clear conscience."

"Yes", said Paul.

"Paul... I want you to destroy Odiari. Kill him with that his adulteration of a goddess. That his goddess is an abberration. I renounce him now ... here. Paul don't be afraid. Don't believe all those stories about how Odiari came about that bitch of a goddess of his, even if it were true. The spirit has long left that joss. Untold evil have been committed in its name. That shrine merely represents an extension of Odiari's will. But I won't be surprised if like many great liars he has started believing his own lie to be true.

199

Now Paul, take Jude and Obuekwe with you. Kill Odiari and go today to that Elesi, that mighty man of valour, the lord is on his side and bear witness against Eze, for his collaborations with Odiari. Make him suffer shame by letting the world see his true face. Will you do this Paul?"

Paul's eyes were suffused with tears and he looked confusedly at his tired friend.

"Paul, I know what you must feel ... but don't think that you can beat this. We must pay for our wrongdoings and you know how long the hands of the gods are. By doing what I tell you, you might be able to pacify them. At least you will die a cleansed man. Will you do this Paul ... Paul? please Paul ..." A sudden spasm of coughing seized Peter and his voice faded. His body sagged.

"Peter ... Peter, please don't give up, I will do your wish." Paul said as he tried to help his now unconscious friend. Peter was beyond hearing. His hand was limp and lifeless.

"Baba Onyedo, please save him." Paul called the old man. "He said that you give back a dying man his life. Please help him, I will give you anything."

The old man kept his distance.

"Are you this heartless Baba?" Paul shouted hysterically.

The old man moved closer.

"In my business son, I don't need a heart. You've seen for yourself what I contend with, all alone everyday. I buried my heart in my back the very first week I came to this house."

"But you can save him, can't you?"

"Who the gods have taken, no longer belongs here. Your friend is dead. I have no power over the dead".

"He is dead then?"

"He is dead".

This verdict from the old man, for the first time seemed to make some meaning to Paul.

Paul looked up at Jude and Obuekwe with bloodshot eyes.

"Did you hear him? Did you hear Peter?" Paul asked Jude and Obuekwe.

"Yes ... we are ready to carry out his commandments."

"Good ... Baba, please make arrangements to have these men buried. You can have one of those cars as your fee for that. Is that okay?"

"It is satisfactory."

As Paul drove off with his friends, Baba smiled. In his business, corpses counted. Seven heavy men to be butchered and sold in parts to his peculiar customers. He felt no scruples. Afterall he had told Paul the whole truth. In his business, hearts did not count.

*   *   *

"I promise to let you know what I feel about Peter and Paul today" Odiari told Bide.

"Yes sir."

"And something else ... remember?"

"Our initiation into the inner cult."

"Do you know that Peter and Paul are not their real names?"

"Well sir ... I heard--"

"But do you know their real names?" Odiari asked confidently.

"No Sir"

"That's the strength of this organization. Secrets, even about simple matters like that. You will learn no more from me until you've been initiated."

Since the disappearance of the hitmen, Odiari had taken to conferring with Bide. He found his thinking absurd, but he liked his physical strength and devotion.

Even more was the look of awe in Bide's eyes everytime they were together. With him, he felt like he wanted to feel. He would have killed him for botching Defo's assasination attempt, but something told him not to.

"Is Sebo back?"

"A long time ago sir."

"With the new man?"

"No sir. The man will be coming later."

"Call him then ... tell him to prepare himself for the initiation. It is almost 6.00 p.m and tomorrow will be a busy day. I'll brief you people after the initiation."

Initially, Odiari had thought that Peter and Paul did not want to come back because they probably failed on the job. They knew that he did not like failures. Even more serious was their reputation which had been perfect and would now be in jeopardy. He had hoped that they would come back when they got over the shock. But they did not come back all through the morning till noon.

At this time, he felt that they had conspired against him in order to desert him. But they did not have enough money and muscle to declare their independence. They would come back. Again time proved him wrong.

Were they caught? How could two of them be caught in two different missions. A rather unlikely possibility. At least one of them, somebody amongst the lot must have survived or escaped to bring him news.

The conspiratorial theory again occupied the centre of his thinking. Afterall, those twosome were queer; hardly interested in women and wordly pleasures. They worked hard and clung to his promise of independence like holding on to heaven's gate. His conviction now, was that they failed his plans in order to make him pay for not keeping his promise.

Odiari was not a man to take perfidy lightly. He wanted to reorganise himself and recoup his losses for the struggle with Elesi and Eze, after which he would think out a more appropriate way to make Peter and Paul pay. He had sent a frantic SOS to his friend, Ovie, in Benin for a supply of men. Ovie had promised to send the men tonight. The task now was to bring Sebo and Bide into his trust. The simplest way to do this was to take them to his shrine. He had always marvelled at the effect this shrine had had on his past hitmen. Today he would have a new set of hitmen and a fresh supply of men.

"Sir we are here," said Bide. Sebo looked excitedly and wistfully at his master.

Odiari pointed them to the lounge chairs in his office. "We must work hard to free ourselves from this evil that is about to fall on us ... If the snake averts his head, the ground carries the wound of the knife. The eldest man in a family is the oldest, as such, family responsibilities lie on his head. In this case you are both old and worthy. But it is necessary to ask you, do you want to work for me?"

"But we've been·working for you sir!" Sebo said, surprised.

"I meant, do you want to work with me? This is an initiation, remember. I want you people to have a stake in my business, to share in it and become my right and left arms."

"Yes sir," said Bide piously.

Odiari looked at Sebo.

"Of course sir ... always," said Sebo bewildered.

"I am going to make you swear to this. I don't write agreements with men because I have a protector. I have a goddess whom I worship. She has kept me through great difficulties in this life and I believe solely in her".

"Today is a special day and I am very happy because I am finally going to make a wholesome sacrifice to my goddess. Do you fear blood?" he asked them.

Bide fidgeted in his seat, while Sebo looked devoutly at Odiari.

"No", he said.

"I am going to tell you a story I have never told anybody in my life."

He cleared his throat.

"I was born a bastard. I grew up with no place to call a home, with no town to call my own and with no relations. I remember that it was in Onitsha that I first became aware of existence. I wandered around the great river taking in the activities of the rogues who operated from there. In no time I was their errand boy and soon a member of one of the organizations.

"But one day changed my life. It was the day our leader took us to a priestess to offer sacrifice to the goddess who now resides in my house. That day, I learnt what cow-love was. I was being fattened and treated well for the purpose of being used as a sacrifice for the goddess. There in the priestess's home, the gang abandoned me and left me at the mercy of the priestess. But the priestess had other ideas. She felt that it was her time to die. So she made me sacrifice her to the goddess instead of me. She made me to take the goddess, to care for her on the promise that I would make her the greatest of all the gods in heaven. I would still offer human sacrifices to her, that way I would be a very successful man, and everybody who associated with me.

"This has always worked for me, a hitchfree operation I have enjoyed since my independence, until I set out to enthrone the goddess as the greatest god of heaven. Eze was a product of the gods. At about this time, he started speaking against idol worship. In him I saw a strong ally in the crusade against other gods. His pronouncements made many people turn against their gods. But these were insignificant gods. I met Eze and told him the idea of using any means possible to destroy these gods. He welcomed this idea with his two hands wide apart.

"Eze is the meanest hypocrite on earth. Tell him that you are going for a business overseas, and that you want his blessings. Even when he suspects that the business is illegal, like drug trafficking, he prays for you and asks no questions. That way, he feels safe. He understood my language, but he felt safe again because I didn't spell every thing out. Not that it bothered me until recently when his greed led him into a grave mistake which led to the disintegration of everything.

"Thus we hunted for the gods, giving them to that greedy Reverend who sold them for money. The day we destroyed Okpoko's shrine, the shrine reputed as the most important of them all. I thought that my goddess would be very happy with me, but on the contrary I have been having problems, the last of which is the desertion of my two hitmen.

"As the protector of the goddess, as her mouthpiece, I believed that there were problems because the goddess needed a sacrifice. But I was not in a hurry since I wanted to make a wholesome sacrifice to her. Like the priestess who bequeathed her to me, I wanted to sacrifice myself. On a second thought however, I saw that the condition was different. I wasn't old and I hadn't found a willing caretaker. I was still contemplating what to do when one morning, the priest of Okpoko walked into my residence with a gun he couldn't shoot. It was a significant event, the complete death of Okpoko realized in the death of his priest, with no survivors. He has been fettered in the presence of my goddess for a long time now and she must be eager to drink his blood. I have chosen this special occasion of the election of my new hitmen to offer the priest to the goddess.

"The very hands of my new hitmen will cut the throat of the priest as a signification of the supreme agreement between us ... Please follow me."

"Since priests are not exempt as sacrifice to the gods, you'll go ... Odiari."

Sebo, Bide and Odiari froze as Paul came in, a cold pistol in his hands pointing at them.

"You bastard, you've come back," Odiari said unconsciously as he made to move.

"Stay where you are ... liar. With every new set of hitmen, you change the story. With myself and Peter, she was a gift from your father. He only could minister to her and be a good business man at the same time. And he wanted you to be like him. It worked because priests and goddesses sometimes had a husband and wife relationship often consumated in dreams. And you could make the goddess do anything ... Oh ... why do you lie to your closest men? Why did you lie to us?" Paul's hands stiffened on the gun and that instant Odiari stared death in the face. The tension in Paul's hands released.

"Peter is dead, with him all his men because you hide under a fake goddess and command the impossible. What haven't we done for you? Why did you have to send him to die like that? Speak now," demanded Paul with a raised voice.

"Why do you use people?"

"I have been used too ... Paul."

"And you profane the name of the gods".

"Who doesn't Paul ... look around you, who doesn't?"

"You will pay for it ... now".

"Paul ... I want power like any other man on earth and there are many ways of having it," said Odiari in a meek voice.

"You do that by asking people to pluck meat from the lion's mouth?"

"Who is this lion? Elesi? You surprise me Paul." Odiari was hoping that by extending the conversation, there was a chance somebody might come visiting. Then he remembered Ovie's men.

"Peter died by his own miscalculations ... I didn't kill him", Odiari said.

206

"Shut up, you magot," bawled Paul.

"Don't talk to master like that," quibbled Bide, trembling. " He is your master? You go with him then," said Paul to Bide decidedly.

They heard a vehicle pull up in front of Odiari's house.

"Don't do this Paul, you won't get away with it. My men are already on their way up and I will forgive you if you change your mind before they enter here."

"Idiot ... your divining powers have left you. You couldn't see who are coming".

"What are you talking about?"

"Your home work. Tell me about lies ... perhaps I would change my mind after hearing it," said Paul.

Odiari was surprised and impressed by what he considered foolhardiness on Paul's part.

"Your time is running out, Paul."

"Yours too ... and faster than you think," Paul replied.

There was a heavy kick on the door and Jude and Obuekwe came in bedecked with assault rifles.

Your men are drinking peppersoup at a joint in Onitsha with my money. They won't be here till at least 8.30. Now, make me change my mind. Why do you lie the way you do?"

" I've already told you that there are several ways of obtaining power. The most common are wealth and words. Great wealth can move men, but great lies are more potent. When you kill for a lie, people believe it."

"And you don't care what happens to the victims of your lies?"

"I don't ... please" Odiari pleaded to Jude as he saw his gun pointed at his leg.

In Jude's eyes, the whole picture of the encounter with the Elesis was replayed. He pulled the trigger and tore Odiari's legs to pieces.

"A slower death would have befitted you more, but we have not time," said Paul.

"Tie them to that goddess ... You will have a feel of the firing squad today ... Odiari".

Bide was too cowered by the sound of the gun to resist. Sebo looked piteously at Paul. "No," Paul told Jude as he made for Sebo. Just the man and his servant. Odiari's eyes were tightly closed as bullets thudded into his brain.

"To the shrine, let's rescue that priest," Paul told his men.

*   *   *

There was a thrill of pleasant excitement in Uda when Ikwu's people saw him. Notwithstanding his gaunt looks, they were happy that he was alive. His uncle, a prudent man had been worried about his disappearance. Ikwu was the only surviving child of his father. Because of this, his uncle had been advising him since he attained the age of sixteen to get married. "What is one is finished," he always said.

Since Ikwu's disappearance, his uncle had been torn between different lines of thought, He had wondered whether their troubles, especially Ikwu's (for he was missing), was Ikwu's making. Those days he had had to wait for Ikwu's return in confusion, he always remembered what his father used to say: "Always do things the proper way, so that even when things go wrong, you won't have to blame yourself." He remembered what he told Ikwu the day he decided to leave the village, a day before the period of abstinence ended at the time he shifted his vocation of priesthood to Okpoko: "Don't be the crazy tortoise who after serving years in prison began to complain of the filth in the place, a few hours to his release." But Ikwu had not heeded his warning. With the encouragement of the old man who was to replace him, he had left only a day to the expiration of the abstention period, so that his uncle had worried, whether the gods were angry for that act of omission.

When the old priest finally got implicated and arrested for aiding those who destroyed Okpoko's shrine, Ikwu's uncle was more confused than ever. Ikwu's return was therefore a great relief to his pained soul. He wanted to tell Ikwu everything that had happened during his absence, but Ikwu had not come to spend time. As he told him, he had some unfinished business to attend to before coming back fully. He had been sick and hospitalized, he told them and therefore had not been able to communicate them since his absence. Now, what was important was getting to Onitsha tonight with Paul's proposal.

"You must take me to Elesi's house in Onitsha this very night," Paul had told him as they turned into the earthen road that led to Uda.

"What for?" asked Ikwu, unsure of what Paul wanted from him.

"Haven't you been listening? We want Eze nabbed. We want him arrested tomorrow. We don't even need to see Okpoko to arrest him, I've decided to go and bear witness against him about dealings with him. I was his Chief Executioner and I stole all those gods for him. There will be many other gods which we stole and which I am going to show the police."

Ikwu was very confused inside. He wanted to say something, but did not know or understand what. Then, gradually, the question began to take shape. Could this be one of the men who destroyed his ancestral shrine?

"So you were one of the men who attacked Okpoko," asked Ikwu, fighting hard to hide his burning anger.

"Yes, I'll recognise the god, if he's still there, I'll show everything, I'll —".

"Hei ... what ... God! What do you think you are doing?" Jude asked Ikwu who had his fangs in Paul's left shoulder. "Man if you are still playing a hero, remember that I saved your life. The past belongs to the past. I've repented from all the evils that I committed against everybody, against every god. And I've decided to pay the supreme price, even for my men's sake I don't care what you think about me ... okay? But don't attack me ... you idiot."

"Obuekwe! turn this car and head to Onitsha," Paul commanded.

"No ... please," said Ikwu "I must see my family in order to have the strength to follow you. I am sorry. I'll go with you, but let me at least see my family. Before eight I will have finished and we will head to Onitsha ... please". Ikwu, pleaded.

Paul looked at him. Paul was not afraid to be lynched at Uda if Ikwu revealed his true identity there, but to be liquidated by an angry mob was to him like stopping at the middle of the road. There was no need for him to die in Uda. He wanted first, to help the police arrest and prosecute Eze before he went in. He could even do better than the police.

"Remember that if anything happens to us, you won't have anything against Eze. I personally, I want him hanged," Paul told Ikwu.

"Don't you trust me?" asked Ikwu.

"Okay," Paul said. "Obuekwe, right back to Uda".

Thus Ikwu had met with his family and left them wondering where he was going again with these strange looking men.

*   *   *

The Elesis were watching television when the phone rang. Ibuego rushed to the box, hoping that the call was for her.

"Hello," she said with a smooth accent.

"Hello," a rustic voice replied from the other end.

"Is Chimezie around?"

"Who is this?"

"Ikwu, please tell him it's Ikwu and it's urgent."

Ibuego covered the transmitter. She looked at Chimezie and said in a bated voice. "Who is Ikwu? he wants you."

"What!" exclaimed Chuby. "Ikwu, the bastard where is he calling from?" Chuby was mad with joy.

"Hello ... this is Chimezie."

"Oh ... Chimezie. It's Ikwu, Chuby's friend". Chimezie was very surprised at the reality of Ikwu's voice. "Chuby is also here," he said.

"Thank God. I have something important to tell you. Can I come over now.. now?"

"Yes of course." Chimezie told him.

"I will be with you in a moment."

"We are waiting."

"He is coming over." Chimezie told Chuby after speaking with Ikwu. "He sounded a bit pressured."

"Forget his voice. He's always pressured. It's good he's still alive. It's funny, we've nearly forgotten that he started all this. Isn't it funny the kind of calls we've been receiving this night."

Betty had called from Lagos to tell Chuby that Annie's boyfriend, Zuby had attempted to rape her. He was also found in possession of cocaine which police said he had wanted to plant in Chuby's home. The whole story had sounded odd and grotesque and had been demoralizing to Chuby, but he was happy that Zuby had not been able to carry out his plans. He had tried to forget about that as he had enough trouble in his lap already. Betty had made sure that Zuby was detained, and she had promised to come over to the East tomorrow, with Annie to spend the rest of the week.

Just then a knock sounded at the door, Chimezie opened the door and Ikwu came in, thin as ever. All of them stood up to welcome him, even Ibuego who had once quarrelled with him now realized how he must have felt the night they were discussing the stolen god at Nkwoko. When Ikwu greeted Chuby, he asked after Betty and Annie to which Chuby said they were alright. They could see that Ikwu's mood was significantly altered. The melancholy and mawkishness were gone. Despite his poor physical condition, he was very excited.

When Ikwu sat down, he spoke, "I have some people with me, people who are important to what I have to say to you. May I bring them in?"

Chimezie was a bit surprised the way Ikwu was talking. He could not imagine what he had in his mind, but he sure must have had a gruelling experience. He looked at his brothers who looked impassively at him. "Of course," he told Ikwu.

Paul and his men were sad and excited when Ikwu came to call them. A strange feeling now engulfed Paul. It was not annoyance, it was not even remorse for he had genuinely and honestly thought the matter over and he had forgiven himself. But God, it was strange that these people through the cutting down of his best friend had opened his eyes to a completely new experience in life, a new life he could not yet explain. It felt so much more rewarding doing good.

The moment Paul and his men entered the Elesi sitting room which was now nearly restored to its former dignity, everywhere became tense. They were maverick in a disturbing way. Their tall sturdy features threatened and assaulted the personality of everybody present. Even the way they looked at people was odd. They stole glances and never looked anybody in the eyes.

When they sat down, Ikwu inquired whether Elesi was not at home, Sylvester went and summoned his father. "Here is Paul. There is Obuekwe and there is Jude. These men saved my life yesterday. They saved me from being cut to pieces by Odiari the thief. Odiari is dead. They saw to that. They were once working for Odiari, but having repented from their sins, decided to come to see you, to beg for the forgiveness of your family and also to help us arrest Eze. They are willing to confess about all the things they did for Eze and Odiari, including the destruction of Okpoko. I've long forgiven them for their terrible action against Okpoko. Maybe they should speak for themselves".

Ikwu's speech was received with mixed feelings. It was unexpected, comforting, scary, incredible. Even the great Elesi had problem managing a cool posture. Ibuego had been pinching Defo wildly in the buttocks. Chimezie was clearly uncomfortable at the import of the revelation. Sylvester looked at Chuby, for the first time taking his eyes off the big man Paul. Lizzy was visibly shaken. She stretched her fingers as she murmured thanks to the Lord. She was so scared of Paul that she started praying for him in her soul.

Paul looked at the Chief and his children and sighed. When he spoke, it was with effort that he spoke. It was the speech of one not used to speech making, but it was honest enough.

"Baba," he said looking at Elesi now, "It is as Ikwu has said except he did not tell you that I am a killer. Myself and my friends here were part of the squad that came to destroy your house. We had been part of the group that caused you pain both in your village and here. We ask for your forgiveness. We are prepared to suffer anything for our wrongdoings, but please give us the opportunity to make sure that Eze is caught, to make sure he pays for his sins too. He must face the law."

"We are sorry," said Obuekwe and Jude.

What Paul said created an immediate physical discomfort in Elesi. His children who knew him well were so afraid of his reaction that they were incapable of forming their own feelings on the matter.

213

Elesi raised his head and stared wickedly at Paul. The sudden appearance of heavy veins in his head and blood in his eyes shook even Paul. If Elesi had magic potions in his hand, he would have reduced these men into worthless ash. Were these the men who a few days ago wanted to destroy him and his children? Were they the men who murdered his own brother Emeruo? Elesi's head was ringing murder. He suddenly shot up from his chair, "You will suffer," he cried and rushed into his room. He was searching everywhere for his gun. His family rushed into the room with him, pleading with him to calm down. Chimezie was so alarmed by his activity that he tried to hold him down. But Elesi pushed him away hard. "You are a stupid boy," he told Chimezie. "Those bastards won't live."

Ibuego had closed the door and now came and knelt in front of his father. "Papa please. They will die but calm down. Calm down, we love you, please." All of his children now begged him with one voice. Elesi sat down on his big bed and tears rolled down his eyes. His children wept bitterly when they saw the tears in their father's eyes. Chimezie noticed Defo start to shake with anger. He quickly went to his side and held his shoulder. "It's okay," he told him soothingly until he calmed down enough. Elesi asked them to leave him alone for a while after accepting their plea that the matter be handled cooly.

When he came back into the sitting room, he was completely changed, calm as he was when he first entered the room. Shaken as Paul, Jude and Obuekwe were, they made no attempt to save themselves. They were relieved to see that the Chief had no weapons when he came out.

"Man," Elesi addressed himself to Paul ... "I am sure you understand my anger. I am the son of my father and the simple truth is that I will not allow the man who shot his gun at me to remove the bullets from my body. That would be a grave unforgiveable stupidity. You are

214

poisonous, dangerous and deadly snakes in a man's roof. Such animals are not played with, they are killed. In the olden days, the likes of you are used in burying real warriors. A man who has swam many rivers as I have must know what he is saying. I grieve for the mother that gave suckle to you, for a sheep that bears a ram has no child at all. Look at yourselves, too many men and yet not a man. You killed my brother by threading him through a tree and shooting his head and you attempted to kill my son Defo and wipe out my entire family and expect me to offer you seat in my house. You are sitting in my house but you are not sitting in it. I thank God for the strength he has given me to continue to endure these hardships, these insults.

"There is one thing you will do now to let me know that you are serious. You must offer yourselves to the police now. From the police station, you may join us to Eze's mission. He is organising an exhibition tomorrow. I will go there with Chuby and the police to assess things for myself".

"We are prepared to do that," answered Paul, "but please allow us to go with you to Okwu to identify those gods to the police."

"That will be done," Elesi said to Paul. He turned to Chimezie. "Call the police." _

"Papa — " Lizzy started to say.

"Call the police," Elesi repeated in a hard voice.

Chimezie dialled the number and spoke with the duty Sergeant. "They are coming," he announced after he had hung up.

"Good," Elesi said. They all sat in silence and awaited the arrival of the police.

215

Chapter 12

In the morning, Elesi and Chuby drove to the police station where Paul and his colleagues were made available with police escort to Orlu.

At Orlu, the Assistant Superintendent of Police there, who knew Elesi well, nursed a lot of misgivings about letting Paul and his colleagues go to Okwu with the Police and Elesi. "These men are highly dangerous," he told Elesi. "They've confessed to murdering people, one of them only yesterday. They may escape."

"Remember they offered themselves for arrest. You did not find them. I assure you that these men are not going to run. I promised them they could go to Okwu with us before they would agree to be arrested." Elesi continued arguing. In the end, the police chief gave in against his will.

When Paul and his colleagues came out of the cell, they threw a happy "Good morning Chief" at Elesi who also replied genially. Most of last night, Elesi could not sleep, his mind was fixed on what had happened between him and those criminals. He had refused to forgive them when they asked his forgiveness. Last night he was convinced that such men deserved nothing less than being burnt soul and body. In the olden days such men were buried with their hearts opened, salt and palm oil stuffed in them to destroy whatever was left of the spirit in them and they were forbidden from reappearing in the clan ever again.

But the act of willingly offering themselves up for arrest had surprised Elesi. Elesi nearly thought it was brave. Again, he thought every act of their kind emanated from a strange quality of character other than courage. But having watched Paul closely, he was beginning to think differently, believing courage, a quality that advanced and rarified as a man enhanced his experiences. The courage of thieves was misdirected. It was wickedly insensitive.

Elesi was surprised last night to observe Paul appear free from the evil cocoon, attaining a fullness that was rare among men. Paul had had a clear appreciation of his difficulties, and he was determined to mend his life at all costs which was to Elesi the criterion of judging wisdom. Elesi had gradually come to the realization that negative experiences should not harden us, but should awaken in us a desire to change and conquer. Thus he had brooded last night until he forgave Paul and his colleagues. He forgave the murder of his brother and the attempt at destroying his family. He forgave everything. Paul had even come to acquire a special significance for him.

The fate that awaited Paul was great, really great, but then the AG was there. If only the supreme fate could be averted, Paul would live well.

*   *   *

"Nobody dey here, no need for you to enter" said the security man at the gate of Eze's mission in Okwu. This was the fifth time he would say this. Elesi restrained the policeman with him in his car from flashing his identity in order to gain them entry into the grounds, not sure what it would benefit them. From the look of things, it was obvious that no exhibition was going on in the mission. An exhibition of the kind planned by Eze was not something that could be made such a secret. If for some reason however they decided to make this one secret, there was no sign that it was taking place here. There were no cars, no sign of people coming and going, in fact there was no activity in Okwu, and they had come early.

Elesi began confering with Chuby. "It means that Defo's informant was wrong or deliberately misled him. Maybe the card was just another trick to make us not take the other day seriously. Maybe they had it somewhere ... Somewhere Sylvester did not know."

"Do you have the card Defo gave you?" Elesi inquired from Chuby.

"Yes. And the Inspector has his."

"Why don't you show it to this man? Make a big show of it. Tell him that you are here for the exhibition and see how he reacts to that," Elesi urged Chuby.

"What if Defo's informant is not trustworthy, and gave him this card in order to give us away, to make our presence noticed?"

Elesi thought the question over properly. "We will find these things out by trying something. Try what I told you, whatever comes out of it, we shall see it."

Chuby then stiffened his shoulders and put on an air that only a good actor can manage. He was suddenly transformed from gentle politeness to aggressive haughtiness. He walked back to the gateman, the card now in his hand. "We are actually here for the exhibition ..." he showed him the card. "All the way from Lagos—"

The moment the gateman saw the card, he was all service. "Oh! Sorry sir" he said. "But you for tell me now. The exhibition no de hold here again. They changed the venue and I sure say the Reverend inform everybody wey get this card about the change. I think say you know." He took the card and examined it.

"I was not informed about anything," said Chuby impatiently.

"Sorry Oga. But the problem be say na only our security staff and some policemen dey here. Who go show you the place now?" The security man said as he cracked his brain. "Make I see whether any of them go gree go with you. The place no far and e'no dey hard to find."

Chuby instantly saw what was wrong with the gateman's proposition. They were lucky so far dealing with somebody who did not know them. To involve somebody else who might recognise them would be risky.

"E, no dey necessary," Chuby told the man in pidgin. "you fit just direct us how we go fin' the place."

"I'm sure somebody go gree go with you".

"Don't worry," Chuby said and gave him a twenty naira note, "just describe the place for us."

The man was overwhelmed. "If you go out of this place, tell the villagers to direct you the way to Oboma village. Okay, it is better to go back the way you came. At the big market, just ask them the way to Oboma. They'll show you. E dey by your right as you go reach the major road. Straight down Oboma road leads to the place. When you reach the place, nobody go tell you. Na the Reverend's new house. The walls high like prison wall"

"Thank you" Chuby told him.

"Oga talk say make we no describe the place to anybody, but as you carry that card ..." the security man said as Chuby and Elesi turned to leave.

"Thank you" Chuby told him again as he strode towards Elesi's car. Eze's security man had described the road to his new residence very well. It was not difficult going back the way they had come to the big market. There, it was easy locating the road to Oboma. A clear sign pointed to it by their right. They followed the road down until they reached the beginning of a very high fence. They could see several cars parked by the fence. They obviously belonged to people who came for the exhibition. There was nobody in sight.

They came in three cars. Two peugeot estate wagons which the police brought. They had been waiting at the market while Elesi and Chuby had gone to survey the Reverend's mission. In all, there were six plainclothes men together with Paul, Jude and Obuekwe. Inside the other car, a peugeot saloon, were Elesi and Ikwu and Chuby. They all pulled up at the very rear of the line of cars.

They decided that Chuby and the Police Inspector, who also had the card should enter the place. The other policemen, with Paul, Jude and Obuekwe should keep as close as possible in order to come to their rescue should anything go wrong. Chuby and the Inspector were advised to raise an alarm in any way possible in order to alert others, in case of any trouble. Elesi and Ikwu waited at the point where they kept their cars.

At the main gate, the Inspector and Chuby showed their cards to a security man who looked at them through a square opening in the gate. The cards earned them immediate admittance into the Reverend's new house, and for a moment, they did not know what to do. When the security man had finished closing the gate, he came to their side and started leading them to the halls where the exhibition was holding.

The Inspector, sensing the danger in moving hurriedly to the hall began to talk in order to defuse the tension building around them. He started in praise of the Reverend's new house to the admiration of the securityman.

"A beautiful house," the policeman said, "Quite big with a lot of space for children ... people," said the Inspector when he remembered that the Reverend had no children.

"It is God's work," the securityman said appreciatively. From the look of things, it seemed that Eze was not expecting any trouble today. Security was minimal, at least from the outside and the securityman talking to Chuby and the Inspector looked anything but tough. Just an old man of the village.

"A very quiet place for the exhibition". Chuby said.

"Many people inside like here, them all outside just now, before the organisers of the exhibition come take them in," explained the security man.

"I hope that we are not late" said the Inspector.

"No ... not too late," said the securityman.

The securityman led them to a heavy wooden door on the basement and told them to go inside. Here, Chuby brought out the photograph of Okpoko and had a good look at it, when the securityman had gone out of sight.

"You needn't worry about that," said the Inspector. "That man, Paul, says that they stole almost everything here. What we are just going to do is to make sure that the exhibition is going on, and then bring our men to arrest the Reverend. We just want to make sure that there won't be any trouble when we move in."

"Okay," Chuby said as he slipped the photograph back into his breast pocket. As they entered the ante-room which the securityman had led them into, they saw another door by the left. Before the door as they came in, was a rectangular glass window from where they could see several objects of art displayed on shelves and stands. To their surprise there was nobody in the hall except one man in uniform, His uniform looked like a security uniform but of a higher taste than that of the gateman.

The man smiled up to them.

"Welcome," he told them.

"Thank you," they replied.

"They are in the other hall. They have covered this place and as you can see, many of the items here have been sold. They buy as they look at each item. There is a bottom price fixed by the organisers of the exhibition on every item, but people are free to bid from that price higher, to any price they are willing to pay. For instance, said the glib talking man in the security gear, "we have two thousand naira on this one, but it was sold for six thousand naira. On this one also we have three thousand, but it was sold for six thousand five hundred." The Inspector looked at the ugly wood carving of a god carrying a mighty plate on its head and wondered why people had to give anything for this kind of thing. He went close, in order to be able to read the words printed on a paper that was clipped to the object. The information on the paper showed that the work was of Nri origin, but it was undated. There was another smaller tag which had the information "sold" on it.

Chuby had already swept his eyes across the hall, looking for Okpoko. When he did not see anything resembling him, he lost interest in the securityman's explanations.

"You may now join them in the other hall," the man in uniform said as he led them towards another door at the far end of the hall. Chuby and the Inspector could see through another rectangular glass window on the wall separating the two halls, a group of people, about fifty of them, gathered around one man who was explaining something to them.

The inner hall was on a lower level than the outer one, so they had to descend a few steps inside another ante-room between the halls before entering it.

As they approached the group, nobody paid any attention to them except another man who was wearing the same kind of uniform as the other man inside the outer hall. He walked up to them and welcomed them with a warm smile and led them to the group who were listening to a man dressed in a well cut English suit.

The speaker was tall, handsome and clean-shaven. He put on a specs of gold and a gold ring shone on his left middle finger as he continued to engage the interest of his audience.

Chuby tried to listen to him, but could not because he was listening to the conversation between two whitemen who were close to him.

"We must buy this item ... at all costs," insisted the shorter of them. "That is our instruction."

"Don't let your eagerness show," the other man told him, "or you'll end up buying it at an outrageous price—"

"You can now bid for it", rang the voice of the auctioneer, "the bottom price is twenty thousand naira. So, now we have twenty thousand naira. Twenty ... twenty ... yes? —"

"Twenty-two," said one man in a white caftan."

"Twenty-three," said another bidder.

Until now, Chuby had not had an opportunity to see the item bidded for. But when the handsome speaker, obviously an agent of the Ramblers International, turned to speak to somebody, he had a clear view of the object.

The familiarity of the object made his heart skip and for an instant, he was nonplussed. He braced himself, fixing his gaze upon the object, to make sure that he was not hallucinating but, certainly Okpoko stared back into his eyes, unmoving, undisappearing, undestroyed. He looked around him and could not find the Inspector who had accompanied him to this place. Chuby wanted to rush out of the hall, to tell the others that at last, Okpoko had been found. This he knew, was unthinkable. In his confusion, Chuby neither heard nor understood what was going on around him.

"Forty-five," Chuby shouted, thinking that the astronomical leap from twenty-something thousands might make the policeman to notice him.

A hand touched his right shoulder and he turned. He saw two men grinning at him, wonderingly.

"Where are you,?" one of them asked him in a friendly tone.

"What —" he started to say when he heard "eighty two."

"Ninety," Chuby shouted, hoping to attract the Inspector's attention to him by making the leap of eight thousand naira.

The shorter of the whitemen now came out fully to show that he wanted to acquire the object.

"Hundred," he said challengingly.

"One ten", said another bidder.

Chuby gave up the challenge and started searching for his Inspector friend once again. When he could not find him, he focused his attention on the handsome agent of the Ramblers. Delightfully, he saw that the man was chatting with Reverend Eze while the Inspector stood very close to them, smiling at everything they said in a bid to edge himself into their conversation.

When Chuby's eyes met the Inspector's, he signed to him with his eyes to come to his side. The Inspector quickly left his position and came to Chuby's side. Chuby was too excited to talk. He started searching in his pockets for the photograph. The Inspector seemed to sense what was on his mind and looked at him questioningly. Chuby understood and nodded. "Let's go outside," he told him. Only the man in security uniform saw them start to move out.

He followed them, but did not make any effort to catch up with them. Inside the other hall, he saw them speak to his colleague there, after which they left.

"What did they say?," the security man inquired from his colleague.

"They were a little late, and seemed to think that everything they would have liked to buy had already been bought...". "Did you see their cards?"

"That is for Okey outside to check," the man in the outer hall told his colleague.

"Then find out from Okey."

"Who will be here?" asked the man at the outer hall. "We were told never to leave our stations."

"I'll stand between the halls," said the man inside. "Just make it fast."

Outside, the securityman beckoned to their member at the gate who came immediately.

"Those men, who just left," he said, "did they show their cards?"

"Yes," answered the old man at the gate. "Is there any trouble?" he asked his colleague.

"No. It's just the manner of their coming in and going out."

"There is no problem," said the old man.

"They came with correct cards signed by the Reverend. They are not bad people," he concluded

"Okay," the man inside answered and made for the hall again.

Outside, Chuby and the Inspector informed their men of their findings. In their excitement, they told Paul, Jude and Obuekwe to go and look after their remaining weapons in the cars which were parked where Elesi and Ikwu waited for them. The whole six policemen with Chuby, went in to arrest Eze.

As Paul and his men walked back to the point where Elesi was waiting with Ikwu, Paul began exhorting them to do what he had told them to do last night.

"We will do it" they told him.

"Be courageous and quick," said Paul. "It seems that God was listening as we talked last night. See now, these stupid men have made weapons available to us..."

Paul changed the topic of their conversation when they saw Elesi's car. Elesi was overjoyed when he saw them. In his mind they represented a different thing altogether, and this strange feeling he felt for them, was it pity or love? He was determined now to encourage them in their ordeal, for only the test of fire they said made good iron. Elesi smiled gravely as they came close to his car.

"What is happening?," he asked Paul.

"They have found Okpoko," Paul answered.

"What?" asked Ikwu, unbelieving.

"They've gone in to arrest Eze."

Ikwu was overjoyed. Until now, life had lost meaning, and purpose to him. He had felt like a man totally disconnected with the earth and heaven. He had been floating through life, and in this trauma had gone through crushing conditions and survived. His ordeal in Odiari's house was the greatest. As Odiari had continued to contrive new ways of ridiculing and soiling his body and soul, he had summoned his reserve courage to block from his mind, all the mental and physical pains which Odiari inflicted on him. Somehow, the world had become dead to him. This news from Paul felt like the flow of ice cold water on a hot dry land. The smoke of it was the joy, the warmness of the land, the new connection with existence and the coolness that followed signified peace. Ikwu had traversed the threshold of the smoking. He was warming up to the reality of this news, but he did not know how to begin. He needed to do something physical to convince himself of it. Thus, he rushed at Paul to embrace him and share this joy with him. He slapped his back several times, and when he did not feel the same warmth, he left him and went to Jude who rudely shoved him aside with the warning that everything was not over yet.

"Go to hell," said Ikwu to the three men and went to Elesi instead. Surprisingly, Elesi was not of much help. There was a gloomy air about everybody that Ikwu felt more than the joy he had felt before. He could no longer bear it and he started running towards the house, to the scene of action.

"Ikwu!" called Elesi. "Ikwu come back here!" Elesi ran after Ikwu.

Paul, Jude and Obuekwe selected good rifles from the lot left by the police in their cars and made for the bush.

Inside the compound, the policemen handcuffed, fettered and gagged the old gateman. In the outer hall, they met nobody, so they all marched into the inner hall assault ready.

"Hold it everybody!" the Inspector's voice droned across the hall. The crowd turned in the direction of the shout to stare death in the face. Confronted by the rifles, almost everybody in the group held up his hands in surrender.

"We are policemen and we want Reverend Eze. We want him only and anybody who does not want to get hurt should be very careful as not to shake an hair."

The Inspector moved closer to the crowd which froze at his advance. "Now show yourself Reverend."

"Yes, here I am said the Reverend from the very rear of the crowd. "What do you want from me?"

"You are under arrest for stealing," said the Inspector.

There was a ripple of laughter from the unbelieving crowd of people.

"You will regret this," said the Reverend who squeezed himself through the crowd of people, who refused to move as he pushed them in order to accost his accuser. "Come out quietly," the Inspector commanded in a hard voice, "unless you don't like your life."

The Reverend showed himself at the front of the crowd and the Inspector commanded him to come to him in order to be arrested. The Reverend walked quietly until he reached within a few feet of the Inspector. From there, he struck out on the Inspector who easily averted his blow and forcibly turned him around to handcuff him from the back.

"This man is a rogue," the Inspector told the crowd again. Everything here are exhibits. We therefore warn all of you not to allow yourself the misfortune of being found with anything with which he may be prosecuted. All of you come out this way and be searched. When you go out, quickly pick your cars and go."

"No!" the Inspector said on second thoughts. "You all wait till we've driven away," he told them.

Nobody made any effort from among the crowd to save the Reverend. The Inspector also had the agent of the Ramblers International handcuffed, with the two uniformed securitymen.

They led them out to the gate. When the Inspector opened the gate, he saw to his surprise, Ikwu and Elesi, perspiring profusely.

"What?" he asked them alarmed. "Have they escaped"

"Who?" Elesi asked back.

"Those criminals."

"What for?" said Elesi. "It seems that your duty is finally completed." Was it a question or a statement of fact? The Inspector did not know. He started leading his captives to where they had put away the cars, his men following behind. Reverend Eze was in the vanguard of the group.

"They are coming," said Paul to his men as he sighted Eze in front of the Inspector. "I think it would be easier to shoot from the side."

Paul, Jude and Obuekwe hurried to the opposite side of the bushes near their cars and waited. Everything seemed to work out mysteriously in their favour. Eze was walking ahead of them all with the Inspector, his head bent in a mournful manner. Suddenly, the Inspector drew back to give orders to his men. When Eze reached within five yards of Paul, Paul whistled softly. Only his men

228

heard him and they all opened fire on Eze. The priest took all the bullets and faltered for a few second before he fell.

"Cover!" shouted the Inspector, jolted out of his wits. His men flattened themselves on the ground waiting for whomever was responsible for this in order to capture him.

Paul and his men, now filled with a sense of fulfilment, came out of the bush, flaunting their guns.

To the policemen, they were dangerous criminals with guns and they had killed yet another person here, and so the Inspector shouted: "fire!" to his men. They opened up on them. Before Elesi could do anything, the three men were down and probably dead. Elesi rushed at their fallen bodies, but the Inspector warned him to move back. He nevertheless defied the Inspector's warning and went to them. Jude and Obuekwe seemed to have died instantly, while Paul struggled to raise his hand when he saw Elesi. Elesi bent down and took his hand.

"Papa," he managed to say before he gave up the ghost.

"My son... my son!", Elesi called Paul as he wept over him.

"Give me a hand," the Inspector told his men as he lifted the bodies into one of the estate wagons. In the same car, he put the officials of the Ramblers International.

Elesi was still crying when they reached the major road. Ikwu was very surprised to see Elesi's eyes streaming with tears. He could not understand why. Those were the men who Elesi wanted to shoot yesterday.

"It is okay now Papa," Ikwu tried to comfort the old man.

"I love that boy ... Paul," Elesi told him between sobs.

*   *   *

It was some days before Ikwu could reach Uda again. He had been to the police station to ensure that Okpoko was never kept a day longer than necessary. The police on their part had been most co-operative. They had informed Ikwu that owing to lack of evidence, the old priest, Are (the one who had been in Okpoko's service before the attack on the shrine) had since been released. Ikwu had therefore arranged for a van to convey the oracle back to its shrine.

Ikwu had travelled at night, having considered it profane and sacrilegious to bring Okpoko back to Uda in broad daylight amidst stares of children and women. Even among the menfolk of Nkwoko, including the chief, no one could claim to have seen Okpoko in the past outside his shrine.

It was a moonless night and the atmosphere was pitch-dark when the van turned into the earthen road that led to Uda. Ikwu found himself brooding more and more about the old priest, Are, what to do with him. Are's admission that some men had broached to him the destruction of Okpoko was disturbing. And why did he not tell anybody? Perhaps he had not considered them serious. His conduct had been unrepresentative of his office, for Okpoko's priest was Okpoko's voice and when that voice uttered a contradiction to the wishes of the Oracle, that relationship must dissolve and dissolution with the deity meant a great deal. Ikwu found himself praying more and more to Okpoko to guide him in resolving the matter.

Uda was as quiet as a grave-yard when Ikwu entered. At that time, it was usual to hear old men having a tete-a-tete with each other. Only the jangling of metals could be heard as tyres moved in and out of the myriad potholes covering the entire length of the road that led to Ikwu's house. Soon they reached Ikwu's house.

Ikwu climbed down from the back of the van where he had been keeping watch over Okpoko.

"Mmn ... mmnnnnn". He made a sound hoping to find his uncle outside their house. There was no reply from the darkness. But as soon as he touched the small gate which demarcated their house from the road, a male voice barked.

"Who is that? "It was his uncle, Nwike.

"It is me Papa ... Ikwu".

"Oh ...".

Some passed seconds during which Ikwu could hear the swish of legs on the cement floor. It was the movement of a leg looking for something. A light suddenly flashed and Ikwu could see the outline of his uncle, holding a match and lighting a lamp. His uncle walked heavily towards the gate to open the door. He was getting very old, thought Ikwu.

As soon as the man could get his hand on Ikwu, he embraced him shakily, touching most of his body as if to reassure himself it was Ikwu. Then he turned to the vehicle. "Is Okpoko back?"

"Yes".

"We heard ... they read it. They told us but we didn't believe it ...".

"Come and have a look" Ikwu told him.

The old man stared at Ikwu intently and then smiled. "The father of the forest has been here ever since the last time you returned".

Ikwu was startled. "You mean the sacred snake?" Ikwu asked in fright. "Yes. I had to make sure. I took it downstream on a stick several times, but every night, it would crawl back to your room. I just want you to know that. We will go straight to the shrine now to welcome back the Oracle ... just the two of us. The people will know tomorrow with great joy I am sure. A lot of misfortune has befallen us since the departure of the Oracle. Wait a minute".

The old man disappeared into the house and soon came out with a rucksack and a white cock in his right hand. "Here, let's go".

When they had carefully laid Okpoko down in his shrine, they both kowtowed. Ikwu quickly took a knife from the rucksack and with it killed the cock. He offered prayers to the Oracle asking for his forgiveness and patience with the people of Uda.

"Why is Uda so quiet?" Ikwu asked his uncle when they had returned to their house.

"People have been afraid," answered the old man. "Many bad things have been happening to us. The worst of it is Are. He has been missing. He came back not quite a few days ago. He got missing on the very night when he entered Uda and the people fear that he has gone for dissolution. That is the reason everybody has been careful not to go out lest anyone finds him and brings a curse upon himself. They'll all be very happy to see you tomorrow. It is your duty as the priest of the Oracle to look for him".

Ikwu shivered a little from what his uncle had said. He would have told him that he was afraid to undertake such a task but after considering the entire situation, he kept quiet.

"It means Ikwu that you are henceforth ... the priest of Okpoko. You can't combine that duty with anything else. The presence of the father of the forest in our house is proof of it".

Ikwu nodded.

*   *   *

In the morning, before cockcrow, a strangely droning sound roused Ikwu from sleep. The sound was mosquito-

232

like. Ikwu thought to kill the insect, but when he struck, his palm fell hard on his cheek. He became fully awake and was instantly overtaken by fear.

From the other side of the room, his uncle was watching him. Ikwu went for the matchet which was leaned on the wall near him.

"You can't go with anything", the old man said.

And suddenly, Ikwu began to mumble unintelligible things. And then he faced the door and walked out into the dark.

*   *   *

The people of Uda woke up to the exhilarating news of Ikwu's return. Uda elders quickly sent news to their Chief, telling him that the day may see the formal installation of a new priest for Okpoko as it was in the beginning.

The Chief made haste to provide the sacrifice. He had been informed by the elders that a propitiatory sacrifice was important as this was the first time in their lives they might probably witness the departure of Okpoko's priest by dissolution. The Chief had thereby provided two white cows, two black bulls, a horse, a dog, a goat, a ram, seven cocks and seven hens, sixteen ducks, several reptiles from alligators to lizards. The wise old chiefs helped to provide important herbs and seeds of potent plants necessary for the sacrifice.

Uda people had all gathered at the gully area. While they waited for the appearance of their priest, they sang their old songs and danced their old dances. Aged women and men wailed to the great Oracle. "The Great One. The Wise One". They called him. "You chiefs and wise men, spirits of those who have led us in the past. Sharpen the eyes of the man who shall be the caretaker of our sacred shrine, the guardian of our sacred things, our good, our

233

shield, his name our safety. Guide him to the way of peace. The living need peace and peace we shall have". Thus the people of Uda supplicated the help of their Oracle and their ancestors. They beat their great drums and their great gongs which could be heard a long distance away.

*   *   *

Ikwu had been in the bush since the early hours of the morning. As soon as he stepped into the dark, he was filled with a great power which he had never known before. Everything suddenly seemed so small. The dark to him was like daylight and even the sky seemed so close. He felt very close to everything and he talked freely to everything. He feared no obstacles on the road. He feared no thorns, no snakes, no spirits. He just roamed the bush until the late hours of the morning when hunger and fatigue came upon him and seized him.

In that tired state, his mind was still centred on discovering the hut, if any. Thus he still traipsed round the bush searching for the palm-frond thatch as he had been told.

At a point, in the centre of the bush, his legs gave way and he lay down and slept. He did not sleep long when a flapping sound startled him wide awake. He stared in horror at a flock of vultures hovering around him. He flapped his hand at the carnivores to chase them away, still struggling between sleep and wakefulness. But the hard-beaked animals unsure whether the carcass was still alive charged still towards it. It was then that he stood up and they all flew away in another direction of the bush. There Ikwu could see more vultures. They were an excited bunch playing a great sport with one another. One of them flew in Ikwu's direction and a few others followed it.

234

As Ikwu observed them in flight, he could see that they all had animal flesh in their horny beaks.

As Ikwu drew close to the vultures, he saw the thatch enclosure and he wondered what kind of meeting Are was having with these birds. And then he tried to think of the effort the priest had made, without his sight to collect the fronds in order to construct the shade and how long he must have waited calmly? For his final dissolution.

He found the vulture – cleaned skull at the foot of the thatch hut and used a heavy wood to sever it from the rest of the body. The head of the priest must be buried in the abode of Okpoko. Are had atoned for his sins.

It was nearly twilight before the people of Uda observed the warrior-like figure of Ikwu in the distance. He danced as he came and they roared with thunderous shouts that sent shock waves over the ends of the earth. They were waiting for the sign that his mission had been successful but he continued dancing. Finally very close to them, he raised up the skull for all to see. The entire village of Uda broke to pieces because of the great shouts of joy coming from the mouths of its people. They kept shouting until Ikwu reached them.

They had never seen more wiser eyes. They had never seen more patient eyes. They had never seen a more confident man. The young face had given way to a pained serious feature only the wisest priests could have.

The Chief moved back as Ikwu led the procession straight to Okpoko's shrine to offer a befitting sacrifice to the Oracle.

*   *   *

As Elesi looked at Chuby, Betty, Annie, the A.G. and other guests who had come to Nkwoko for marking the one month since his brother, Emeruo's burial, he felt comforted. Now that their friends were here, in the midst of all the people of Nkwoko, Elesi felt good. Only in death did we recognise our true brothers and friends.

He was also happy to see that Egondu, Emeruo's wife was strong. It would have been tougher for her in traditional time. At that time, she would have been kept on a mat strewn with ashes, with the hair shaven from her head, and not allowed a bath for an entire month. She would have been dressed in rags and she would have kept constant guard against her husband with a knife knotted with *omu*. During this time, she would not be expected to go out to any other place except to use the toilet. She would see no titled man, nor would she have dealings with anybody around her. After *izu asaa*, one month, she would then be led up and out of the mourning mat and she would be allowed a bath, after which she could visit with her friends, and she would then mourn her husband for three years in dark clothes.

Today, there had been a mass said for the repose of Emeruo's soul. The village priest, with a solemn face had dwelt on the qualities for which he claimed Emeruo was known. These qualities were bravery and uprightness. "He was brave during his life, and he.was honest about his nature, and with every man he dealt with," the priest had said. Elesi had considered this and believed that the priest was right. To him, the events that led to Emeruo's demise rightly belonged to those experiences one could call accidents of destiny, for Emeruo had been faithful to his tradition and culture and to decency before he got mixed up with the bad crowd.

After the mass, every person had retired to Emeruo's house where Elesi had hired a good caterer to provide refreshments.

"Papa, we must go," Chuby told Elesi when he was ready to go. He and his wife and sister had stayed till evening and they had a long way to go.

Elesi looked at his watch. "If you must go, this is the perfect time," he said.

"We will go at the same time," said the A.G.

"Good dear friend," Elesi told him. "Thank you very much for coming. I'll see you off then". He rose as he spoke, with him most of his children who were familiar with his friends. The villagers now started waving good bye at the visitors who did not forget to greet the elders before they left.

They walked their friends to their cars. Inside Chuby's car sat Betty and Annie. Annie was occupying the rear seat by the left of the car. She kept straining beyond the crowd waving at them like somebody who was missing something very important. And then, "wait," echoed Defo's voice from behind the crowd.

They all made way for him as he pushed his way to where Chuby's car stood. He rushed to Annie and handed her a white envelope while everybody watched, rather surprised at the exchange between him and Annie. He was whispering something into her ears and Annie's eyes fluttered like the wings of a butterfly. Before she knew it, Defo bent down and gave her a peck on the forehead. Her entire face flushed. Everybody was further surprised. From Annie and Defo's shining faces, it was clear that something was happening between them. Nobody knew when it all started. Ibuego watched it all with joy. She had told Defo to announce his intention to the family in this fashion and he had done it. Chuby could not say anything more to the Elesis. He waved quietly at Chimezie as he started rolling the car.

All of Elesi's children were now looking at him, knowing his feelings about such indiscreet behaviour as Defo had manifested. He turned to Defo. "Young men of nowadays," he said. His face was a mysterious mask like the indecipherable faces of the *ozoebila*.

237

At the security counter at the Lagos Police Station, Chuby stood facing Zuby. They were separated by an iron screen. They have become tired of arguing over a matter that in Chuby's mind proved that Zuby was a nut.

For how could Zuby claim that his attempts at hurting Annie was caused by the pain and disappointment that Chuby had caused an imaginary sister of his, Asa? .He had described this sister as "dark, tall and beautiful". He had insisted that his sister had attended the same university with Chuby.

At the risk of a heart burst, Chuby had protested that he had never known any girl by the name Asa, nor did he go out with any tall dark and beautiful girl while in school. There had only been Rosa and Betty. He would have turned to go but considering the seriousness of the vindictive attempts by Zuby at his sister, he decided to wait to the conclusion of the matter as Chuby had said that his sister would be coming.

Before long, Chuby saw a tall dark girl walk into the hall. That moment he heard Zuby say, almost in a whisper, "that's my sister". The girl had no sharp looks and she was dressed in ugly taste. The moment she saw Chuby both her hands went up and covered her mouth in fright. Slowly, she drew close and said, "Is it you Chuby?" Her voice was as familiar to him as his own. And suddenly the face began to fall into picture. This must be Rosa's twin sister. But Rosa never spoke of any sisters.

"You are Rosa's sister?" Chuby asked her "Oh ... Chuby. You've forgotten me so. You can't even recognise me ... your Rosa," the girl said between sobs.

Chuby felt terrible at the shocking revelation. This was truly Rosa. What could so alter a person's appearance from reverent beauty to stark ugliness? Frustration? No ...

no. It had to be those tubes, those tubes of toning creams which she used to buy in large quantity. How benighted she was now.

"You've destroyed my life," Rosa said falling in Chuby's direction, but Chuby let her fall to the ground, whereupon she began to weep seriously.

"I've always loved you all my life —" She started to say "Is that why you sent your brother to destroy me?"

"After all you did to me, you went and married Betty. My own girl friend, Chuby. You have no shame at all. And she is there straddling her legs in your bed, ready to suck your anus at the flick of your hand. That devil —".

"Stop it", Chuby shouted at her." I love that girl a million times more than I ever loved you —"

"Did you loved me at all?"

"Yes —"

"Everything will still be okay. After all you've not wedded her."

Chuby felt like he had been jolted with a naked wire. "I loved you because I thought you loved me, Rosa. But your hate towards me was like the darkness of your skin now. All those days you were seeing Alhaji Mohammed Suleiman, you thought I didn't know. Because I loved you greatly, I felt that part of loving you was leaving you to look for material comfort which I was not able to give you, and you used me. I didn't tell anybody about your affair with Mohammed, only my friends who saw you with him in Lagos knew. I was reading a book which opened my eyes to what an untrustworthy whore, you were. In Betty, in her discipline, control and understanding, I saw the perfect woman for me. Even after we left school, I could not find any other woman as good as she was until God brought her back to me. I don't think you deserve any pity from me."

At this, Rosa drew back her head, and let fly a wad of saliva in Chuby's face. It was Zuby who returned the insult on Chuby's behalf. He coughed up a lump of phlegm and spat on his sister's face. Asa was so enraged that she started fighting her brother through the screen, where she cut her hand. In a mad rage now, she started rummaging in the heavy bag which she had brought with her. From it, she took a white plastic container. Immediately her brother saw the container he shouted. "Acid!" at Chuby.

Before Chuby could duck, Rosa had spattered him with the liquid. Within seconds, he tore his jacket and shirt ripping off buttons as he did so. He was beginning to feel a burning sensation in his chest. He rushed to a sink by the door. Turning on the water, he washed his chest till he felt the sensation no more. When he turned, he saw the burly Sergeant slapping Rosa. He watched him slap her three times before he intervened. Chuby's only regret now was that Zuby was nowhere to be found. He wanted to thank him for saving him. His actions had proved that he had been misguided in doing the things he did.

When Chuby finished writing his statement, he marvelled at the accuracy of some of the words he used in describing Rosa, "frustrated bitch, deceiver,"etc. As he left the station with Rosa behind bars, he remembered one of Elesi's frequent thoughts: "Better to win in truth than to kill in vengeance."

Printed in the United Kingdom
by Lightning Source UK Ltd.
1370